# DAYS OF DOOM

# DAYS OF DOOM

## APOCALYPTIC VISIONS & UNEARTHLY NIGHTMARES

## OWEN OLIVER

COACHWHIP PUBLICATIONS

Landisville, Pennsylvania

*Days of Doom: Apocalyptic Visions & Unearthly Nightmares* by Owen
  Oliver
Copyright © 2012 Coachwhip Publications
No claim made on public domain material.

Owen Oliver, pseudonym of Sir Joshua Albert Flynn (1863-1933)

ISBN 1-61646-110-1
ISBN-13 978-1-61646-110-2

Cover Image: NASA / Goddard Space Flight Center & JPL Caltech

CoachwhipBooks.com

# CONTENTS

The Black Shadow (1903)      7

Out of the Deep (1904)      21

The Pink Madness (1904)      36

The Plague of Lights (1904)      52

The Gray Weed (1905)      66

The Dark Days (1906)      83

The Long Night (1906)      97

The Shadow (1906)      111

The Annihilator (1910)      124

The Cloud-Men (1911)      143

The Soul Machine (1911)      160

The Sleep and the Awakening (1911)      179

Platinum (1916)      211

# THE BLACK SHADOW

### The Mark Upon the Floor

The chemicals in the retorts were still hissing, and the multiple wheels still kept the mouth of the conical receiver following the invisible moon; but Professor Flint sat back in his chair and heeded them no more. Twenty years of deep study, twenty years of original thought, ten years of ingenious contrivance—and the experiment had failed!

He could scarcely believe in failure even now. Twice he half rose to try the tests again, but shook his head. There had been indications that the receiver held something, but they were very faint; probably nothing more than electrical disturbances due to some by-play of the agents used. At any rate, no effect had been produced on any of three hundred elements and compounds that he had tried, or upon some dozen animals that he had introduced into the yawning cone. Either his vast net had missed aim or its prey would not manifest itself in a form that man could understand. The practical effect was the same. He had failed.

He stopped the machinery, rang for his man to take the useless cages away, and looked out of the window with a frown. The discovery would be made in the end, he knew, but it must be by others now. The further researches which he foresaw meant another twenty years. It was not likely that so long remained to him.

"Not half so long," he muttered, as he sat down again in his chair. He was feeling old and ill. The excitement had evidently played upon his nerves.

"I thought," he reproached himself, "I had more stamina. Naturally I should be disappointed; but this feeling of collapse and dread— It must be nerves."

He looked uneasily round the room. Something seemed pulling at his heart-strings—something that he could not see, or touch, or hear.

"It is an atmospheric disturbance," he pretended to believe. "Perhaps if I could remove it I might yet— I seemed to have allowed for everything."

He put his hand to his forehead and considered for a long time. The blue veins stood out on the pale, ascetic face, as he reworked the experiment in his mind.

Suddenly he gave a start, and a stifled cry. There was something in the room. He was in a cold sweat from strife with the invisible presence.

"It is the odour of the chemicals," he assured himself. "I never noticed it so strong before."

He rose hurriedly and stumbled to the door. When it was nearly closed he glanced over his shoulder, like a man who must look because he is afraid. There was nothing.

In the quaint, old-fashioned drawing-room he composed himself in the rocking-chair, and rang for some tea. When the housekeeper brought it, he kept her talking for half an hour, much to the worthy dame's surprise. He was all right, of course; it was only nerves. But he did not care to be alone. When she went, he took up the paper and tried to read, but could not find anything to interest him. "Eighty surrenders." Good news, but small. "Discovery of Ancient Pottery at Addington." What was the use of ancient pottery? "Von Kuren's Experiments." *That* should expel his fancies. What folly they were! *There was something in the room!*

Something! He could say no more of it. It touched no sense that he could name, appealed to nothing that he could think. It was just a presence.

"If I could only perceive it," he muttered excitedly. He was not afraid. No, no, not afraid! But his voice sounded almost like a sob. He rose with sudden decision, and returned to the laboratory. His armour to face the unknown was there, and he meant to face it.

He turned a strong electric ray into the receiver, and examined it with the microscope—vainly. He applied powerful acids with heavily gloved hands, but they found nothing. He covered himself in a strange insulating garment, and used great currents; but there was no result.

"If there is anything," he declared, "it must be in the receiver."

He rubbed his chin thoughtfully. Then he went to a cupboard and took out some clumsy spectacle frames without glasses, such as opticians use. He fixed curious transparent substances in them, increased the electric light, and peered into the funnel. There was nothing there—nothing. He turned impatiently away. . . . What was that mark on the floor?

He stared blankly for a moment laughed hysterically.

"It is—a shadow," he said. "Just a shadow. When I move the light it will go."

His hand trembled so that for a moment he could not raise the glowing bulb. He set his teeth, picked it up, and waved it over his head. The shadow did not stir! He stood the lamp down, and staggered to a chair. The shadow followed him. He took off the strange spectacles to avoid seeing it; but he knew it was coming upon him. When he put them on again it was hovering by his side; a black shadow, twice the bigness of a man's hand. He spoke to it, entreated it, but it did not answer. He struck at it, but it clung to his hands. He turned from it, but it crept round him!

"My God!" he cried. "My God!"

## II
### THE ERROR IN THE FORMULA

*From Professor John Flint to his friend and fellow scientist, Herr Karl Von Kuren.*

"Your observations upon my unfortunate experiment are marked by even more than your usual insight and brilliancy. I pay you the best compliment by deferring reply until I have given them adequate consideration. Meanwhile I write to ask your help.

"Since I succeeded in ridding myself of the lunar influence, which so unexpectedly threatened me, I have been haunted by a fear that the matter is not yet at an end. Lest you should think this foreboding merely the result of disordered nerves, I will state the case exactly as it presents itself to me.

"The object of my researches was, as you are aware, the study of the lunar inhabitants, of whose existence we are both convinced. The quasi-electrical signalling, upon which you and other experts rely, seemed to me inadequate. Granted that, in the course of generations, you established an alphabet of signs, and built the signs into a rudimentary speech, no real first-hand knowledge of lunar life would be obtained.

"The bodily transfer of beings from one world to another, if ultimately feasible—which I doubt—is not, at present, within practical range; but I deemed it possible to create upon earth what would be virtually a being of the moon. If I could capture the principle, or form, of lunar life, which would certainly be some kind of undulation or vibration, it would probably select for itself a suitable habitation, since earthly elements are not very different from those of the moon. I therefore aimed at this.

"My experiment divided into three portions:—

"(1) To ascertain the lunar 'life wave.'

"(2) To devise an apparatus to absorb it, much as the earth absorbs solar heat.

"(3) To re-embody the 'wave' in terrestrial material.

"The result of my experiment proves that the wave formula differs little from that which I communicated to you some months since. The difference, though slight, was material. It rendered the receiving apparatus incapable of holding the 'waves' after the failure of my attempts to transfer them to an earthly body. Hence the 'black shadow,' as I have called it, escaped, invisible to ordinary sight, but distinguishable by my lunar lenses, invented for a different object.

"Since I succeeded in severing the connection of this 'shadow' with myself, a disturbing reflection has occurred to me, viz. that only a human organisation can here support a principle of intelligent life. Consequently, this poor spirit seeks to dispossess some human soul from its body. Now that I have driven it away, it is out in the world seeking whom it may devour. It is my duty to prevent harm to an innocent person even by the sacrifice of myself.

"I am, for the moment, too unbalanced to approach the question with the power of thought which it requires. Our friendship has, I hope, a human as well as a scientific aspect. Will you, my dear Von Kuren, come over and help me?"


## III
### THE DARK LIGHT

The birds were singing, and the little brook was babbling and glistening beyond the trees. The roses made a glory of red and white and sweet odour along the avenue, and the blue sky was faintly flecked with white. Professor Flint saw none of these things as he rode up to The Laurels. And Mrs. Thornton, who came to meet him at the open door, did not notice that in the last few days his grey hair had become almost white.

"I knew you would come," she said, with a choke in her voice. "She has been asking for you again." He nodded, and his keen old eyes flickered.

"How is she?" he inquired. Mrs. Thornton turned her face away. He could see the tears on her cheek. "Surely not worse?"

"She is dying!" cried the mother. "Dying! My little girl!" His lips moved, but no words came. So he took her hand and held it for a few seconds. They did not look at one another.

"Little Vera!" he murmured at last. The voice did not sound like his own.

"She was always so fond of you."

"Ah!" he groaned. "And I— My will would show—but it does not matter now." Mrs. Thornton shook her head. There comes a time when things on which we have set store matter so little. "When did it begin?"

"The day before yesterday; about three in the afternoon."

"Three in the afternoon," he repeated, mechanically.

That was when the shadow left him.

"She was playing in my room while I dressed. We had been talking about her birthday. She would be six next Saturday as you know."

"I had—sent to town—for something." The Professor's breath was short, and left gaps between his words.

"She expected you would. You have taught her to look for such things. 'There will be a present from the Professor, of course,' she had been saying."

"Of course," he said. "Of course." They were silent for a full minute.

"What form does the fever take?" he asked at length. Mrs. Thornton sighed wearily.

"The doctor thinks it is brain fever; but he does not seem to know."

"We must have a specialist."

"I have telegraphed to London for one: but if he does not come soon, I am afraid—" Her lips refused to say the words. "It is terrible to hear her raving."

"What does she rave about?"

"It is so vague and strange. I can scarcely tell you. Something is creeping upon her—frightening her—trying to steal her away, she says. She calls it the dark light."

"The dark light!" The Professor shivered.

"Sometimes she imagines that the moon and stars are calling her. You are ill, Professor."

"It—is—nothing." He paced up and down the room, muttering to himself. "Let me see her."

Mrs. Thornton rose, and he followed her unsteadily and slowly. His years had come upon him in the last few days. When they reached the landing they could hear the babyish voice babbling incoherently. When they opened the door she was tossing wildly upon the bed, and waving her round arms at nothing.

"I don't want to," she wailed. "It is my house, not yours. Take it away."

The Professor sat down by the bedside and held the child's hand. His own shook violently.

"What is it?" he asked. "Tell me, dear."

She stared with vacant eyes that grew gradually to understanding.

"Make it go away," she entreated. "Right away, Professor." She clung excitedly to his arm. "Ever so far."

"Yes, darling," he soothed her. "Yes."

"It s'an't have my nice room," she pleaded, "shall it?"

"No, dear," he promised. "No."

"Not my dolly. It mustn't hurt dolly."

"No, dear," he repeated. "No."

She laughed a pitiful little laugh that hurt them more than a cry.

"It s'an't have anysing. You'll send it away, tause it's frighted of you, isn't it?"

"Very frightened of me." He brushed the hair back from his forehead. The child looked over her shoulder, and clung still closer to his arm.

"You got to go, nasty sing," she declared, with simulated confidence. Then she buried her face in his sleeve.

"You's not frighted of it, is you?" she whispered. The Professor stiffened slowly.

"No," he said. His face was grave and stern. She drew a long breath of relief.

"*I* was," she said.

"Frightened of what?"

She looked up with dilated eyes.

"It will hear if we're not careful. I want to whisper."

He bent his grey-white head over the golden curls. The child put her lips to his ears, and her little arms round his neck.

"Don't tell anyone," she said faintly. "It is my shadow!"


IV

THE TWO LAMPS

For an hour after little Vera had fallen asleep on his arm the Professor sat motionless by the bedside. He feared to disturb the child, he said; and he could think as well there as anywhere else. The nurse went to lie down, and after a time Mrs. Thornton fell into a doze in the armchair. When she was quite asleep the Professor looked round stealthily several times. Then he drew from his pocket the spectacles that were not ordinary spectacles. Twice he half lifted them to his face and laid them down again. Suddenly he put them on.

For a moment he gasped. Then his breath came regularly and hard, like the thumping of an engine. Five—ten—fifteen—twenty minutes passed, and he had not stirred. At length he raised his hand slowly, like one feeling in the dark, and removed them. His eyes had the look of some hunted creature, and he hung his head. Nearly an hour went by in silence, except for the breathing of the sleepers and the audible beating of his heart. Then Mrs. Thornton woke. He drew his arm slowly from the sleeping child and rose.

"If the worst comes to the worst," he said, "I will try a remedy."

"Why not now?" asked the mother, quickly.

"It is dangerous."

"Anything," she said desperately. "Anything." He bowed.

"If need be—anything." He bent over the little one and kissed her gently. "Should the delirium return put a lamp in the library window—I can see it from my room."

"And then?"

"If it becomes very violent, and she shows signs of exhaustion, put two lamps."

"And if—if—" Mrs. Thornton turned suddenly to the mantel-piece and put her head upon her hands.

"Do not be afraid," he said earnestly. "She shall not die." At the door he turned again. "She shall *not* die."

Then he went.

When he arrived home he found a foreign telegram:—

> "Starting now. Do nothing rash.
> Von Kuren."

He smiled a faint smile.

"It is not rashness, but prudence, to be ready."

He went to his laboratory and arranged various apparatus, filled retorts with curious mixtures, and stood long phials of liquid at hand. Also he set the great cone facing the moon, and started the complex of wheels. When these things were done, he went to his

THE BLACK SHADOW

15

lonely dinner. During the meal he talked a good deal to the atten-
dant, which was strange; and he took a second glass of the old port,
which was stranger. Also he had the rose-shaded candles removed,
because they threw such long shadows. The man mentioned these
circumstances to the housekeeper later, and they concluded that
the master had something on his mind. "It is the child," the dame
said. "He was always so set upon her."

As the twilight came on the Professor retired to the laboratory,
giving directions that he was not to be disturbed. He sat at the
great desk, adding a few words to some notes, until he could no
longer see to write. Then he went to the window facing The Laurels.

It was the beginning of darkness, when a hush comes in the
air. An old man was lighting the lamps in the avenue. There was a
white spot on the gravel from the lamps at the front door of The
Laurels; and a faint glimmer on the shrubbery at the side. That
would come from the child's window. The end of the house facing
him was unlit as usual. They had used it rarely since his old friend
Thornton died.

"She is sleeping," he muttered. "Sleeping. Perhaps I have drawn
it away." He put on the strange spectacles and looked round the
room. The black shadow was not there. He sighed with mingled
regret and relief. Presently he put his elbows on the tall window-
sill and placed his hands together as if he prayed.

The darkness grew darker. He could no longer see the house—
only the lights. The slow old man had reached the lamps in the
road and gone by. Spots like glow-worms came out on the left from
the distant village. Quivering specks of fire were growing in the
skies above. There was a pale brightness on the fields to his right,
where the moon was commencing to shine, and a feeling of thunder in the air. He opened the window to let in the scented breeze.
There was a soft sighing of the trees outside, and down the lane
some shepherds were singing on their way home.

"She is better," he told himself. "She must be better. There is
no light."

The moonshine crept slowly across the green cornfields and
the white cottages. It glimmered in the pool among the elders, and

lit up the white Cupid, standing one-legged on the fountain at the bottom of his garden. He always set it playing for the child when she came. She loved to watch the spurting water, and to catch the spray upon her laughing, upturned face and rosy cheeks. The Professor sighed again.

The sound of an organ came faintly, and then the voices of singers. They were practicing for Sunday in the village church. If the child was awake, she would be glad to hear them. She "made-believe" that it was the singing of pretty little white-robed angels, she had once told him. She was full of dreams—full of dreams. They go with golden hair and pale blue eyes, and the loneliness of an only child. This "dark light" that she spoke of, what was it but a fancy of hers—and his? When she was better—

There was a light in the library window!

The Professor nodded calmly several times, and walked over to his apparatus. He adjusted a few wheels, tested a few coils, mixed a few liquids, moved a stand a quarter of an inch, and an index the breadth of a hair. Then he returned to the window, and fixed his eyes upon the dim light afar. Beyond, in the darkness, he seemed to see the child tossing and waving her arms, fighting with a shadow. It was, he thought, the shadow of the great valley—but not for her.

It was hard to die so soon. A week ago he had seemed to himself a young man, though his beard and hair were grey. There was the great work so near its finish; and the essay for the Royal Society, that promised so well. The next few years were to complete so much that he had begun. His death would be a loss to science. Everybody would call it a loss.

A loss to science was a loss to the whole world. Compared with this, what was the life of a child? Nothing! He laughed at his own answer.

"Everything," he said, softly, "to her mother and to me." Also there was the dead friend who had left them to his care.

But was there need of any sacrifice at all? Why should she succumb to this invisible foe? It was only the substance of a shadow. If she held out till Von Kuren came, perhaps he would find a way!

A flickering glow appeared behind the far-off light. He raised himself a little on his hands. . . .

There were two lamps in the window!

## V

### THE PASSING CLOUD

The child's delirium had grown to a frenzy. It was dying out from sheer exhaustion now. The cries had ceased to be passionate, and were only frightened. The mother sobbed fearlessly, and kissed the hot, restless hands between each outburst. The little one was sinking fast, the nurse said. The specialist could not arrive till the early morning; and, in spite of the signal, the Professor had not appeared.

"Take it away," pleaded the faint voice. "Oh, mamma, take it away. Take it away!"

"God of mercy!" prayed the mother. "She is all I have left. My child! my child!"

Still the quavering voice went on. "Take it away! Take it away!" But the words grew fainter and fainter, till they could scarcely hear them. Once they feared that the laboured breathing had stopped, and bent over her; but she roused again.

"The light!" she cried. "Want the light!"

They thought that she tried to point to the window, so they pulled up the blind. She lifted her head a little, and fixed her eyes upon the side window, where she liked to stand and wave her handkerchief to the Professor. He was the slave, he used to say, of the flag.

The moonlight was bright upon his house, and its five quaint gables stood out clear against the hills beyond. A heavy cloud was driving over The Laurels, and the shrubbery and lawn were in shadow—dark as ever a shadow could be. Vera tried to sit up, and her mother raised her on her arm.

"See!" cried the child, pointing with her small hand. "The dark light! It is here." The shadow crept from the lawn to the privet hedge. "He is calling it. Make it go. Make it go!"

"It is a cloud, darling—only a cloud!"

"No, no; it is the dark light. Send it away."

The shadow crept on to the brook, and the dance of the moon-beams on the rippling waters disappeared. The child clapped her hands.

"You must go, dark light," she called, with sudden energy. "You must go! The angels are here!" On the window-sill, and the light green shrubs, and the close-cut lawn the pale moonlight appeared.

"Go sleep, mamma," she said, drowsily. "Dark light all gone. Not come *any* more." She sank back on the pillow, and the nurse darted forward and looked at her.

"Oh, thank Heaven!" she cried. "Thank Heaven! The child will live!" Then she went over to the window to hide her unprofessional tears. Presently Mrs. Thornton went and stood beside her and held her hand.

Out in the night the black shadow crept away—away till the Professor's house was swallowed up in the darkness.

There was a rumbling in the distant hills. It grew nearer. Presently there came a mighty clash of thunder, and a great light.


VI

THE COUNTRY OF GOD

*From Karl Von Kuren to Gustave Jeike, Professor of Philosophy at Munich. {Translated literally from the German.)*

"I have somewhile delayed thy much valued letter to answer. There are times when the soul-bitterness beareth not telling, and thy kindly meant congratulations have deepened the bitterness, dear friend.

"Truly, success in a measure has crowned my life endeavour; but set, like a palisade, before me is a not-to-be-passed limit. The greatness of what is done is dwarfed by the greatness that might have been.

"As in my former letter recounted, the Professor Flint was bodily uninjured by the lightning stroke, and his marvellous instrument happily escaped. Only the mighty intellect that made him master of us all was gone. He spoke the gibberish of an unknown speech, fragments of which, for future study, I have retained in phonographic record. Also had changed his nature that aforetimes always was gentle and kind. Wherefore all living creatures were to be removed from his hand. Especially was he antipathetic to the before-mentioned little maiden, whom, by his will, whereof I am executor, he held in great regard. He was, dear friend, the body of John Flint, with the soul replaced by a lunar soul!

"To solace my mind, by these untoward happenings much distressed, I prosecuted in his house my researches in stellar and lunar signalling, even to noised-abroad result.

"Upon him these experiments had a strange effect. He became docile, and would sit by the instruments with his ear against the Flint-receiver, to the use of which, for other purposes intended, I attribute my success. In some unexplained way his presence there aided the communication. I can only suppose that the spirit which inhabited his body had power to draw the lunar rays.

"Never-to-be-forgotten results were approaching when it became plain that the principle which animated him would destroy the frail body, unless speedily set free. The way to release it had become evident; whereupon there was the faint hope that the soul, formerly so revered, might reappear. But the greatness of my experiments would be gone.

"This, then, was my dilemma. On one part the certainty of between-world communication, such as had never been dreamed. On the other the bare possibility of rescuing a soul straying homeless and hopeless in space.

"I will not pretend to thee to whom my thoughts are known that I weighed these things in a balance. The World Disposer will give in His good time such wisdom as it is meet for us to know. Meanwhile, He places men's souls in this sphere for some not to-be-laid-aside end. Also, the soul was my friend's soul. Of these things I will write no more.

* * * * *

"At the end of my experiment I feared that no friendly spirit had replaced the spirit released; but slowly he came back to life. To-day he can even sit up in bed, and to thee most kindly greetings doth send. First of all he asked for the maiden, and she is sitting by him now, holding his hand. To me she hath a childish toy given, for that I am the good doctor who her uncle—so she calleth him—made sound again; and this I shall ever hold dear.

"He is smiling as I write, and disposing events in his old impulsive way.

"'To-day,' he says, 'we will play. Tomorrow the world of science!'

"But the world of science has only to-day. To-morrow is the country of God!"

# OUT OF THE DEEP

The Adolf Karl brought the first news of the evil that had come upon the earth. She was a Norwegian timber-ship, and a coal-brig running from Newcastle found her waterlogged in the North Sea, and towed her to port. There were only two tall, light-haired sailors left alive. The older man said one phrase over and over again, and nothing else. "Fishes—fishes! O Lord, the devils of fishes!" The younger sailor kept laughing and sobbing, and clasping and unclasping his hands for hours after he came ashore; but by degrees they got a rambling narrative from him.

He said that a great company of big fishes had come out of the sea in flying machines, and taken and eaten the rest of the crew; but he and the other man had hidden under an old sail. The sea-devils, as he called them, had pulled up the decks and torn open the storehouses, and eaten all the food aboard except a few fragments of biscuit. He and the other mad had lived on these for two days till they were rescued. He shivered and clung to those around him whenever he saw a bird flying in the air, thinking it was a sea-devil afar.

The old-fashioned papers ignored the wild story, and merely said that the men had lost their reason through privations; but the halfpenny papers happened to be short of news. So they expanded it into two or three columns, with glaring headlines. They pointed out, also, that three other ships reported having seen afar "enormous flocks of enormous birds," and that nearly twenty vessels were overdue at East Coast ports. This was on Thursday, 26th July, 1906.

On Friday, the P. & O. *Alamanzar* drove ashore near Plymouth, with the furnaces just burnt out. There was no one aboard, and no feed except in the refrigerators. Her decks, upper and lower, were burst open. It was noticed that all the planks were broken upwards.

A question upon the subject was put to the Home Secretary in the House of Commons that night; but the Home Secretary considered that the matter came within the province of his Rt. Hon. friend the First Lord of the Admiralty, and his Rt. Hon. friend had "no official knowledge of the matter."

On Saturday morning the *Maplin Castle* came in at Southampton with only a third of her passengers and a fifth of her crew remaining. They told a plainer tale.

They were nearly two days out from Madeira, they said, and two from home, when what appeared to be a cloud of remarkable blackness and size was observed ahead. The captain, who had been forty years at sea, had never seen anything like it, and feared a hurricane. In about half-an-hour, it was close upon them, and looked more like an incredibly great swarm of large black birds.

At this time a multitude of huge fishes, with six wings, three on each side, began to show themselves upon the surface of the sea. The cloud proved to be composed of similar monsters flying by machinery, and with a paddle-wheel arrangement, revolving with enormous velocity, on each side of their heads. Professor Thorne, who was aboard but did not survive, surmised that these were contrivances for supplying their gills with oxygen from the air to enable them to breathe in our thin atmosphere.

As they bore upon the ship, the fishes in the water rose and joined them. The crew and a few of the male passengers prepared to resist them with hatchets and revolvers. The rest rushed to their companions. While they blocked one another in their struggles to get down, the fishes angled for them with lines which seemed to adhere to whatever they touched. The majority of the passengers were borne shrieking into the air and devoured, before the remainder succeeded in closing the entrances. The crew, and the bolder passengers who had joined them, suffered still more severely. Meanwhile the captain had ordered full speed ahead; and as the pace proved too great for the monsters, the vessel ultimately escaped. The third officer brought a piece of one of the "fishing-rods," which was broken in a door when it was closed. Major Dunne shot its owner in several places, and the beastly creature fell upon the deck, but two other "fish-devils" had carried it away. The rod was made of a curious, flexible metal unknown to science, but akin to iron. It was apparently used to transmit some attractive force, for it had no adhesiveness in itself.

A dozen torpedo-boat-destroyers were at once sent out to scour the seas. Two only returned. The *Leopard* reported having put a head of some five thousand sea-devils to flight with its quick-firing guns as they were rising from the sea. The *Myra* had been attacked by a multitude flying overhead, and half the crew, including the commander, seized and devoured; but ultimately escaped by its speed. Portions of the deck and bulwarks had been torn away by the fishing-rods.

The *Myra* returned on Monday, 30th July. On the next day cablegrams reached England that several villages on the Bay of Biscay had been attacked by the sea-devils, and nearly all the inhabitants carried off. The following morning Lisbon, and several other Portuguese and French ports were reported devastated. The evening papers had huge placards:

BRIGHTON, HASTINGS, AND PLYMOUTH
ATTACKED BY SEA-DEVILS.
CHANNEL FLEET DESTROYED.
INDIA AND CHINA INVADED.

After that there were no newspapers.

A continuous service of trains was run night and day from the Southern Coast to London; and trains left London every few minutes for the Midlands, with every carriage and truck carrying double its proper number. Seats were booked for a week ahead. It was understood that millions of monsters were making their way slowly to London, clearing out every town and village as they came. People who could not get in the trains left in carts or on foot.

The Government sent officers down to the coast to report, but none returned; and telegraphic communications was rare. Wires came, however, to say that the monsters were approaching from Hythe, Chatham, and Ashford. It was pretty well established that all the towns on the South Coast were destroyed, and some on the East, and in the North of Scotland; and there was an authenticated statement that a cargo of refugees had arrived from Holland, and stated that the country was completely wiped out. We knew these things from "town criers" sent round by the Home Office. They ceased to come round on August 8th.

The next morning, I walked along the Strand, and saw two shops open, and counted eighteen people. The buses and cabs had long since departed with passengers inland. I stayed in town myself because I had no money, and could live gratis at the deserted restaurants. In one of them I met a slight, ladylike girl. She had no money either, she said, and no friends in town, and she was very frightened. We kept together afterwards. Her name was Elsie, and she was twenty-two. She had been a typewriter before business stopped. We joined company with a man and his wife for two days. They had three children, they told us, and had sent them to Derby in a County Council train. The Council ran forty a day for children only, before the train service ceased. They could not get in the trains themselves, and the woman was weak and could not walk far. On the third day the man found a wheelbarrow and took her off in it. We never thought to ask their names.

On the 10th August we met a wild-eyed man running in the Mall. He would hardly stop to speak to us. He had come from Wimbledon, he said, and the air was thick with the sea-devils there. A woman who came on a horse told him that they were breaking open every house systematically, and gathering up the people and cattle. They seized her father just as he had placed her on the horse. Elsie and I decided to go inland on foot the next morning. We had found money in some of the empty houses, and we thought that with that and a bag of provisions we could live on the road.

We slept at the Army and Navy Club that night, as we had done for two days previously. There were five old officers there, but they were hospitable, and placed two rooms at our disposal. They'd never run away from anything yet, they said, and they were too old to learn sense. Four of them played Bridge all day, while the fifth, in turn, kept guard at the front door with a revolver to stop the three club servants who remained from flight.

Elsie woke me by banging at my door at about seven o'clock.

"They're coming," she cried. "They're coming, Fred!"

"Run!" I shouted. "Don't wait for me. Go up Shaftesbury Avenue. I'll catch you!"

When I had dressed, however, I found her waiting outside the door; and when I reproached her, she smiled and tucked her arm in mine.

"I thought we'd make a better dish together," she said with a little laugh—and a little shudder.

The veterans were growling in the front hall because the cook had escaped out of a window. We advised them to fly, but they said they might as well be eaten if they would get nothing decent to eat; and they were going to stop and have a final hand of Bridge. So we left them.

We had intended going North, but there were black objects in the sky in that direction. So we made for Charing Cross. The morning was exceedingly dull. It was probably raining; but I do not remember.

When we came to Trafalgar Square we found that the black things were converging upon it from every point of the compass, and driving in the remnants of humanity from the outskirts of London. There were more left than I thought, perhaps five thousand in all. A shrieking mob was rushing up Whitehall, and another along Northumberland Avenue, and another down the Strand, and another down St. Martin's Lane. In the air behind each crowd, and from every other direction, came troops of the sea-devils. The foremost were so near that we could hear their breathing-wheels and distinguish a white line of teeth in their heads. We stood still and gazed helplessly at them.

"It is the end," Elsie said. "You—you have been good to me, Fred." She touched my shoulder softly with the side of her head. It is strange, the power of little things—an old phrase—a glance—the breath of a woman's hair. If she had not done that I should have stood rooted there till we were taken. As it was I caught her by the hand and pulled her along.

"The National Gallery!" I cried, "They may want to preserve it as it memorial of our art—who knows?" I chuckled a metallic chuckle. "Run!"

We knew that a lower door was open, as we had been in there the day before. We reached it just as the forerunners of the crowds came to the square. There was a dark shadow over the doorway; the shadow of an overhanging monster. Its wings were making a slow, clapping clatter as it descended, and the whirr of its breathing-wheels was loud in our ears. Elsie gasped, and staggered. I seized her in one arm, and carried her to the door and fumbled at it. It was perhaps two seconds before I turned the handle the right way. It seemed hours. My teeth chattered, and my hands trembled so that I could scarcely fasten the door.

We wandered aimlessly through the galleries and tried to talk about the pictures, but our words broke all in the middle. At last we stood still, holding one another's hands. Elsie's face was ashy white; and I felt cold and moist and sick.

"We'd better hide in a cellar," I suggested. "They mightn't find us there."

"Anything is better than waiting like this," she said suddenly. "Let's look out and see what they are doing."

We found a room, at the end of the water-colours, looking into the Square, and stood in the corner behind a screen, and peered round it. Sometimes when I am in the middle of a jest the scene comes back to me and I am struck dumb. Sometimes Elsie will pause in her laughter, as she plays with her baby, and put her face in her hands; and it is years ago now.

The crowd had huddled together in the Square and the empty basins of the fountains—a sea of white upturned faces, with the statues in between. A few—very few—were screaming. A few were laughing insanely. Others were contorting their fines horribly. Some had fainted, but still kept their feet, wedged in by the crowd.

Most of the women had their heads on men's shoulders. Some held children in their arms.

A guard of the sea-devils had settled on the roadways round the Square. A countless multitude were poised in the air overhead. It was proved afterwards that there were some twenty varieties, but they all looked of one devilish pattern—fishes, about ninety feet long, with disproportionately large heads and disproportionately short, broad tails. They were covered with blackish-green scales that looked like armour. They had light-green, phosphorescent eyes, about twice the bigness of a liner's port-hole, and terrible mouths, ten or twelve feet wide, shaped like a shark's, and showing immense jagged teeth. Their scales crackled and rustled as they moved.

The front half of their body was girt with a framework of black-grey metal, since called *marium*. It extended along their backs towards the tail, like a skeleton deck. This deck carried three pairs of wings with marium ribs, and an inky-black membrane stretched between. The front of the framework supported the breathing-wheels, or artificial gills, as they are accepted to have been. These were composed of concentric circles of a substance now termed *pelagium*, which scientists say is neither metal nor nonmetal, but a new class of element. Each circle revolved upon that within it, so that the velocity of the outer circle was enormous. The outermost layer was a soft leathery material, which has been named *philoxon*, from its extraordinary powers of drawing the oxygen from the air. The few remains of this, however, were so charred by combustion that nothing definite can be said about it. The "fishing-line" was a thin, flexible, marium rod, which operated from the front of the "deck," and was coiled there when not in use. It was about two hundred feet long, and the thickness of a very stout clothes-line.

How this machinery was controlled, or how it had been made by these creatures, who had no members, like our hands, capable of graduated pressure and contact, remains unknown. Most people, however, accept the conjecture of the learned Von Raben, that they manipulated matter by means of what he termed "piscian magnetism"—a force generated by the fishes themselves, and which they were able to graduate and control, to the finest degree. The experiments upon the scales of the monsters (which ended with his unfortunate death) proved that when electrically stimulated in a certain manner, some portions of a scale would attract, and others repel, and so work a wire, or a thin plate of metal into various shapes—portions being held firmly, while the neighbouring parts were driven away. So that each scale was virtually a many-fingered hand.

As we watched the monsters, the long fishing-rods came slowly forth, wavered in the air, dipped among the crowd, that ceased to sway, as if fascinated. There was a shriek—shriek upon shriek—men, women, and children were lifted up in the air as if they were bound to the fishing-lines, though there was no visible means of attachment. Some of them hung limply; others beat at it with their hands—and could not draw them away again. Then it carried them to the shark-like mouth.

Elsie buried her face under my jacket, and we shrank behind the screen. The shrieks grew fewer and fewer. Presently they ceased. Then a series of crashes began. I laid Elsie down (she had fainted) and peeped round the screen again. The long metallic lines were tearing out the windows and sides of the houses across the Square, by adhering to them and pulling them outwards, and searching the premises. Now and then one brought out a man or a woman. They would fish for us, I thought, next.

I lifted Elsie up and staggered away to the galleries, till I came to the end room of the Dutch-Flemish school. I pulled a big screen covered with small pictures close to the wall, and sat huddled on the floor behind it, with her head on my knee. We were just under a man's portrait by Rembrandt, with a painting of a fish and poultry shop beside it. I have forgotten the name of the painter, and I would not, for worlds, go there again to look. I listened with my ear against the wall for the approach of a clinging line; but I heard nothing. Possibly they wished to preserve some specimens of our art, for throughout the country they did very little damage to churches, museums, or galleries.

A lean, half-starved cat came round the screen and mewed piteously. I screamed aloud at the sound. Then I held my breath, wondering if *they* had heard. A spider made its way slowly down a cobweb, and dropped on the floor. I could hear it drop, everything was so still. I shook Elsie to try and rouse her, to hear her voice. I half rose to fetch some water to restore her, but sat down again. Her unconsciousness was so merciful! I stroked her face gently. She had been so cheerful, and so contented, and so kind. Poor little Elsie! There was a sound of distant thunder outside, and a flash of light invaded the darkness. I saw the cat standing there with its back arched. I called to it, "Puss, puss." There was another flash and rumble. Elsie sighed, turned her face a little closer against my hand, and looked up.

"Are—we—dead?" she asked in an awed, halting whisper. "Dead?"

I told her briefly what had happened. She was silent till another flash startled her.

"I thought they were coming," she whispered. "If they took us it would be over. I must see what they are doing. I *must!*"

"Very well," I agreed dully. It did not much matter, I thought. Nothing mattered. I lifted her on her feet and half carried her to the stairs that led down to the Turner water-colours. There was a good view of the Square from there, and we stood some way back, a few steps down the stairs.

It was thundering heavily now, and jagged streaks of lightning were darting across the yellow sky. The rain was pouring down in streams. The sea-devils were bellowing to one another. I could not tell whether in pleasure or fright. Some were marshalling the rest, and those on the ground were rising into the air. One stared in at our window as he passed, but he did not pause. His eyes looked like great green lamps. The bellowing grew louder and more urgent, and the rain became so heavy that one could scarcely see through it. Then a sea of light covered the place, and a hurricane of thunder. The windows shivered in fragments, and the wet air rushed in. Nelson's Column tottered. I was blinded and deafened for a few moments. When I could see again the Column was down and the monsters were falling headlong on the Square and the houses. In a few seconds the place was heaped with their mangled remains. I thought I was mad or dreaming, because I heard no sound as they fell; but when I did not hear my own laugh, I knew that I was still deaf. We stood staring at the ruins—staring—staring!

"God has delivered us!" Elsie said at last—her voice sounded faint and a long way off. "God!"

"God!" I echoed—He had been only a name to me—before.

We stood looking out of the window in silence for a long time. The yellow fog melted away and the sun came out and the sky was blue. Then Elsie borrowed my handkerchief and wiped her eyes. "'If only we could forget," she said. "If only we could forget!"

We went back to the galleries. A dozen dead and mutilated monsters lay in them. The glass roofs were broken where they fell in, and most of them had crashed partially through the flooring. It shook as we walked over it; but we had been too frightened to fear any more. We found some biscuits and tinned meat and brandy and water in a room below, and ate and drank and washed. Then we slept for it couple of hours; till Elsie woke and woke me.

"They are all dead everywhere," she said confidently. "Let us go."

She tidied her hair with a brush and comb that she always carried, and put her hat straight before a glass. There was a pink bow at her neck, and she retied it carefully. I laughed suddenly—a jarring, unmirthful laugh.

"I thought the whole world was altered," I said; "but you are still a woman."

She drew a slow, deep breath.

"I suppose it *is* foolish," she said, "but I don't like you to see me look as if—as if I didn't care how I looked to you."

I took her hand and we went out. We found every way blocked with the corpses of the sea-devils. After several attempts to find a passage through, we decided to climb over them. It was then that we learnt that the scales were not armour, but tough hide, like that of a hippopotamus. We climbed by holding on to the metal framework, and finding footholds in the crinkly hides. I mounted first and pulled Elsie after me, and lowered her down before me.

The air was full of a fishy odour, and we felt faint. We thought at the time that this was due to the smell; but now I believe it was owing to the partial exhaustion of the oxygen of the air by the breathing-wheels. A few that were not broken or hampered still revolved slowly, and one or two of the monsters were breathing feebly. Their hides rose and fell a foot or so as we walked over them. Some of the "fishing-lines" were dangling in the air. One of them touched Elsie's dress, and I had to cut a piece with my penknife to get her away. She pinned the skirt carefully together to hide the rent. The green eyes were all open, and some blinked at us helplessly, malevolently. The journey across the Square was a waking nightmare of three hours, from one till four. In Pall Mall East we had to climb over several more dead monsters that lay across the road.

Dozens of the monsters were lying in St. James's Square. So many had fallen on the War Office that it was crushed like an egg-shell. The front of the club was broken out and none of our friends were left. The cards were scattered over the card-table, and on the floor there were a couple of cigar-cases. One of them bore the silver monogram—C. V.—of General Vine, the courteous, bent old warrior, who had invited us in as we wandered by.

We found food and drink in the basement, and laid down and slept. We did not wake till early in the morning. I put on some clean clothes that were lying in a dressing room, and Elsie found a new dress in a house in Pall Mall. Her hat did not match it, she said with a sigh. We took some money, in case there was still use for money in any part of the world. Also we took a big bag of food. We could get water anywhere.

Then we wandered to St. James's Park. Dead monsters lay all over it. Their breathing-wheels were all still now, and smoking as if they burnt. The oxygen had doubtless set up combustion, when the creatures no longer assimilated it.

Buckingham Palace was a heap of bricks, and most of the houses down Buckingham Palace Road were ruins. We reached Victoria Station without meeting a soul. Elsie gripped my arm suddenly with both hands.

"Suppose," she cried, "there is no one left, but you and me? It is the end of the world!"

"The end of the world!" I echoed with a groan.

"There *must* be someone left," she said after a pause of frenzied silence. "There *must!* We will find them. Come!"

We went into the S. E. & C. Station. The roof was smashed in, and the whole station badly damaged. There was a heap of luggage on the platform, and a guard's cap. A little further on there was a child's ball and doll. Elsie picked up the doll and kissed it. I did not look at her, but walked away down the long, main-line platform.

About, fifty yards beyond the platform there stood a solitary engine and tender. I walked out to them and inspected them while I waited for Elsie. The boiler, I saw from the gauge, was full of water, and the furnace was laid. I lit it, and we stood on the platform till there was enough pressure to start. Then I turned the steam on cautiously and we went forward at six or eight miles an hour. Luckily the points were set to a clear road out of the station. We passed slowly over the bridge (the river was full of the bodies of the sea-devils), through Battersea, Clapham, and Brixton. There was no sign of life anywhere, not even a dog, or a cat, or a bird.

"There is no one left," Elsie said. "No one. I used to think people uninteresting, and now—and now—"

"We shall find them presently," I assured her; but I doubted it.

We passed Herne Hill and came to the long-gardened houses of Dulwich. There was a tent and a table laid with an unfinished meal in one. In another a bicycle was turned upside down for cleaning.

"That is Thurlow Park Road," I said, "where the station is. I used to know the man that lived there."

"Call to him," she suggested. "The people may be only hiding."

I stopped the train and shouted. Elsie cried out at the sound of my voice. We had spoken under breath for the last two days. There was no answer.

"Call again," she implored.

I shouted wildly; but there was only the echo in reply. The she called in her clear, high voice:

"People! Dear people! The monsters are dead—dead! We are friends—friends to everybody in the world—. They are all gone. And they live; and loved. Fred, we are all alone!"

"Perhaps—" I began; but she looked at me, and the hopeful words died on my lips. "If there is only me," I said, "I shall be good to you, Elsie."

"Oh, *yes!*" she cried. "It isn't *that!* I am glad it is you. Only let us go on."

We went slowly on till the houses grew fewer and the country more open; and still we saw no one—nothing—alive; only the dead monsters lying here and there.

Then we saw the Medway like a silver snake afar. At about three we came to Rochester Bridge Station. The water was getting low in the boiler and we were tired of standing on the platform. So we got out and walked on to the public bridge, and looked up and down the river. There was no smoke from the tall chimneys, or from the dockyard at Chatham below; no sound or movement anywhere. There were boats at the pier and boat raft, barges at anchor or run ashore; but no crew to any one. Great black bodies were floating on the tide. A number of them had jammed and blocked up two spans of the bridge.

We wandered along the banks of the river, and up into the Borstal Road. We found a house that had a couple of bed rooms undamaged, and stayed there for the night. The stillness was terrible—terrible! There was a half packed portmanteau in one room, and a litter of children's playthings in another. Some leaden soldiers were set out for a mimic battle. Elsie told me she should never smile again.

In the morning, however, she found a hat that matched her costume, and came down to the dining-room to show me.

"We *must* find people," she said with a gay little laugh, "if it is only to admire my hat. Oh! but she who wore it—she who wore it!"

She flung it suddenly on the ground and buried her face in her hands. I picked it up and put it on her.

"It makes you look nice," I said. "You are all I have to look at now, you know."

She put on the hat silently, and we went out together. As she passed the hall mirror she glanced at it and took my arm.

"It *does* suit me," she said, "and—you'll like me to look nice, won't you, Fred?"

"You always look nice," I told her.

We tramped out into the country and saw two birds. They were ungainly, flapping rooks, but we watched them lovingly. The air was sweet, and the sky was blue, and the sun was shining.

Presently we tramped back to the town by way of Watts's Avenue. The rents in the houses, and a long row of water-carts—some of the shafts had been broken evidently in tearing out the horses—made us depressed again. We went down the Maidstone Road, into the High Street, and turned to the right. We went as far as Luton Road, and found no one. Then we turned back to Rochester. We raided a few shops, and I offered Elsie some jewelry; but she would not have it. It did not matter what she were now, she said.

"We shall find people further down the line," I declared.

"But they will be changed," she said. "Life will be different—everything will be different—no one will laugh or sing or smile—no one will care how anyone looks. But if only we could find a few people to cry with. Hark!" She clutched my arm.

We listened, and heard the sound of a man's voice afar. We took a hasty step forward. Then we stopped and looked at one another. It was a man's voice—and we feared!

"We must be careful," I warned her. "We do not know what manner of men they are. There is no law, no order, no police. We are in it state of nature."

"Yes, yes!" She clung to me. "We must be careful. But their 'nature' may be good."

I shook my head.

"In the state of nature," I told her, "life is solitary, hasty, brutish, and poor. Everyone takes what he wants, and keeps what he can."

"Fred " she whispered. "You won't let them take me!"

I smiled grimly and drew a revolver from my pocket. I had taken it from a shop in town some days before.

"Not while I live," I vowed fiercely. "What I have is mine!"

"Yes," she said quietly. "I am yours."

That was our love-making and our betrothal.

We walked stealthily down the street, keeping close under the houses, till we came in view of the courtyard outside the town hall. About two dozen people—men, women and children—were standing there. They looked hungry and travel-worn and fierce. A tall, gaunt clergyman was preaching.

"The Lord," he said, "has taken much; but He has left us one another. The Lord has swept away the past; but He gives us the future. The Lord has given us sorrow; but He gives us work. Dear friends, our work is to comfort and help one another. Let us begin. And now to God the Father—"

We came out from the shadow and stood with the others for the benediction. When it was finished, the clergyman held out his hand to us.

"Dear friends," he asked, "what can I do for you?"

"Marry us," I said.

And we knelt down in the square, and were married there and then; and when we rose and would have joined in the day's labours, the others pushed us laughingly away. We should not work on our wedding day, they vowed, and they would make ready a house for us. And we went and stood on the bridge, and looked up the river and down the river—on the ruins and the black monsters turning in the tide. And we smiled—and smiled.

To-day, though there are so few of us on earth—handfuls of men and women and children (and our children among them)—toiling in the ruins of town and country we have still a smile. For here on earth we have one another; and afterwards there is God!

# THE PINK MADNESS
## A STORY OF THE YEAR 1920

One by one those who saved the world from the Pink Madness have died at the hands of those whom they saved. I do not think that any one who knows the truth is left but myself, or any one who knows that I know; but I lie awake at night, hearing an assassin in the rattling of the windows and the creaking of the stairs. In case the fate of the others may fall upon me I write the story down for posterity.

It was a Wednesday morning early in August. I was sitting in a beach-chair on the crowded sands at Broadstairs. My children were paddling, and my wife was knitting beside me. I could hear the click-click of her needles as I dozed over my newspapers, and presently I heard the newspaper rustle from my hands. My wife woke me by clutching at my arm.

"Harry!" she cried. "Look!"

I blinked at the water for a moment. Then I rubbed my eyes sharply and sat up. I rubbed them again before I would believe them. A curious pale pink fog was closing in round the bay from every direction.

"It must be the wind, or the sun, or—something," I said doubtfully. I did not like the look of it.

"It isn't the wind," my wife cried, "or the sun. It isn't *anything* natural. Harry, the children!"

I stood up and looked more carefully. The pink fog, or whatever it was, was nearer than I had thought. The outskirts were barely half a mile away, and they were scurrying towards us, over the sea, like huge pink waves. A paler pink foam was rushing in front of them. People were gathering their children together and running from the sands. Some of them were joking, but the majority were evidently frightened. I ran down to the edge of the water and carried our two children back, one under each arm. Bob was seven and Francie was six. They cried at being taken from the water, but I quieted them with a promise of ices.

"It is only a mist," I assured my wife, "but it may be malarial. Don't stop to put on their shoes and socks. Come!"

I put Bob on my shoulder, and she carried Francie. We stumbled up the soft sand towards the steps, but could not get upon them on account of the crowd. Some of the people had lost their nerve and were pushing violently. Two or three children were hurt in the crush, and several women fainted. One had hysterics. In a few moments we were wedged in by people behind us pushing frantically towards the steps. I looked over their heads, being a tall man, and saw the pink foam coming across the shallows in great sheets over-running one another. Then it crept silently up the sand. My wife clung to my arm. Bob caught at my head and knocked my hat off. Little Francie clapped her hands and cried "Pretty!" In a few seconds the vapor ran over us, climbed the steps and spread over the people. Their faces, their hands, their clothes, all seemed to have turned pink. The bay, the pier, the sands, the white cliffs were all pink, too. There was a great shriek, and then a great silence. I expected to be choked, but I tasted nothing, smelt nothing, felt nothing.

"It doesn't hurt, anyhow," I said, drawing my breath. "There's nothing to be frightened of. It makes people look pretty, Francie, doesn't it?"

Francie clapped her hands again and laughed a shrill laugh. My wife laughed, too, strangely and uncontrollably. The sea of faces looking down from the steps was moving with laughter. There was something in the sight and sound of the laughter that made me shudder. Suddenly it stopped, and the people held their breath as if to listen. In my dreams I still look up and see the hundreds of expectant faces smiling strangely through the strange pink atmosphere.

"The music!" my wife cried. "Hark!"

"Music!" the boy on my shoulder shouted.

"Music, daddy. Pretty music!" Little Francie held up her chubby forefinger for silence.

"The music!" cried the crowd on the stairs. "The music!"

I looked round in bewilderment. There was no music that I could hear; but some were keeping time with their heads and others with their hands. Bob was drumming with his bare heels against my breast. Francie was beating time with her finger and my wife was swaying her as if to a tune. All the crowd were smiling foolishly, and the vapor was swirling round us in great pink waves. A woman collapsed on the coping just above me. Her eyes were closed, but she still nodded in time. Two old boatmen were dancing grotesquely on the pier—I could see so far through the pink clouds. The donkeys on the sands were braying and capering round in circles. The truth flashed upon me. Whatever the pink vapor was, and however it came, it sent living creatures mad! I had escaped for some reason that I did not know. I do not know now.

Presently the crowd began to move slowly up the stairs. I pushed my wife along with them. She still swayed to the music that I could not hear, and Francie jigged in her arms. Bob danced on my shoulder so that I could scarcely carry him. I was almost exhausted by the time that we reached the top, but my wife did not seem to feel the exertion, though she was a delicate woman.

The pink vapor covered the promenade. The clock tower, the bandstand, the shops and Bleak House on the cliff all looked pink through it. My wife rushed up to strangers and shook them by the hand; and they came and shook hands with us. Every one was smiling vacantly and babbling in an ecstasy of foolish delight. A "blessing" had come upon us, they said, and everything would be right for the rest of our days.

I got my wife and children back to our lodgings. They capered and sang all the way up the High street. The crowd going along with us were dancing and singing too. The woman of the house grinned and beat time when she opened the door. Her sleeves were tucked up. She had evidently gone mad at the washtub. When I asked for dinner she said she wasn't going to cook or work any more, only listen to the music. It was better than a hundred bands, she declared, and I must be stone deaf not to hear.

I went for a doctor, but he refused to come. There was no more work for doctors, he said. The pink vapor was the cure for all ills. The people in the shops had gone mad, too, and would not serve me. I could take what I liked, they said. There would be no more buying and selling now that the blessing had come. The trams had stopped. One place was as good as another now, a conductor told me. The railway station was deserted except for one old porter, who informed me that the trains had stopped running. He had been on the line for thirty-five years and heard nothing like the music, he declared, "and everythink sich a wonnerful color, sir! An all our aches gone!" I found later that the madness produced insensibility to pain.

I tried to wire to London for advice, but the telegraph office had closed. So I went back to the lodgings and persuaded my family to eat some food. Then I packed up some victuals and drink, and a few clothes, put them on a barrow that had been left in the street, and told my wife and children to come with me. I had decided to make my way inland, in the hope that we should escape from the pink vapor, and their reason would return.

We went up to St. Peter's Church, and along the country roads, towards Canterbury. I pushed the barrow, and my wife and children laughed and sang and gathered flowers. They made wreaths of poppies and cornflowers and wheat and put them on their heads and mine. I thought it best to humor them.

"We'll live in the country," my wife stated, "now that you won't have to go to that horrid office. There will be no more work or trouble. We shall all be happy."

She seemed to have grown very young and pretty. I thought then that the change was in her, but I learnt afterwards that it was only in the light. It made everything look different. The country people were dancing in circles, holding hands. My wife and children joined every party of dancers, and I had difficulty in getting them away. The day was hot, and the barrow was heavy to push. I grew very tired, and almost screamed with the horror of it.

At Monkton some people came out from a villa and dragged us in to a tea party. An old gentleman with white hair (it looked pink) made a speech. He wore a garland round his head, and smiled vacantly.

"All the days will be summer days," he said, "and all the summer days holidays, and all the holidays holy days," and he thanked God for the blessing that had come upon the world.

We walked some way beyond Grove Ferry that night. The children grew tired and we put them in the barrow. My wife helped me push it, smiling up in my face.

"It's absurd to take all this trouble, Harry," she declared, "because it doesn't really matter whether we are in one place or another now; but I'll humor you tonight. You have got so used to work that you can't leave off, but you'll soon learn to. How good it is to think that the little ones will never work, or worry, or feel pain!"

We spent the night in an open shed, covered with the rugs that I had brought. My family rested well, smiling in their sleep, but I could only doze. I was frightened by the pink moonshine that came streaming in upon us. The cursed vapor would go in the morning, I told myself; but the day dawned pink! Pink-blue in the skies, pink-white in the clouds, yellow-pink on the corn, a shimmer of pink-green on the grass and the leafy trees; and every face we saw was pink—and smiled insanely.

We reached Canterbury in the forenoon. The vapor was thinner there, and the madness took a milder form. A train had come down in the morning and brought the papers. The "blessing" had not reached London yet, the news agent told me; and the papers were enough to make a cat laugh. "They speak of it as if it were the plague, sir! Well, well! I suppose we shan't want newspapers any more. Please God, there's enough of it to reach London!"

I learnt from the papers that London was still sane, so I decided to get there as soon as possible. They were going to run a last train up, "to carry the good news," the station master told me. He was capering with delight on the platform, and he wore a garland in place of his uniform cap. They refused to take payment for the tickets, and crowded round us to shake hands before we left.

My wife and children sang and laughed at nothing. I sat in a corner and read my paper. I have the summary by me now.

A curious Pink Vapor which appears to produce mental aberration settled upon England yesterday morning. It has now attacked the whole of the South and East coast, and some parts of France, Portugal and Spain. Several deaths are reported to have occurred from overexcitement. The train and telegraphic services from the afflicted parts have stopped, and the reporters sent down to them have not returned. They are supposed to have been affected by the Pink Madness, as it is generally termed. (Page 3.)

We publish special articles by Dr. Thorne and Professor R. Smythe, F.K.S., upon the origin and nature of the Pink Vapor. The former ascribes it to volcanic eruptions of oxygenic gases. The latter attributes it to an upheaval from the bottom of the sea and to its volatilization by the sun. Both gentlemen ascribe the disturbing mental effects to the presence of a gas akin to etherine, the new anaesthetic produced by Dr. Long by the action of radium upon chloroform. (Pages 5 and 6.)

Dr. Long, who is considered by authorities the only person capable of coping with the epidemic, has disappeared and cannot be traced. When last heard of, three weeks ago, this eminent scientist was contemplating an excursion to some remote locality in order to pursue his experiments (which involve considerable risk) in seclusion. Any persons having knowledge of his movements are requested to communicate immediately with the Prime Minister. (Page 4.)

The hospital authorities are quite at a loss in regard to the treatment of the Pink Madness, but they believe that it is only a temporary "exaltation" which would soon cease upon the disappearance of the pink vapor. (Page 7.)

Three or four cases of persons unaffected by the vapor are reported. They include the Prime Minister, who was attacked at Seaford, but escaped in his motor-car. He is anxious that persons who have proved immune should communicate with him, in order that their services may be utilized in the event of the epidemic spreading. (Page 4.)

The pinkness of the air became paler and paler as we traveled up the line, and at Faversham we passed completely out of it. I cannot describe how beautiful the world looked to me in its homely brown and green. My wife and children, strange to say, did not seem to notice the change, and there was no improvement in their mental condition.

We were delayed at Sittingbourne for an hour. The driver of the Sheerness train had been attacked by the pink vapor at the Ferry, and had run past the signals into a goods train. The line was blocked by the debris. At Chatham we were overcrowded by people fleeing from the vapor, which was said to be coming up the river. We alighted at Herne Hill at four o'clock, and took a cab to our house at Tulse Hill. I obtained an evening paper, and learnt that the "Pink Madness" had appeared in Scotland and Ireland, and was spreading, from the Mediterranean, over Italy and the South of France. It had stopped the progress of the French expedition in Morocco, the two armies fraternizing and refusing to fight. There had been a number of wrecks through the fog and the delirium of the sailors. The P. & O. *Sahara* had run aground on Drake's Island, and every one on board was lost. The vapor had been analyzed and proved to contain a peculiar and concentrated form of etherine. It had been found that insensibility to pain was one of the features of the attack. The Prime Minister urgently entreated all persons who had proved immune to call upon him at once.

I should have gone that afternoon, but the behavior of my wife and children caused me great anxiety. Their gestures and antics and the wreaths of flowers which they wore, and would not remove without violence, attracted a crowd at Herne Hill; and my wife seemed quite incapable of attending to her household duties. If left to themselves they would probably have starved—as many who were attacked by the madness did. Our servants were away and I spent some hours in finding and engaging a charwoman.

They went to bed early, and after I had cleared away some of the litters (they got out everything they fancied and put nothing away) I retired also. I woke soon after two. The Venetian blinds were half opened, and the moonlight shone in through them—pink! I laid staring at it, with my lips moving dumbly, till the dawn. Then I drew up a blind and looked out upon a pink world. A rheumatic old watchman was dancing stiffly in the road.

The charwoman was affected like the rest, but not so violently. She seemed to have enough sense to get the meals. So I decided to go to the Prime Minister and offer my services. I impressed upon my wife that they must stay indoors till my return, and must take food and drink. She promised to do her best to remember. "But these little things slip my mind," she said. "It is so full of lovely thoughts! Do you think you could write it down on pieces of paper and pin them up where I shall see them?"

So I wrote the directions down and stuck them up in conspicuous places. Then I kissed my family and went. I little thought that I should not see them again for nearly two months.

All public conveyances had stopped running, so I walked up to Downing street. The Prime Minister saw me at once. He looked pale and worried, but he was very resolute to fight the evil.

"It is spreading very rapidly," he said. "I can only find fifty cases of immunity up to now; forty men and ten women. I propose that twenty men and the women should stop here to assist me, and that the other twenty should go in search of Dr. Long. I know nothing of any of you, so I am compelled to trust to blind instinct in selecting a leader. I select you. I think you have brains and courage."

"I have courage," I replied, "and I hope I have brains; but I have also a wife and children. If I leave them they may starve or do themselves a mischief."

"If this is not stopped," he retorted, "all the world will do itself a mischief or starve. The frenzy will increase till they die of sheer exhaustion—unless they starve first. No one is working. The food supplies for which we draw on all the world are not coming in. The police are mad like the rest. There will soon be no protection for life or property. My dear friend"—he leaned forward over his desk—"it rests with you and me to save the world. I must stay here and try to minimize the evil and keep them alive. You must go and fight the evil at its source. A naval officer and several sailors and stokers are available. You must take a torpedo boat and go instantly. Every minute is important. I will look to your family. You have my word. You will go?"

"Yes," I said. "Now tell me about it. What *is* the evil? How did it come? Where does it come from? What am I to do?"

"The evil is etherine. Dr. Long—who is half genius and half madman—discovered it in seeking for an anaesthetic which would destroy sensibility to pain without destroying consciousness. To the best of my belief he has deliberately loosed it upon the world with the idea of benefiting suffering humanity."

"But surely he could not generate this enormous quantity."

"Oh, yes! I saw an experiment of his on Windermere a month ago. An almost invisible particle of matter dropped on the water produced miles of pink cloud. He could do it; and he has. I have information that he is on one of the deserted islands of the Madeiras. Lieutenant Harrison, the young naval officer of whom I spoke, can find it.

"Long has about three assistants and half a dozen mechanics with him. I don't know how they make the stuff, but they fire it off from long stages running into the sea. We found the plans in his rooms. The vapor is formed when the etherine particles fall upon the water. I suppose the stages are used to avoid the risk of handling them, or of explosion when they are projected, but I don't know. Anyhow you must blow them up, and seize him and his followers. I don't suppose you will have much difficulty with them. They will probably be as mad as hatters. Long will be dangerously sane, I suspect. He's pretty sure to have protected himself from the vapor. From some notes that he left I gather that he can counteract it, if he will. I don't think he *will*, but you are a sensible man, Mr. Canning, and I can speak plainly to you, I think? Then I say that it is not, in my judgment, a case in which you should be over-scrupulous as to means, if you think you can induce him to undo the mischief."

He looked hard at me, under his eyebrows, and I nodded.

"I shall not be squeamish as to means," I promised grimly. I thought of my wife and children babbling vacantly.

"No! If they do not succeed, you can at any rate stop any further production of the pink vapor. You had better shoot him unless he will dissipate it. It would perhaps be best to shoot him even then. He will always be dangerous while he lives."

"I will shoot him," I promised, "but what good will it do, if the vapor is left?"

"I hope it will gradually die away if it is not reproduced. God and nature provide the remedy for most ills in time. May He reward you, if I am not here when you come back. If you do, we are friends and comrades for the rest of our lives, I think. Anyhow, I will look after your family. Now I will introduce you to your crew."

My followers appeared to be a very ordinary, average set of men, and I did not discover then, or afterwards, any special characteristics in them or others who escaped the madness—unless it was courage. They all had plenty of that, and they were young and well-disposed to every one but Long. They were very bitter against him.

"I see my pritty little donah ravin' like a maniac," one of the stokers said hoarsely. "An' if I lay my 'and on the man wot done it!" A young carpenter blubbered when he told me how his father, who was seventy-two, and had his own shop, and had always "been looked up to," was playing like a baby in the backyard.

The officer—Lieut. G. R. Harrison, R. N.—was a blue-eyed, frank-faced lad of two and twenty. I liked him very much. He had seen his "little mother" taken with the madness, and his gray-haired old father, the admiral, babbling like an imbecile, he told me; and whether we destroyed the vapor or not he wanted to shoot Long. "You don't know how I feel about it, sir," he said.

"I've seen my wife and children, Harrison," I told him. "Yes. We'll shoot him! But first we've got to save them and the world."

We went down to Portsmouth in motor cars, and arrived about five. Several torpedo boats were lying idle. Harrison selected the *Flight*, as it had the new electric engines, and would not require coaling, which would have been a great difficulty. There were plenty of arms on board, and we helped ourselves to whatever we wanted from the storehouses, which were left open.

We started at daybreak on Saturday morning. The dense pink atmosphere made navigation difficult, and Harrison stopped on the navigating platform for forty-eight hours without sleep. I scarcely saw him during this time, for I was down with seasickness, and so were those of the crew who were not sailors. We had recovered by Monday morning, when Harrison said that we were well over the Bay of Biscay. He had gone at full speed after we got out from the Channel, trusting that the sea would be clear of ships. On Tuesday morning he reckoned that we were within a hundred miles of Funchal, the capital of the Madeiras. I was standing on the platform with him when a vague shape loomed up ahead. It was about a mile off, he said, and that was as far as he could see. It turned out to be the Union Castle liner, *Sandwich Castle*. We hailed her with a megaphone, but obtained no answer. Apparently the passengers and crew had gone ashore at Funchal and abandoned her.

A few hours later the pink vapor grew denser. After we had run for half an hour at half speed it became so thick that we could scarcely see a hundred yards ahead. After another half hour it became like a thick pink wall, and we could not see from head to stern of the little vessel. Harrison reduced the speed to bare steering way, and we held a council with the crew.

"So far as I can make out, sir," Harrison said; "we are about twenty-five miles from the island we want; but I can't be sure to ten miles or so. We shan't see the land till we are aground. She is nothing but a thin plate of iron, and a touch will rip her. What shall I do?"

"How would it do to go on slowly for another ten miles, and then send a boat out to reconnoitre?" I suggested.

He shook his head. "It would never find us again."

"Then," I decided, "you must get the boats ready, and go on till we strike. At least, that's my view. It's life and death, boys, so you're all entitled to a vote."

The men looked at one another and then a huge navvy stepped forward.

"I vote as there ain't no votin'," he said. "Wot the cap'n sez is good enough for us, ain't it, mates?" The men cheered lustily and I shook hands with them one by one. There was a choke in my voice when I tried to thank them.

We went slowly on for four hours, running straight into the thickest of the pink vapor. It was so dense that one could almost feel it, and it had a sweetish taste. "Like laughing-gas," Harrison said.

The suspense got upon my nerves, and I was silent and gloomy, wondering what would become of my wife and children if I perished without executing my mission. Harrison and the crew, however, jested and laughed as if they were going to a picnic. I don't think they had more courage than I, but they had less foresight. Wisdom is the parent of fear.

We had some tea at five. Just as we had finished there was a grating noise; then a sound as of silk being ripped, only a hundred times louder. Then we stopped.

"She's got it," Harrison pronounced calmly. "She'll go down within five minutes. Lower the boats, boys."

The boats were in the water, and we were in them in less than two minutes. The *Flight* was already leaning over heavily. Harrison alone remained on her.

"May I fire a torpedo before she sinks, sir?" he asked. "It might shake the vapor off, or blow up one of their infernal stations. It won't take a minute."

"I don't want you to run any risk," I protested doubtfully.

"*I'm* all right, sir," He waved his cap gaily and ran down below. We waited anxiously while one might count twenty, resting on our oars, under the side of the vessel. Then suddenly it reeled over upon us. I felt myself crushed down into the water—down—down— I am a good swimmer; but the vessel was over me in every direction. I caught at a rope hanging from one of the davits, and pulled at it till I could not hold my breath any longer, and the water began to ooze into my lungs. I gave a desperate pull and came out from the ship. The few seconds during which I was floating up to the surface seemed an eternity, and I was swallowing water all the time. When I emerged I was almost unconscious, and I should have drowned after all, for I had no strength to swim; but a piece of grating floated near me and I clung to it. I heard a terrific crash afar, as I panted with my head on the grating. Then I was sick from the salt water that I had swallowed. Then the water suddenly whirled me round and round, and the pink fog between me and the shore was torn away. The torpedo, the firing of which had overturned the little vessel, had struck home, and one of Long's stations (as I learnt afterwards) was destroyed.

The water whirled me round till I was giddy and almost choked with the swell that washed over me. When it quieted down I saw a sandy beach with a great hollow in the sand where the torpedo had exploded, and the ruins of a building and a small pier. The sea around me was green again, and I caught a glimpse of blue sky above, but walls of pink vapor were closing in on me from each side and from behind, and creeping down the beach to the shore. There was no sign of any of my brave comrades. I called them by name and none answered. God rest them.

I was tempted to let myself sink after them, but the sight of the cursed mist brought an angry resolve to fight it, and I struck out slowly for the shore. I was badly bruised in landing and could hardly stand. It was lucky for me that Long did not find me then. I stole into an empty hut in the night and found a long knife, and some food and water, and slept till the morning. I came upon Long suddenly, round some bushes. There was no parley. He fired at me twice with a revolver and missed. The second time I struck up his arm. My knife went in just underneath—

I dragged him away and buried him. The six men who were left on the island (three had perished in the explosion) were too mad to suspect me, or even to miss Long. They were friendly enough, but they guarded the stations for producing the vapor jealously. There were three of them still. They were all arranged in the same way. The etherine was made in huge vats in sheds at the edge of the water. From the sheds, platforms about fifty yards long ran out, over the shallow sands, to the edge of the deeper water. Pipes ran along the platforms, and the etherine was wafted through the pipes and up a hollow iron tube forty feet high at the end of them, by electric fans. At the top of the tube it passed into what appeared to be a sort of air-gun, which fired it out into the sea. When it touched the water huge mountains of dark pink cloud formed rapidly and rolled away from the shore in all directions.

The vats were fed from piles of yellow and gray dusty material; six feeds of gray to one of yellow. There would be a fearful explosion, the attendants told me, if a gray feed were five minutes late, till the yellow feed was exhausted. I fought the two attendants at each station in turn to prevent them continuing the gray feeds, and killed them all. God knows I was sorry, but it had to be done for the sake of the poor mad world, and my poor mad wife and children. The stations blew up as they said. On the last occasion I was dangerously near, and the explosion stunned me for some time. After that I was in a fever for about a fortnight. I had just strength enough to crawl to a brook and lap some water, and back to my hut, where I had a store of fruit. The pink mist grew fainter and fainter, till at last it was only a dim haze on the sea afar. I don't remember exactly how it went, and I did not know that a fortnight had passed till the *Sarah Dillon* took me off, and the captain told me.

We called at several ports before we reached England, and the voyage took a long time; but I cannot say how long, for I was very ill till the last few days. Then the fever went. The crew were very kind to me, but they seemed terribly depressed. I thought it was the reaction after the madness. This evidently lasted for some time after the vapor departed, for at Lisbon they were praying in all the churches for the return of the "pink blessing," as they called it.

I thought the madness would have passed by the time that I reached England, and in my vanity I pictured myself being hailed as the rescuer of the world. But when I landed I found all the people sombre and sullen. The "blessing" had gone, they said, and suffering and sin had come back to the world. Most of them were very pale and feeble. In addition to the nervous exhaustion of the frenzy, many of them had been half starved during the epidemic, as they neglected the common necessities of life; but they ascribed the evils which were caused by the madness to its cessation. It was out of the question to proclaim my part in removing it, and I judged it wise to pretend that I, too, had suffered from it.

The trains were running again, and I went up to London. On the way I learnt that several of those who served the Prime Minister during the epidemic had been assassinated. The *Times* deprecated the occurrence on the ground that, "although these unfortunate persons, having proved unworthy of receiving the 'blessing,' were not unjustly regarded as outside the pale of humanity, still they were not shown to have done anything to remove it." It also reminded its readers that the Prime Minister had not had an opportunity of being heard in his defense, and that upon recovery from his present extreme prostration he would possibly be able to disprove the horrible charge of endeavoring to disperse the beneficent vapor.

My wife and children received me affectionately. I pretended to have succumbed to the vapor and to mourn for it as they did. My pallor and weakness after my illness prevented any suspicion, and my wife said that a weight was removed from her mind now she knew that I had benefited from it.

"I could not bear to think that you were an outcast, dear," she said," because I *knew* that you did not deserve it. Indeed"—she lowered her voice to a whisper— "sometimes I think that those poor people who did not receive the blessing are more to be pitied than blamed. If it rested with me, I wouldn't have them killed, only locked up. Unless, of course, they actually helped to remove it. *They ought to be executed, ought they not?*"

"Certainly," I said; "certainly, my dear!"

I found a letter from the Prime Minister, which, luckily, she had not opened. It enclosed bank-notes for £10,000. "I am doomed," the letter said. "Do not try to help me. It would only mean that you would be sacrificed, too, and I should lose the comfort of thinking that one sane person is left to help a stricken world. Dear friend and helper, do not grieve for me or them. We are all in the hands of God!"

The note was not signed. I locked it up in my desk, and at the risk of my life I keep it yet.

I disregarded his warning, of course, and started to go to him the next morning; but a mob was round his house, and I could not get near. They had torn him limb from limb, I heard; and some one standing at a window held up something on a pole. It was his head, I think—the head which held the brains that saved the world.

# THE PLAGUE OF LIGHTS

The Official Blue Books just published, as the result of the Royal Commission on the Plague of Lights, contain the evidence of some two hundred scientists, and an exhaustive report by the two peers, three M.P.'s, and four Fellows of the Royal Society, who formed the Commission, upon the terrible calamity that recently devastated the earth. It may seem presumptuous for me to add to the testimony of such authorities; but I notice that all the learned gentlemen who gave evidence either obtained their facts at second-hand (having themselves escaped the plague by flight or going into hiding), or confessed that during the actual attack their faculties were obscured. As I am one of the very few sufferers who escaped with memory unimpaired, I think it well to set down the events which came under my observation.

It was on the evening of the 12th of June, 1906, that the "lights" first appeared, among a chattering and laughing crowd that was pouring out of the Strand Theatre into Surrey Street. Phyllis Brand was leaning upon my arm. We were newly engaged, and I was looking only at her till I heard cries from the people around us. Then I saw that the air was full of pale yellow lights. Most of them were some distance above, standing out clearly against the dark houses and cloudy sky; but a few were fluttering down among the crowd; round lights of about the bigness of a shilling, and much the same thickness. When they came quite near, it was seen that they went in threes, each at the corner of an equal-sided triangle, some eight

52

or nine inches apart. Someone called "Fire" and the crowd began to sway dangerously.

I put my arms round Phyllis, and forced our way through, with some damage to our clothes and a few bruises, and watched the crowd from a dark doorway a little distance down the street. The excitement increased, and several of the crowd were thrown down and trampled underfoot. Seventeen people were killed, we learnt the next morning. Afterwards they were accounted among the lucky ones.

The treble lights dropped steadily among the fighting mass at the doors, and darted swiftly at some who escaped from the outskirts, always fastening upon their breasts. A white-bearded gentleman beside me declared it was only a meteoric shower, and there was no real harm in the lights. They were luminous, like electric light, he explained, but did not burn. A man with a hoarse voice suggestive of drink remarked that they had sent for a fire-engine, and when it came the crowd would be worse; and anyhow, it wasn't his business, and he was going home. He had taken a few unsteady steps, when a triangle of lights dropped noiselessly upon him. He howled like an injured animal and ran. A woman in evening dress rushed by with the lights upon her cloak. She threw the cloak aside, but the lights had penetrated it, and adhered to her dress. She tore away the flimsy muslin, but they remained on the underwear; and when she plucked this away they were still left—three pale yellow spots upon the flesh. She tore at them with her fingers, till her nails made long red weals, but the fiendish spots remained. A man, hatless and coat-less, with three spots upon his shirt-front around a glittering diamond stud, seized her arm and hurried her away. Phyllis's hold on me relaxed, and I found that she had fainted. I walked stealthily along the pavement, keeping in the shadow as much as I could, carrying her in my arms, and reached the Temple Station safely. The booking-clerk and ticket-collectors had fled, and I carried her down to the platform below.

The people who had the yellow spots upon them were gathered at one end of the platform screaming, and trying to tear them from themselves and from one another. Those who had escaped attack were huddled together at the other end of the platform. A man with the spots upon him tried to join us, and refused to go away. Another man who stood before his children brandishing a big walking-stick felled him. Several women had fainted. A train hustled in, and we crowded wildly into the already crowded carriages, elbowing each other fiercely out of the way. A somber-looking man in a corner woke up and grumbled about the crowding, and asked what was the matter. Somebody told him that hell fire had dropped upon earth. He snorted and offered us some pamphlets upon "The Curse of Alcohol." It is evident that the rest of the passengers also thought that we were all drunk.

I got out at Blackfriars and carried Phyllis, who was still in the faint, into St. Paul's Station. I tried to get some brandy from the buffet, but it was full of wailing people branded with the lights. They did not hurt, they said but they frightened them, because they would not come off. The lights penetrated the clothing and stuck to the skin; but when the clothing was removed they left no mark or rent upon it. In other words, it was the flesh on which they settled, but they showed through the clothing.

I obtained half a pail full of water from the lavatory to bathe Phyllis's hands and face, and she revived. She was very brave, and wished to try to help the sufferers, but I persuaded her that she could do no good. I would have run the risk of contact with them myself, but, of course, I could not let her.

The officials assigned one end of the train to those who were attacked and their friends, and the other to those who were not, and we got back to Dulwich about twenty minutes after time. All the doctors of the locality were at the station, waiting for sufferers who had telegraphed for them. I did not stay to hear what they said, as Phyllis was very weak, and I thought it best to get her home. Also, I confess, I was a little frightened of the light. Phyllis's father pooh-poohed the matter as an optical delusion, and advised me to go home and get to bed, and I went.

The morning's paper, however, treated the matter very seriously, and gave two whole pages to it. The lights had appeared in most parts of the City and West End at about eleven o'clock; it stated, and had fastened upon people in the way I have described. There had been some hundreds of fatalities through panics in the crowds, and several persons had died of fright. Professor Morden, F.R.S., the great authority upon physical astronomy, considered that a disembodied asteroid, in the form of luminous vapor, had fallen upon the earth; and that, owing to chemical affinity for living tissues, its particles had adhered to the people with whom it came into contact. He could not explain why it attacked only adult human beings, and not children, dogs or horses; but he was sure that it was too unsubstantial to do any real harm, and that the lights would fade away gradually. Dr. Maurice Ray, the specialist for skin diseases, held similar opinions, and pointed out that the perpetual dying out and regeneration of the tissues would in a short time, rid those who had been attacked from the objectionable spots. He gave a prescription for a lotion that would expedite this result.

After calling to inquire about Phyllis, I went up to town by the train that should have started at 9:19. It was late owing to a special having been run to convey those who had been attacked by the lights to the London hospitals. At the Elephant and Castle we came into a swarm of the yellow spots, faintly visible in the light of day. A porter and three passengers had been attacked on the platform, and many people alighted to return by the next train. I went on, as I had an important business engagement. The lights were flitting about most of the streets in the City, but they bore no large proportion to the number of people. An early edition of the evening papers said that there was to be a question in the House, and that Dr. Ray's lotion had been issued to the police, so that they could render first aid to sufferers. A little later placards were stuck up, by order of the Home Office, directing those who were attacked to report themselves immediately to the nearest police-station.

"In view of the uncertainty as to the effects of the plague lights, and their infectiousness or otherwise," the placard said, "it is considered desirable that cases should be isolated and kept under observation. No permanent ill effects are, however, anticipated."

The lights, as I have said, were not very numerous, and they seemed to be flitting about like butterflies in search of something, rather than settling indiscriminately. Some of the newsboys were chivying them with their papers, and throwing their caps at them, and I went about all day without being attacked; but I saw at least a dozen people seized upon in the streets; and a man and woman who were together were branded at the restaurant during luncheon.

The evening papers reported that pairs of the light-triangles appeared to have an affinity for one another, and to endeavor to attack couples, so that infected persons must be carefully avoided. The people who had been first attacked, the report said, were beginning to show signs of mental derangement, talking a strange gibberish, manifesting a marked antipathy to their former associates, unless these were also attacked, and frequently showing demonstrative affection to some one of their fellow sufferers of the opposite sex— "in which case the lights, which differ microscopically from one another in marking, are found to be identical."

"From the manner in which the plague lights select their victims," the report went on, "and work in pairs, and from the forced, and often apparently unwilling attachment between the persons so attacked, it is impossible to avoid the conclusion that the lights are intelligent, but malevolent, beings, seeking to obtain an embodiment in human form; and that those which have been associated in their former sphere seek to associate those upon whom they seize here. It is noticed that, as the afflicted persons grow weaker, the spots grow larger and brighter. Dr. Lurnaker, the great philologist, maintains that the gibberish, which the sufferers frequently talk, manifests the characteristics of rational speech, and conjectures that it is inspired and understood by these evil visitants."

I found Phyllis sitting with her chin on her hand, a newspaper lying on the floor beside her. She was very pale, and she trembled a little in my arms.

"If this evil has come upon the whole world;" she said, "it may come upon us, Frank. It will not matter so much if we are taken together. Promise me that, if you are attacked, you will come to me at once, so that the fellow lights may take me and no one else. I shall not flinch, or worry you with complaints, dear!"

I promised what she asked, but, of course, I had no intention of keeping the promise until I knew how much or how little harm the lights did. I made her promise also that, if she were attacked first, she would come to me, but I fancied that she would not keep her promise either.

I spent the evening at her house. About 10 o'clock her father came in with a late edition of the *Evening Standard*. They called it the "Plague Edition." It stated that the lights had appeared in great force in Paris, Berlin, and New York, and to a less extent at all the great centers of life.

In France the effects of the attack were much more rapid than elsewhere, probably owing to the excitable temperament of the people, and in several cases sufferers had died within a few hours. During the progress of the disease the lights grew in size and upon death detached themselves from the body. In some case the detached lights simply departed; in other instances they seized upon the doctors and nurses.

Sufficient time had not elapsed to record the progress of these secondary attacks. In the primary cases the lights had grown as follows:

Diameter of circles 7/8 inch to 3/8 inch.

Thickness of circles 1/4 inch to 1/2 inch or 5/8 inch.

The distance between the outer edges remained constant, so that the inside edges of the circles approached one another as they grew.

The lights were unaffected by electricity, heat, or the action of any chemical agent which had been tried upon them; but they gave a dark skiagraph, like a solid substance, when photographed by the X-rays, from which it was inferred that they possessed substance, though of a kind unknown to us. The general theory was that they were disembodied spirits trying to reincarnate themselves in human bodies.

In the morning my own newspaper did not appear, but I obtained one at the station, and learnt that the lights had spread all over England, and that many deaths seemed imminent. I started for town, but at Herne Hill I found that the up traffic had been suspended, and that extra down trains were being run to take home the people who had started earlier, many of whom had been attacked In most cases another set of lights was hovering about the sufferer, doubtless waiting for the second victim. A few who had been seized in pairs were holding one another's hands, and some of these were talking in an unknown tongue, in which a phrase which may be represented in our characters as *La-Lu-Le* constantly recurred.*

The City was swarming with the lights, I heard, and a bright swarm of them was visible hanging over Brixton. People were running from that direction into Herne Hill. A hatless man with the lights on his vest was standing on the top of a cab outside the station praying aloud, and a crowd was kneeling in the street.

As I could not get into a train I walked back to Dulwich, and went to Phyllis. People were leaving their houses, in cabs or on foot, for the country. Probably we should have fled likewise, but her mother was ailing and unable to be moved. I did not ask her. Her father had started for town earlier than I. He did not return, and we never heard of him again. Many people disappeared like that in those days.

An early evening edition, hastily printed on a small portion of a single half-sheet, related that all the hospitals and public buildings in town were full of sufferers, and that whole streets had been commandeered for those who were crowded out. A local Plague Committee was hastily formed to make arrangements in West Dulwich. I offered my services, and worked all the morning at getting one of the houses in order, and laying in provisions, etc. As I was going back to Phyllis's to lunch, along Thurlow Park Road, Doris Fane rushed out from her house. She had the triangle of lights

---

*Appendix LVI, of the Blue Books gives a few fragments of this speech and conjectural translations. It seems to be established beyond doubt that *La-Lu-Le* was a profession of affection, but its exact force is thought to have differed according to the syllable accented.

upon her blouse, and another was fluttering behind her. They were much the same color as her pale yellow hair. She was white and half distracted with fear, and she ran to me and clung to my arm. We had always been friends, and I think, if I hadn't met Phyllis, I should have grown fond of her.

"See!" She cried, pointing to the light following behind her— "See! It is looking for its mate. He will be my lover, when it finds him. I shouldn't be so frightened if it were you. Didn't you know that I cared for you, Frank? I can tell you now, because I am going to die. Take them away—Oh! Take them away!" She tore wildly at the fiendish lights upon her breast.

The other lights hovered around me—brushed my arm. I closed my eyes and shuddered. It was the thought that Phyllis would wait for me, look for me in vain, that frightened me most; but when I opened my eyes again, the lights were fluttering away, up the hill, towards the high school. Doris released her hold upon my arm and followed them slowly, looking backward with her eyes fixed on me.

I went on to Phyllis's house in Croxted Road. A number of the lights were flitting about the road. When they came near me I ran. I did not hope to escape them, but I wanted to get to Phyllis first. When I reached her gate I heard Dr. Hallam's voice through the open window. We had been rivals for Phyllis, and I had won. He was a better man than I, but there is no accounting for a woman's fancy.

"Let them take me too," he cried. "I am willing to die with you. I always loved you, Phyllis."

"Hush!" She said gently. "Hush! I love Frank. I always shall while I am myself." Then she saw me and flung out her arms, and I saw the yellow spots on her dress. They looked like golden ornaments; and the others looked like a halo of stars over her dark hair. "Frank! Frank! Run away, dear. It has taken me. It wants you—the other one. You are safe from the rest. I know. Run away from me and you will be saved. God bless you, dear!"

I vaulted in at the window and took her in my arms. I did not notice when the other lights settled on me, or anything but the tears in her eyes. She smiled at me through them. Presently I looked down and found the three yellow spots on my breast. They did not burn, or hurt in any way, but they seemed to be drawing my very soul out of me. After a few moments Hallam came up and touched my arm.

"You must go to the hospital," he said huskily, "both of you. I will come quickly and do what I can. I will arrange with the nurse to look after your mother, Phyllis. I was mad just now, and you must forget. I don't think it's much use, the treatment that they recommend, but I'll try it. I'd save you for one another if I could. Anyhow, you are together. You are lucky."

We went together to the hospital. It was in the high school and the houses adjoining it. A number of fellow-sufferers were there, and others were thronging in. Those who came singly were excited and restless, and some of them called wildly for their stars—meaning, doubtless, the "mates" of the lights that had seized upon them. Those who were in pairs mostly behaved like lovers, as some of them had previously been, we knew. Some, however, were evidently strangers, or unfriendly. These were sullen, or reviled one another.

We found a quiet corner in a garden, and sat there for a time holding hands. We did not feel any pain or illness, only very weak; and I think, perhaps, this was the effect of excitement rather than the stars. At length it occurred to me that we could help those who were more afflicted than we. So we went in again. We found Hallam and Doris Fane sitting together in the hall, looking at one another with set faces—hers flushed and angry, his pale and grave. The twin lights had bound her and him!

We went a little nearer to speak to them, and I felt the lights leap on my breast. At the same moment Phyllis started and seized my hand, and he and Doris suddenly rose.

"Frank!" Phyllis cried. "His stars are calling mine. Don't let them take me from you."

"They shall not take you," I said; and I seemed to hear the lights that held me hiss. Then we walked up to them and shook hands. And a struggle took place that I cannot describe or wholly understand, but I know.

I cannot give any reason for the thing that saved us, but I know. So does Phyllis. So do Hallam and Doris. The twin lights that held us four had been wrongly mated. Mine wanted those of Doris, and hers wanted mine. Hallam's wanted those of Phyllis, and hers wanted his. But they were bound otherwise, and having seized upon us they could not leave us, and struggling to leave us they did not take any great hold upon us or do us any great harm. That is how I have escaped to write these things.

We did not lose our faculties, or talk gibberish like the other sufferers, and we did not fail utterly in body as they did, and die; and for two days and nights we toiled almost without cessation to minister to them; toiled till we were giddy and almost dropped. At first we had the help of a few elder children who had not gone to the homes established for them. The lights did not attack the children, as I have said before.

Few people came into the hospital after the first day, as most of those who were not attacked at the beginning had fled into the country, where I fear those who were attacked perished more miserably, no homes having been established for them. Two or three, however, came in singly, drawn by the triple light to its mate on someone with us. Two of our patients also left, beating their breasts, and saying that they must seek their stars—the "love-lights" some of the poor, demented sufferers called them.

Those who remained with us—some sixty originally—were helplessly inert for long periods. At other times they gesticulated wildly and talked in the unknown tongue. *La-Lu-Le*, they kept crying, with the accent first on one syllable and then on the other, and in times varying from love to despair. *La-Lu-Le!*

They had intervals of reason, but those grew fewer and shorter. After the first day they made no attempt to take food or drink, even in their rational moments, and they lost the power of their limbs and lay in long rows on the beds and couches. We worked unceasingly to minister to them. The supply of food grew short, and Phyllis and I went out and raided some of the shops that had been hurriedly left with the doors open, and we brought what we had found back in a baker's barrow, that the two of us had scarcely strength to push. I have no words to describe the awful silence of the deserted houses and streets.

The lights seemed to have more power to weaken us while we were separated from the doctor and Doris, and similarly they were more affected while we were absent. So we kept together in the evening. We were all too exhausted to say much. Phyllis and I sat hand-in-hand the others sat a little way apart, but they had ceased to quarrel.

"You have gained my great respect and admiration, Miss Fane," the doctor told her, and she bowed and wiped her eyes.

"I am glad that I shall die with a man," she said.

We had little sleep that night. Several of our patients died. Their stars grew larger and brighter and more substantial—they felt like a spot of mist if you touched them—and at the end they went off together.

The third day more died, and the rest were in a stupor. The air was fill of showers of lights that fell in a long rain of triangles. They were the outskirts of a dissolving world that was falling upon us, a shriveled old gentleman, who had escaped attack, declared. There was probably a more material core, he said, that would come soon. That would be the end of things. He was a scientist whom men had called great, he told us, but his name did not matter. These things did not matter now. He went on slowly, leaning on his stick, towards Beckenham. Someone whom he loved had been buried there for thirty years, he told us, and the "love-lights" (he called them so) would be waiting for him on her grave, he hoped.

More of our patients died in the afternoon. Phyllis and I went always arm in arm when we were not attending to them. The doctor and Doris kept away from us as much as possible because their ghostly masters struggled with ours, and they wished to save us from annoyance during these last sad hours.

"You lucky people!" Doris said. "Don't look like that, doctor! You and I are luckier than some. Let us do our work together, dear friend, and hope for the best."

"God bless you, dear, brave girl," he said, and kissed her hand.

THE PLAGUE OF LIGHTS

There were only twenty-two of our patients left at the close of the afternoon, and these did not understand anything that we said. Doris fainted from overwork, and Phyllis seemed in a sort of coma. The doctor and I had to feed them also. He and I were so weak that we could scarcely move, and, the four of us seemed bound closely together by the lights. He and Doris were unable to resist them any longer, and drew closer and closer together as they sat on the sofa, after she had revived from her faintness.

"It isn't my fault, Miss Fane," he apologized. "I am sorry if it causes you annoyance."

"No," she smiled up at him. "It doesn't. I think it is near the end, doctor. I am glad to be with you."

He drew her head down on his shoulder. "It is near the end," he said. You will be more comfortable so."

We sat very still for half an hour. There was no sound except when the stars of those who had died fluttered by. We could hear them now. They seemed growing into substantial bodies, and we into unsubstantial spirits. Then gradually everything seemed to change. We found that we could move more freely, not that we were stronger, but because our bodies had less weight. The air seemed fill of something that we could not see, only feel; and it grew swiftly dark, an hour before sunset.

"What is coming, Frank?" Phyllis asked, in an awed whisper.

"The end of all things, dear," I said. "I suppose it is the 'core' of the dead world coming upon us, as he said. We are together, dear. It has not been without its happiness, this sad time."

"No, dear. I have been with you."

The darkness grew suddenly darker, and looking out of the open window—we were in the long room where most of our remaining patients were—we saw a shapeless mass overhead, shutting out the sight of the sky; a bluish, ashy grey, with portions bulging out like low mountains, and black gaps between, where seas might have been. The Blue Books say it was from ninety to a hundred miles away; but it seemed almost to touch us then. Why it did not touch us quite, even the Royal Commissioners do not know.

The weight seemed now entirely gone from our limbs. I suppose because the attraction of the other world counterbalanced the attraction of gravity. There was no light, except the faint shine of the plague-lights on our breasts, and as we watched, holding our breath, these suddenly floated upward.

"They have left us!" Phyllis cried. "The love-lights! Don't love me any less."

"I shall always love you, Phyllis," I assured her, "if there is no light left in the world." But she fainted and did not hear me.

I think I must have fainted too, for it felt as if time had passed when next I remembered anything. Through the window I saw the dark world still hurrying by, escorted by battalions of tiny twinkling lights. I could not see if they were still in triangles of three. They were—thank God!—too far. In the room it was inky dark. A few of the patients, come to their senses, were calling in feeble, frightened voices to ask what had happened, and where they were.

"The lights have gone," the doctor was telling them. "I do not know what the darkness may bring. But we are in the Hands of God, dear friends the hands of God!"

It was the morning of the 19th of June when the sun shone again on the pale, enfeebled people who were left—humans, men and women as before. The Royal Commission has narrated in Appendices xxiv to xxxii how the work of the world was put together again, like a map that had been dissected for a puzzle. I only know the small happenings around me. We tottered about getting food and drink. Some who had met during the plague settled down where we were, and many who had parted went off to seek those they had lost. Children came down from their homes to find their parents, and parents went off to look for their children, and we smiled and wiped our eyes. Presently some went off to the churches and set the bells ringing, and all of us gathered there.

We shuddered still as we looked after the black mass passing away in the sky above, drawing after it a misty aurora of light; the plague-lights that had invaded our earth, struggled with us, and slain; and failed after all. Henceforth we were left our own little world, and the world of each is small. Mine is larger than some for I am Phyllis's and she is mine.

Indeed I am tempted to say that ours is a world of four since the doctor and Doris and we are almost as inseparable as if we were still bound by our stars; but they struggle no longer since the evil went.

It was in a pause from our work of helping those who were feebler than ourselves that we understood this. We were sitting down together to the crusts and water that we had collected for lunch, and the doctor placed Doris a chair touching his.

"You aren't bound to sit beside me now," he said, laughing cheerfully, and wiping his forehead with his handkerchief he had worked very hard among the sick. "You can order me to the opposite side of the table—or the world if you wish."

"But I can't wish." Doris said softly; and suddenly he put his hand under her chin and lifted up her face, and she looked up at him smilingly, and held gently to the sides of his coat. Phyllis and I took up our fragments of lunch, and went out in the garden and ate it under a tree. "God bless them," I said, "and all on earth that live and love."

"Amen!"

Phyllis put her arm through mine, and gazed where the dead world, with its trail of pale light, was growing dim afar.

"Perhaps He sent them—the love-lights—to teach us to love. Who knows if they were a blessing, after all!"

That is the lesson that we have learnt from the plague of lights. It is not included in the forty-three recommendations of the Royal Commission, and that is why I have written this story.

# THE GRAY WEED

Owing to the lamented death of Professor Newton, to whose wisdom and courage the world owes its deliverance, I have been asked to contribute to the first newspaper issued in the new era some account of the terrible weed which overran the earth, and threatened to stifle out mankind.

The professor had intended dealing with the origin of the weed, its relations to ordinary plants, the nature of its growth, so far as this proceeded, and the forms which it would ultimately have assumed. Unfortunately his notes upon these points are so abbreviated and technical as to be unintelligible to me; and personally I possess no qualifications for dealing with the scientific aspects of the case. So I must confine myself to a plain narrative of the occurrences which I witnessed.

It was nine o'clock in the evening of November 10, 1908, when I left my office in Norfolk Street, letting myself out with a duplicate key which the hall-porter had intrusted to me. I thought at first that it was snowing; but when I put out my hand and caught a few of the particles, I found that they were flimsy white seeds, something like those of melons, only less substantial. Where they lay in heaps—as I thought—in the road, their color appeared to be gray. At the Embankment end of the street the "heaps" were larger; and when I came to them I discovered that they were not seeds, but a growth of gray weed, which fastened round my shoes as I tried to walk over it.

66

I stooped and took hold of a piece to examine it; but, when I attempted to pluck it, it stretched like elastic, without breaking off. The tendrils were round, and about one-fourth of an inch in diameter when not stretched. They had, at intervals, spherical bulges which, at a distance, bore the appearance of small berries. These appeared to be of the same substance as the tendrils. The latter began twining round my fingers, and I had some difficulty in releasing them. The road and the Embankment were deserted by people, but three or four horses at the cab stand were plunging with fright as the weed wound round their legs. It had grown perceptibly in the few minutes that I had been observing it, and, feeling somewhat alarmed, I made my way back along Norfolk Street.

The weed had spread a good deal there also; and I noticed that wherever a white seed fell a fresh plant sprang up, and grew with marvelous rapidity. In the Strand the weed was nearly a yard high. The 'bus drivers were whipping their frightened horses in a vain attempt to drive over it. The foot-passengers were unable to move, except a big man, who, with a small axe, hacked a passage through the growth for himself, his wife and his daughter—a pretty girl of about nineteen.

They were making their way down to the Embankment, but I warned them that the weed was thick there. The young lady then suggested that they should try to get into one of the houses, and I invited them to come to my offices. The tendrils were seizing people and pulling them down and binding them like flies in a spider's web. We could hear cries and screams all along the Strand, and a cab was upset by the struggles of the horse. The weed had spread over Norfolk Street, while we were talking, and it clung to our feet as we ran. The lady tripped and fell. The tendrils seized her immediately, and we had great difficulty in freeing her. When we had entered the door of the house we could not close it until we had chopped away the tendrils that followed us.

I turned on the electric light in the halls, and took my new friends to my rooms, which were on the fifth floor. The elder lady was faint, and I gave her some brandy and soda and biscuits. I had a good stock of these fortunately.

The gentleman's name was George Baker, his wife was Marian Baker, and the girl was Viva. They had been buying curiosities in the Strand, and the axe—a roughly engraved Moorish instrument—was fortunately among their purchases. Some people whom they met in the streets had told them that the weed was growing all over London, and that the Guards had been ordered out to cut it away. A learned old gentleman had conjectured that the seeds were the atoms of some dissipated planet, or the elements of some world that was to be, and that they contained the raw elements of life, which set them growing when they came into contact with suitable matter.

"It's diabolical!" Mr. Baker said furiously. "The vestries ought to send round water-carts with weed-killer, or—or something. I don't know what they ought to do; but they ought to do something." He wiped his face excitedly with his handkerchief. "Diabolical!" he repeated. "It grows through the flagstones, the wood paving, everything. It—it seizes people!"

"Seizes people!" his wife repeated, wringing her hands. "We saw it."

"It clings to you," the girl added tremulously. "*Clings* to you. If it goes on growing—!"

Her mother gave a sharp scream, and her father groaned.

"If it goes on growing—!" they said together.

"It won't," I assured them, with an indifferent appearance of confidence. "Those things that grow like—like fungi—never do. It will shrivel up suddenly, and let people go again. I don't suppose they're really hurt, only frightened. In an hour or so you'll be on your way home, and laughing about it; and I shall be thanking the—the fungus—for some pleasant acquaintances. I look upon this as a little surprise party."

The girl wiped her eyes and forced a smile.

"A little surprise party," she agreed. "What are you going to do for our entertainment, Mr. Adamson?—I saw the name on the door-plate."

"Henry Adamson," I said, "and very much at your service, Miss Viva— I have some cards, but—"

I paused doubtfully. Her mother held up a trembling hand, and her father shook his head.

"We won't have any fool's games," he said. "Let's talk."

Viva and I talked in broken sentences, and her mother and father in monosyllables. We kept glancing at the window, but no one had the courage to draw up the blind for nearly an hour. Then we opened the window and looked out. The weed was fully six feet high in the street, and higher in the Strand. It had overrun the 'bus that stood at the opening. If there were people on the 'bus, it had overrun them, too.

"It doesn't seem to hurt," I said. "There's no screaming now." I shuddered as soon as I had said it.

"There is no screaming now," Viva repeated. "I suppose they—they are all—"

Her voice broke. Her father shut the window sharply and drew her away.

"It will be gone in the morning," he asserted, "as—as our friend said. We shall have to impose on your hospitality for the night, I am afraid, Mr. Adamson."

"There is no question of imposing," I assured him. "I cannot say how glad I am to have your company."

We made a couch for the ladies by putting several hearth-rugs on the table in the clerks' room, and laying two rugs of mine to cover them. Mr. Baker and I dozed in front of the fire in my room in chairs. Toward the morning I fell into a sounder sleep. When I woke he had pulled up the blind.

"It's fifteen feet high at least," he told me. "Halfway up the second windows. God help us!"

I joined him and saw the roadway filled with a sea of gray weeds. They looked like india-rubber reeds. The largest were as thick as my little finger, and the bulges were the size of damsons. We opened the window and listened. Presently a caretaker opened a window nearly opposite and called to his wife.

"Here's a rum go, Mary," he shouted, with a laugh. "Bulrushes growing to the street! We sha'n't have any clerks pestering us today."

The woman joined him, and they laughed together because they would have a holiday. They treated the matter as a joke, and evidently disbelieved us when we told them of the terrible events of the preceding night. So we closed the window and called the ladies. I made some tea on my ring-burner, and we breakfasted on that and biscuits. The ladies avoided the window, and so did I, but Mr. Baker went to it every few minutes. After each visit he whispered to me that it was still growing. Mrs. Baker seemed in a stupor, but Viva tried hard to cheer us. She sang little snatches of song under her breath as she washed the tea-cups; and once she said that it was great "fun." Her mouth trembled when I looked reproachfully at her.

"Mother is so nervous," she whispered. "I have to pretend, to cheer her. Do you think it will—grow?"

"Heaven knows!" I said. "But you are very brave."

After this she and I sat at the window, watching the tendrils growing and growing, and clutching incessantly at the air. I thought, at first, that they were swaying in the wind, but there was no breeze. Also there was an indescribable air of purpose about their movement. A number of long branches spread themselves over a window opposite. Their swaying ceased, and they pressed on it steadily, till at last it broke with a dull crash. Mrs. Baker fainted, and her husband lifted her on to the sofa. Viva clung to my arm. The malicious tendrils broke down the window-frame, piece by piece, and spread slowly into the room, winding themselves round the tables and chairs.

"If anyone had been there," Viva cried hoarsely. "If—if—" She looked at me. Her eyes were big with fright.

"They must be doing something to stop it," I said— "the—the authorities. If we could find out! I'll try the telephone."

After several calls I obtained an answer. It was a girl's voice. Six of them had stayed all night in the exchange, she said. They were in communication with the police and the Government Offices. The soldiers had been out since the previous evening, and had cut their passage from Chelsea Barracks to Victoria Street, and along this almost to Westminster Bridge. They had intended coming on to Whitehall and the Strand; but the stuff grew almost as quickly as it was cut down, and had overpowered many of them. Over a hundred had been crushed to death by it, and they had sent for gun-cotton to try and blow it up, as a last resort. It was known, through the telegraph, that the weed had appeared all over England and on the Continent. It was also growing out of the sea. The English Channel was choked in places, and several vessels had been bound by the weed in sight of the coast. "It's alive!" she wailed; "alive! Its eyes are watching us through the windows!" (The bulges had the appearance of eyes.)

I was unable to obtain any further answers, although I tried the telephone several times. By one o'clock the third-story windows were covered. The thickest tendrils were then nearly the diameter of a florin, with the bulges the size and shape of exceedingly large plums. The stems and bulges seemed to be of one homogeneous material. There were no leaves or fruit or flowers at this time, but branches were beginning to sprout from the main stems. There did not appear to be any communication between one stem and another; but, according to Professor Newton's notes, this undoubtedly took place at the roots, which interlaced so as to form a gigantic nervous system or brain.

We made another meal of tea and biscuits. Mrs. Baker seemed stupefied with horror, and her husband was evidently overcome by his anxiety for her, and scarcely spoke. Viva and I tried to talk, but our voices broke off in the middle of words. We listened vainly for any explosions, and concluded that the attempt at rescue had failed. By four o'clock the weed was up to the window-sill. Mrs. Baker was in a prolonged faint. Her husband sat beside her, with his head on his hand. He did not look up when I suggested carrying her out on the roof.

"The cold would rouse her," he said. "It is best as it is. You're a good chap, I think. Do what you can for my little girl."

I put on my overcoat, crammed the pockets with biscuits and a flask, and persuaded Viva to accompany me to the roof to look for a way of escape, for us and for her parents. We never saw them again.

Some people from neighboring houses were on the adjoining roofs already, two old caretakers, a man and a lad. We saw about twenty more on the roofs in other streets. Some of them were raving and singing. The caretakers who had spoken to us in the morning flung their window open. They were laughing as if they had been drinking. They brought two pailfuls of boiling water and emptied it upon the weed. There was a soft hissing sound. Then two—four—six quivering tendrils reached slowly toward them. The man and woman seemed fascinated. They did not attempt to move, only screamed. The tendrils seized them; bound them round and round. Viva buried her head on my shoulder, and I shut my eyes. It was about half a minute, I think, before the screams ceased. Then there was crash after crash as windows were broken in. The weed had its passions, it seemed.

"Take me back to my mother and father," Viva begged. "We can all die together—if you would rather die with us?"

"Yes. I would rather die with you, Viva," I said. "I should have liked you very much if we had lived."

We returned to the trap-door, but the staircase was choked with the weed. As we looked down it seemed to be a pit of twirling gray snakes. We called to her mother and father, but there was no answer. Viva would have flung herself among the weed, but I held her and carried her back to the roof. The weed was beginning to crawl over the gutters. Long ropelike filaments were surrounding the other people who were on the roofs. They huddled together and did not attempt to escape. The tendrils overran, them and bound them round and round. I think they had mostly fainted. There was only one cry.

The tendrils lashed one another and fought over their prey. Their struggles made a repulsive, "scrooping" noise—a noise like the sound of stroking silk, only louder. There was also a sound of crunching bones.

I did not notice the weed closing round us till Viva clutched my arm.

"Hold me," she begged. "Hold me tight! I thought life had only just begun—"

I supported her on one arm, and backed toward the Strand end of the roof, where the weed had encroached less. We stumbled against a skylight. The attic below was empty. I opened the frame, lowered Viva and jumped down after her. We crouched in a corner watching the window. One—two minutes passed. Then the gray weed, with the bulges that simulated eyes, pressed upon it. The glass shivered upon the floor. I lifted Viva in my arms—she was too faint to walk—and carried her out on the landing.

The light was bad, and I saw no weed till we reached the next landing. Then it stretched toward us from the broken window-frame. A dozen gray ropes crept toward us from the stairs when we approached them. The lift was standing open. I pushed Viva in, jumped after her, slid the steel railing to and lowered us. A tendril caught at the lift as we started. I heard it snap.

In my excitement I lowered the lift too fast. We were thrown against the sides and almost stunned when it stopped. There was barely a glimmer of light, and we did not know if we had reached the bottom of the shaft or had been stopped by the weed. We listened for a long while and heard nothing. Then we let ourselves out and advanced a few inches at a time, feeling round us with our hands. We seemed to be in the hall of the basement. We came upon a table and found a tray on it with biscuits and milk. We drank the milk and Viva stuffed the biscuits in her pockets, as mine were full. There was a dim, barely perceptible light from an area window. We peered up through the grating into the forest of huge weeds. The trunks, which had grown to the size of young elms, only swayed a little; but the branches above twisted and twined incessantly. Viva shuddered when she saw them, and I took her away.

"We are safe down here," I assured her; but she pressed her hand over my mouth.

"Hush!" she whispered. "Hush! It may hear."

We wandered about in the darkness till we found a caretaker's room. We sat there on a sofa, holding hands. We never lost touch of each other all the time. I do not know how long it was. It seemed years. The basement was very quiet, but the sound of the india-rubbery motion came down to us. Once or twice we thought we heard a human cry. Once a mouse squeaked, and a spider dropped on the couch beside us with a thud. We were always listening.

After an unknown time we groped our way into the scullery to get water. We had just drunk when we heard the sound of india-rubbery tentacles dragging themselves over the walls. Something clung to my hand. Something held her skirt. It tore as I pulled her from it. Something was in the way when we tried to close the door. It followed us across the room and into the passage. We felt along the walls for the door that we thought led to the cellars—found it—fastened it after us—groped down the stairs. It was darker than the darkness of the basement above—darkness that could be felt. We stumbled over some coals—and a rough, hoarse voice came out of the darkness.

"Give us your hand, guv'nor," it said, "just a touch of your hand. I've been alone here for—for a thousand years!"

Something staggered toward us—stumbled against us; and a huge rough hand gripped my arm.

I put myself between him and Viva and pressed her arm for silence. The voice and grip were not reassuring, and I hoped he did not know she was there. "Here is my hand," I said.

"And mine," said Viva eagerly. "You are a friend—of course you are a friend. God bless you."

"God bless you, lady." The rough voice softened strangely. "I—I'm sorry to intrude."

He drew back a little way from us and sat down. I could not see him, but I could hear him breathe. Another unknown time passed. Then Viva whispered that she was thirsty.

"There's a pail of water," the man said, "if I can find it." He moved about in the darkness till he kicked it. Then he brought it to us. We drank from the pail and ate a few biscuits. I offered him some, but he said that he had a crust left. Viva and I explored the cellar and found a shovel and a pick. I suggested that we should try to break through into the next cellar, on the chance of finding food; but Viva and the man feared that the weed might hear us.

She and I sat on an empty packing-case, and she laid her head on my shoulder and slept. After a time I slept too. The man woke us.

"There's something moving, guv'nor," he said hoarsely. "I think it's growing out of the floor. Strike a match, and give me the shovel."

We found forty or fifty weed plants growing. He beat some down with the shovel, but others clutched him round the legs. He was a strong, rough-looking man and he fought furiously, but they pulled him down. I gave Viva the matches and went to his rescue with the pick. The weeds seized me too, but he cut us both free with a clasp-knife, and at length we destroyed them all.

We saw by the match-light that the wall was cracking in one place. So we resolved to try to get through it. The man dislodged a few bricks with the pick, and we pulled others away till our fingers bled and the last match gave out. At length he managed to crawl through.

"You come next, sir," he proposed. "The lady would be frightened of me."

"Dear friend," Viva said, "I am not in the least afraid of you."

So he helped her through, and I followed. We discovered a passage, and along the passage another doorway—and people. I do not remember our words when we found one another in the dark—only the gladness of it.

There were about twenty of them—men, women and children. They had food and drink which they had collected before they fled to the cellar. Professor Newton was among them. He seemed acknowledged as their leader, and he proposed me as his second. He wanted the aid of an intelligent and educated man, he whispered, in fighting the weed.

"We *must* fight it," he declared, tapping me on the arm with his finger, "but I don't know how. I—don't— know—how!—I can't even guess what it is; still less what it is going to be. It may be mere vegetable life—a man-eating plant. It may be brute animal life—a *carnivorous* animal! It may be intelligent—diabolical intelligence. Whatever it is, it will develop as it grows, develop new organs and new powers, new strength and new weaknesses. We must strike *there*. What weaknesses? Ah-h! I don't know! It may outgrow itself and wither. It may perish from the little microbes of

the earth, like the Martians in Wells's romance. We thought that
an idle fancy *then*. It may grow into an intelligent—devil! It may
be one now and merely lack the organs to carry out fully its evil
will. On the other hand, its malevolence may be purposeless—a
blind restlessness that it will outgrow—after we have stifled in the
darkness at its feet. We must fight it anyhow. To fight it we must
understand it. To understand it we must study it. Will you risk your
life with me?"

"Yes," I said.

Viva cried softly when I told her I must go; but she did not try
to keep me from my duty. The professor and I crawled up the stairs
into the basement, and finding nothing there went up in the lift in
the dark. We heard the weed moving about on the second landing.
I jumped out, turned on the electric light, and jumped in again.
The tendrils followed me and clutched at the steel curtain, but
could not break it. We hacked with our penknives at those that
crept through. The juice which ran out from them had an oily smell.
They beat furiously on the curtain. The professor studied them
calmly with a microscope. The bulges were the beginning of eyes,
he thought. He pronounced some feathery sprays sprouting from
them to be the rudiments of organs like hands. I do not know
whether he was right, but he always maintained that they would
develop organs of sense. Anyhow the character of the weed was
clearly changing. It had grown harder and drier, but without
losing its flexibility or strength.

After a time the professor decided that I should return to the
others. He went up again in the lift when he had lowered me. Viva
was waiting for me in the dark just inside the door.

I had obtained some candles. We lit one and stuck it in a bottle.
I shall never forget the group in the low, wide cellar, huddled together on boxes or on the floor. The man we met first was nursing
an ailing child. Lady Evelyn Angell had gathered a young flower-
girl under her opera cloak. A policeman was binding up a wounded
hand with his handkerchief. A shivering old match-seller wore his
cape. Viva took a little boy on her lap and told him about Jack and

the Beanstalk. Steel—a card sharper, I learned afterward—who had been indefatigable in helping everyone, was chatting to Lady Evelyn. Some ill-clad youths had draped themselves in sacking. A rouged and gaudily dressed woman was mothering some younger ones. She had comforted Viva while I was away, I heard, and had offered to accompany her in a search for me, but the others had persuaded them that they would only be a hindrance to us.

After a couple of hours—I had wound my watch again—the professor reappeared. His clothes were torn and his face and hands were bleeding.

"They broke the steel curtain at last," he explained, "but I got away. Good heavens, how it grows! I can't make up my mind about it."

After a time, when most of us were dozing, a portion of the roof and the wall fell in. The growth of the roots under the street had pressed the earth upon it, the professor conjectured. A faint light streamed down the tall weeds and through the opening. The branches overhead were still moving, but the lower stems seemed inert. The professor decided to venture among them in search of knowledge. I went with him. There was just room enough between the weeds for us to pass.

The houses upon the other side of the street were all down. So were many in the Strand. In Fleet Street we saw the way it was done. The huge weeds leaned upon them, till they fell with a crash. The Law Courts went so. We found the clock among the weeds. Sometimes the branches pushed themselves through the windows and walls of houses which were still standing. Once or twice we heard human cries. We found a woman, with a baby and a dog, walking among the weed-trees, and took them with us.

The light which straggled down through the waving branches overhead was feeble and patchy, and we lost our way for a time. At length we found Norfolk Street; but as we were entering it, some of the tendrils, which seemed to be fighting one another viciously overhead, broke off and dropped at our feet. They writhed upon the ground like huge gray snakes, and wound themselves round the weed-trees and lashed out blindly. One of them caught the

woman and dashed her against a trunk. We pulled her away from
the tendril as its violence lessened, but she was dead. The baby
was not hurt and still slept. I carried it in my arms.

A moment later a broken tendril dropped right upon the dog.
He howled loudly, and in his fright bit at an unbroken tendril hanging down among the trees. (There were a good many such, but we
had succeeded in avoiding them hitherto.) It shook as if with rage
and pain, wrapped its extremity round the dog, and bore him aloft,
still howling. Hundreds of tendrils stretched toward it, and fought
with it for the dog. They still fought after his cries ceased; and other
tendrils began reaching downward, in every direction round us, as
if searching for further prey. The professor watched them intently,
oblivious of danger.

"They make a different sound now," he remarked abstractedly.
"It is no longer the scroop-scroop of clammy india-rubber—they
*rustle*. It doesn't seem like decay. They are stronger—stronger.
There is always weakness in excess of anything—even strength. Let
me think!"

"Quick!" I cried. "Quick! They are falling upon us. Run!"

We dodged rapidly among the weed-trunks. He was slow and I
pushed him. Tendril after tendril rustled downward, and the trunks
themselves swayed. Two almost fixed the professor between them—
he was a stout man—but I dragged him through. The light from
above was entirely shut out by the descending tendrils, and we must
have been lost but for an electric lamp burning in one of the houses.
As it was, the descending tendrils must have caught us but for their
struggles among themselves. Broken pieces dropped and wriggled
madly all round us, and we had to dodge them. One caught at my
foot, and dragged my shoe off as I pulled myself away. Several
touched us as we slid down the debris into the cellar. They followed us there.

A few of the people screamed. A few fainted. The rest backed
in a huddled, wide-eyed crowd toward the farthest wall. Lady
Evelyn stood in front of the children, holding out her arms as if to
shelter them. Steel came and stood in front of her.

"Dear lady," he said, "these have been the best days of my life—since we met. I should have been a better man if I had met you before." She smiled very sweetly at him.

"I like you greatly, Mr. Steel," she said.

The rouged woman came and took the baby from me, and I tried to pull the professor back; but he would not come. Viva ran out from the crowd and put her arms round me. The tendrils drew nearer and nearer. Some came along the ceiling, hanging their heads like snakes. Others crawled along the floor, raising themselves as if to dart at us. I do not know whether they saw us, heard us or smelt us, or how they knew where we were; but they *knew*.

They were within a yard of the professor, and still he did not move; only took the burning candle from the bottle, and railed at them as if they could hear. I thought that he had gone mad.

"Do you think man has learned nothing in his thousand generations?" he shouted. "That you can crush him with the brute strength of a few days? Come and see! Come and see!"

The foremost tentacle wound round him; began to lift him. He felt it carefully with his hands. "It is dry," he shouted— "*dry!*"

Then he put the candle to it!

There was a wilderness of white light. Then a purple darkness. I heard the professor fall. When our eyes recovered from their dazed blindness the weed was utterly gone. The daylight was streaming into the hole in the wall, and the professor was picking himself up from the floor. His hair and beard were badly singed, and his eyebrows were gone.

"It dried too fast," he told us, with a queer angry chuckle. "That was its weakness. It dried—dried—"

He kept on repeating the word in a dull, aimless tone. The rest repeated it vacantly after him. Viva was the first to speak coherently—a faint whisper in my ear.

"My dear!" she said. "My *dear!*"

Lady Evelyn spoke next—to ex-card sharper Steel.

"The world begins afresh," she said; "and—you *have* met me, Mr. Steel."

The tears rolled down her cheek and his, and they stood smiling at each other.

"The world begins afresh," the professor called in a loud voice. "Come with me and make it a better world." He strode toward the light, but some held back.

"The weed!" they cried timorously.

"The weed has gone—burned in an instant, from the end of the world to the end of the world!" he assured them. "Follow me."

We followed him out of the darkness into the sunlight. It was a mild, bright day for November, and a pleasant air.

The weed had disappeared entirely, as the professor predicted; and, speaking generally, the conflagration had been too sudden to do much harm; but most of the buildings had subsided upon the sudden destruction of the weed-roots which had undermined them. Here and there houses, stones and timber had caught fire; and in many districts the fire spread, and lasted for days.

The statistics, which are being prepared in the New Department for the Service of the People, over which I have the honor to preside, are not yet quite complete; but I may mention that seventeen per cent. of the buildings on the north of the Thames are found to have been destroyed, and ninety-three per cent. on the south— the wind having blown mainly in that direction; and that the destruction of property in Great Britain and Ireland generally is roughly estimated at fifty-five per cent.

The adventures of our little band, after we came out from our hiding-place, scarcely belong to this story; but I must set down a few events which stand out in red letters in our calendar of the world after the Gray Weed.

Upon the first afternoon we learned that there were other survivors—which we had not dared to hope—by finding a man, woman and child nearly dead with hunger and fright, hiding in a basement. We formed ourselves at once into small parties to go round London, wherever houses yet stood, and rang the church bells, and blew trumpets, and beat drums, and shouted to all those who remained to come out. Here and there frightened groups of white-faced, famished, disheveled people answered the call. As our numbers increased we sent parties to search the cellars and other hiding-places, and rescued many at their last gasp. The total number of survivors in London, where the percentage of deaths was highest, amounts to some 35,000.

Upon the second day we obtained several replies to our calls by telegraph to the provinces; and the next day we were in telegraphic communication with most parts of the United Kingdom and even the Continent. In almost all towns at least one or two persons had escaped. In some parts the Gray Weed had left open spaces, or a few houses, to which people could flee, and only a portion of those who reached them had died from starvation. In a few instances it was alleged to have refrained from injuring those with whom it came in contact. Also it failed to crush many of the ships which it seized at sea—the sea-growths generally being less virulent than those on land. So far as our statistics go at present, we hope that nearly one-eighth of the population of Europe has survived.

On the fourth day the first train from the provinces to London was run; and several ships, which the weed had overgrown without injuring, came into port. After this, traffic was rapidly re-established.

A fortnight later our present government was provisionally established. The professor, whom all hailed as their deliverer, refused office himself; but upon his nomination I was appointed to my present position. Several of our little band were assigned important posts, including Steel—now known by another name, and married to Lady Evelyn—and Viva, who is presiding over the London Homes for Orphans, until our marriage. The day after tomorrow a newspaper appears.

We have toiled unremittingly to reconstruct the social and commercial life of the country, and not without success. We have few luxuries, but no wants; fewer workers, but no drones; fewer to love—but we love more—I think the world will go well, now, because we love one another so much.

"The Gray Weed has solved the problems of poverty, envy, crime and strife, which have puzzled mankind for ages," the professor

said, just before he died. "Don't cry, little Viva. Ah! But I felt a
tear on my hand! There is nothing to cry about, my child. *They*
have gone; and *I* am going; but *you* have learned to love. It is all
for the best!"

"All—for—the—best," he repeated at the last, and smiled. That
is his message to you to whom I write, dear friends.

# THE DARK DAYS

There was a time when none would speak of the horror which came upon the world; but now that three years have passed men talk about it openly and ask one another what it was and how it happened.

Their questions are rarely answered; for some of the survivors have lost their reason; others have lost their memory; the majority remember nothing but silence and unseen hands grasping at them out of the dark. Few of the few who have any distinct recollection possess the gift of expressing themselves clearly. I am one of those whose memory is tolerably clear, and I am a writer by profession. So they have asked me to set down my experience.

It was on the afternoon of the twenty-second of June, 1910. I was hurrying down the Strand to call upon my agents, who had telephoned to me about an offer for my last novel. It was a hot, bright day and I was shading my eyes to look across the street, when suddenly the sun went out. I thought I was smitten with blindness and flung up my arms and gave a great cry. I heard the beginning of it. Then all sound stopped. The rumble of vehicles, the scurry of feet, the cries of the street venders, the shouts of the newspaper boys—all the hum of life—ceased in an instant.

I thought at first that I had died; but I could feel my limbs; feel my lips moving as I cried for help; feel the vibration of the traffic that I could not hear.

"I am blind!" I shouted. "Blind! And deaf! Hold me, someone—
*Someone!*"

I heard no call, and no answer. I groped wildly in the darkness, and met other hands that were groping too. I seized someone by the shoulder, and others seized me. Their hands twitched convulsively. They were crying out as I was. I knew by touching their open mouths and faces contorted with fright. A woman whom I held slipped away from my grasp, and a man whom I grasped in her stead fell too. I suppose they fainted.

It is possible that I, too, fainted, but was held up on my feet by the pressure of the crowd, for I seemed to lose myself for a time and to come back to myself in a swaying, clutching mass of unseen, unheard people. I felt sick and almost suffocated, and tried vainly to push my way out, till the crowd was scattered by a plunging horse which brushed against me as it passed. I took a few hurried steps and found myself somewhere—alone! The perspiration was running down my cheeks, and my throat was dry and swollen with cries that I had not heard. I was more afraid of the loneliness than I had been of the crowd.

I swept the air with my arms till I struck my hand against a wall. I could feel that I had cut my wrist. I felt myself sobbing with utter fear, and felt the tears running down my cheeks. I touched people again; but they were dancing and gesticulating as if they had gone mad, and I was too afraid of them to hold them. When they were gone I beat the empty air again, and wished I had even the poor mad people for company. I stumbled on, and presently I stumbled against a man. He held me, and I held him, both of us shaking horribly. He put his lips to my ear as if he shouted—I felt his breath—but I heard nothing. He smelled of strong drink and I did not like him; but I dared not be alone, so I clutched him as he clutched me. I could not have freed myself from him if I had wished, for he was a powerful man and grasped me violently. His fingers twitched on my arm and he walked unsteadily. We staggered about for what seemed a long time. I did not consider what I was doing at first; but gradually I began to think. Perhaps, I told myself, the darkness and silence would pass away as swiftly as they had come. Even if it lasted forever it might be possible to live in the strange, dark, silent world in some new fashion of life—a life that was only touch and smell—and possibly taste. I wondered whether there were still taste in anything. The idea of taste reminded me that I was hungry and thirsty—terribly thirsty. I decided to find something to eat and drink.

I tried to make my unseen companion understand my purpose by touching his mouth with my fingers, but he still swayed and clutched senselessly. I made signs of cutting with a knife upon his cheek, and indicated a fork with three fingers, and pretended to put things in his mouth, but still I could not make him understand. I invented an alphabet and spelt out messages with taps upon his shoulder; one tap for A, two for B, and so on, but he showed no sign of comprehension. So I dragged him slowly along, feeling about me with one hand.

I found what felt like shop-fronts, and after a time I touched what might be the entrance to a restaurant. I succeeded in dragging the man inside and fumbled at the counter, but found only show-cases. My companion struck his fist angrily upon the glass and shivered it. I could feel the broken glass in his hand. That was how I knew. He steadied himself a little after this and pushed me along. I think he had realized my object, but I could get no intelligible sign from him.

We got into another crowd for a few moments when we re-entered the street, and they drove us almost underneath a horse. Then we stumbled over a number of prostrate bodies. They had evidently fainted, or died of fright. Then we nearly tripped over a dog which snapped at me and tore my clothes. I think it bit my companion, for he kicked out and we lost our balance and fell on the ground. He embraced me so closely that I could not rise. I grew angry and struck at him and he struck at me. He was a very strong man, and I think he would have killed me if he had not been afraid to release his hold for fear of my escaping and leaving him alone. I feared him more than the darkness, but less than the silence.

At last we got upon our feet and after a deal of groping found a public-house—I could tell it by the cut-glass doors. We made our way behind the counter and secured some sandwiches and ate, and filled our pockets. I drank some water. My companion found the

beer engines. I could not get him away from them. He bound my
arm to his with a ball of twine, winding it round and round and
tying it tightly so that he could have both his hands free to drink
without releasing me. He drew beer and drank till the place reeked
with the liquor. Soon he rolled about so that he could scarcely keep
upon his feet. I took out my penknife stealthily and cut the twine
from my arm. Then I gave him a push and he fell. I knew he had
fallen because I felt his hands grasping at my ankles. I eluded them,
clambered over the counter and got back into the street—alone. I
reached out with my arms to try to find someone—anyone. I should
have gone back to the wretched man in my loneliness, but I could
not find the house again. I knocked against cabs and horses in the
streets. The horses were kicking with terror and one bit my arm.
So I went back to the pavement I started from, or across the road—
I did not know which!

At the corner of a side street I ran into some people standing
together. They were gentlefolk by the touch of their clothes; some
men and some women—I was not sure how many—and a little girl
with silky curls. I seized their hands and shook them; but the
women shrank from me and hung upon the men, and the men
hustled me aside. I tried to make them feel my clothes and my
smooth palms to show that I was of their own class, but they could
not or would not understand, and pushed me so violently that I
fell. I picked myself up and tried to find them again. I was ready to
go on my knees to beg for their company, but they had moved or I
mistook the direction. I could not find them or anyone or anything,
and a great terror came upon me. I shrieked and heard no sound,
and staggered on, pawing at the air.

Presently I found buildings, and walked along touching them
with one hand, till the air felt more open. I imagined that I was
coming to the Embankment or to Trafalgar Square—I did not know
which way I had gone—but I ran against houses whichever way I
turned. At last I came upon a drinking fountain, and drank, and
ate some of the sandwiches from my pocket and sat down and
rested till I felt so cool that I judged night had come. Then I rose
and groped about till I found an open door. I entered what seemed

to be a private hotel, found a sofa, and slept on it till I was seized roughly and thrust out into the street. It was still cold, and I thought that the night had not yet gone—if there were now day or night. It seemed to me that there was only time—and silence—and space for the stretching out of a hand. I grasped myself to be sure there was something in the space—grasped myself till it hurt. I walked blindly on, not caring what became of me so long as I came to something, till I fell over a prostrate body. It felt stiff and cold! I screamed silently and went on.

I seemed to lose my senses and find them again as I discovered that I was on the Embankment. I knew the feel of the parapet, and that I could drown if I threw myself into the water below. The thought that there was this refuge comforted me strangely. I fell over more people lying on the ground, and when I knelt down and examined them I felt that they were breathing. I tried my alphabet on them, but they did not understand it, and those who made any movement pushed me feebly away. I walked on till I met a man who tried to hold *me*. I pushed *him* aside. Fear seemed *alive* in the darkness. When the man had gone I was sorry that I had not stayed with him, and I decided to join company with the next person whom I met, whether I feared him or not.

The next living being I touched was a woman sitting on a seat. I sat down beside her, but when I put out my hand to hold her she had gone! It seemed that all feared all who tried to make dumb acquaintance with them. I rose and went on again till I touched a hansom cab. The horse in the shafts was pawing restlessly. I supposed it was hungry and thirsty. I had kicked a pail of water previously, so I went back and fetched it. I stood beside the horse some while for company, but resolved at length to move on. I had an idea that if I could make my way over one of the bridges and get out of London, I might find the sun shining. It must be a city fog, I assured myself—just a fog. Anyhow it would be more tolerable if I could find my way to Blackheath, to my own rooms, and to people who knew me—if anyone knew anyone now.

Presently it grew warm again, from which I inferred that the sun still rose, though I could not see it. Soon afterward I came to a bridge. I took it for Blackfriars. When I had gone some way across two hands clutched my legs. They were such small hands that I did not fear them greatly. I stooped down, and felt a small child lying on the lap of a woman. The woman's hair was loose and hanging over her face. I thought she was young. She shivered at my touch, but I sat down beside her. She laid my hand on the child as if she appealed to me for help. I felt its mouth moving, as if it cried for something. I tried my alphabet on the girl, spelling F-R-I-E-N-D, but she put my hand to her head to feel that she shook it. I could tell by the way she held my hand that she did not mean to refuse my friendship, but to show that she could not understand my signs.

After this she put my hand to her mouth and made motions of eating and drinking. Also she put it to the child's mouth and it nearly bit me in its famished eagerness. I gave them the few sand-wiches I had not eaten and they ate them ravenously. She then made signs of drinking. I plucked at her sleeve to rise and come with me, and she came. She was scarcely able to stand, so I took the child from her and carried it. She hung heavily on my arm and the child kept feeling around my face with its dry lips. I thought there was a drinking fountain at the end of the bridge, but could not find it. My search was greatly hindered by having the child on one arm, and its mother—as I supposed her—hanging upon the other.

We came to shops, but most of them were shut or had the living-rooms locked up. We could not find water for a long time, though I obtained some dry biscuits. At last we brushed against a man and a woman in a furniture shop. I made signs of drinking and they led us within—it seemed unwillingly—and gave us a large jug of water. After we had drunk and eaten my biscuits, the girl lay on a sofa with the child in her arms, while I sat on the floor beside them, and we all went to sleep. I woke to find the girl passing her hands softly over my face. When she had finished with my face she felt the texture of my clothing carefully and my scarf and watch chain and even my handkerchief. She evidently wanted to know what manner of man I was. Apparently she was satisfied, for she held gently to my sleeve when she had finished her inspection.

After a few minutes I stretched myself, as though I woke, and took her hand and tried my alphabet again; and this time she understood and answered. This was the conversation, spelt out slowly, letter by letter:

*I.* F-r-i-e-n-d.
*She.* F-r-i-e-n-d.
*I.* J-o-h-n C-a-r-t-e-r. F-r-i-e-n-d.
*She.* Y-e-s. F-r-i-e-n-d. A-l-i-c-e T-h-o-r-n. W-h-a-t i-s i-t?
*I.* D-o-n-t k-n-o-w.
*She.* S-h-a-l-l w-e d-i-e?
*I.* D-o-n-t k-n-o-w.
*She.* W-h-a-t s-h-a-l-l w-e d-o?
*I.* F-i-n-d y-o-u-r h-o-m-e.
*She.* F-a-r-q-u-h-a-r R-o-a-d, N-o-r-w-o-o-d.
*I.* W-i-l-l g-e-t f-o-o-d d-r-i-n-k f-i-r-s-t.
*She.* D-o-n-t l-e-a-v-e u-s.
*I.* W-i-l-l c-o-m-e b-a-c-k. T-r-u-s-t m-e.
*She.* C-o-m-e b-a-c-k s-o-o-n. S-o f-r-i-g-h-t-e-n-e-d.
*I.* B-e b-r-a-v-e. W-i-l-l c-o-m-e b-a-c-k t-o y-c-u a-n-d y-o-u-r
    b-a-b-y.
*She.* N-o-t m-i-n-e. F-o-u-n-d h-i-m. C-o-m-e b-a-c-k s-o-o-n.
*I.* I w-i-l-l. T-r-u-s-t m-e.
*She.* I d-o. C-o-m-e s-o-o-n.

I gave her hand a long, strong pressure, and went on my search. I felt every piece of furniture several times, arranged the chains in a row, cut notches on the doors and doorposts and scratched a mark along the wall to trace my way back to them. At last I found the man and woman and made signs of eating and drinking. They gave me more water, but no eatables. I could smell that they had food, but when I tried to get some they pushed me away. I suppose they feared to exhaust their supply. The man threatened me, touching my head significantly with a hammer. I would have fought him for the food, but I feared what might happen to Alice and the child if I came to harm. So I felt my way back, by the marks, taking the water, and told her in our alphabet what had happened.

We went out again into the street, holding one another and carrying the child in turn. We talked with our fingers as we walked. Every now and then we met people walking as we were, one foot before the other. They were usually in groups, clinging to one another. From their motions I judged that many had lost their reason. We stepped on some lying upon the ground. At certain places the pavement was covered with prostrate forms. At one of these places a man caught hold of Alice and nearly dragged her away; but I struck him furiously till he released her. We learned to know the dangerous spots by the smell of liquor, and went out into the road to avoid them. On these occasions we frequently knocked against horses and vehicles, many of the latter overturned.

We were very hungry, and at last we "met" some policemen who understood our new language. One of them took us to an eating-house. I offered him money, but he refused.

"N-o u-s-e," he tapped. "E-n-d o-f w-o-r-l-d."

Alice was holding our wrists to feel the conversation, and she answered him. I could feel what she said:

"G-o-d c-a-n s-e-e a-n-d h-e-a-r a-n-d s-a-v-e."

The policeman tapped back:

"G-o-d b-l-e-s-s y-o-u. H-e-l-p u-s a-l-l."

The three of us put our hands together in prayer, Alice's slender hands between his and mine.

We had a good meal and lay down to sleep in an inner room.

"G-o-o-d n-i-g-h-t," Alice tapped out. "K-i-n-d f-r-i-e-n-d. T-h-a-n-k G-o-d f-o-r y-o-u."

I thanked Him very sincerely for her.

In the morning—if it were morning—when we awoke we found a basket, filled it with food and bottles of water, and started again. We were nearly knocked down by a restive horse in crossing a road, and some rough men seized us violently. I struck out and dispersed them; but I lost Alice and the child. I groped about wildly, crying cries that I could not hear, till I tripped over something. I was going on, when a hand tapped my ankle. "F-r-." I knelt down and found Alice. I knew her hair and the ribbon and locket at her neck. We wrung hands excitedly and both "talked" at once. "T-h-e c-h-i-l-d!" We groped about, holding one another firmly, and at last we found the child. It was trembling and sobbing. Alice kissed it passionately and wiped its tears. She gave my arm a pleased squeeze, and put my hand to her face to feel her smile!

"I a-m h-a-p-p-y n-o-w," she spelled out. I began to spell out an answer, but the letters would not come quickly enough for her and suddenly she caught at me and wrote with her finger on my cheek. I could read the writing easily, and it was much quicker than the taps. We were so pleased with our quicker conversation that we stood still writing on one another's faces as fast as our fingers would move. (We always used this way afterward.)

We discussed at length the calamity which had come upon the world. The sun still rose, we thought, because of the changes in temperature, only something in the air would not let us see it and prevented us from hearing one another. "It must be some change in the ether," I wrote; and then I had to explain what ether was.

"Perhaps," I concluded, "it is a sort of fog over London. Shall we try to reach the country?"

"I will do whatever you tell me," she wrote back. "You are very clever and very, very kind. I should not mind so much for myself, but I want the sun for the dear baby. It must be so lonely for him because he cannot write as we do. I keep kissing him to let him know that we love him. Think if all the love had gone from the world instead of only the sun and the sound!"

Only the sun and the sound! I laughed at first at her words; but she put out her hand and felt me laughing, and when I went to write my answer on her cheek I found tears, and she pushed my finger away and wrote on me.

"Suppose you could recover sight and hearing by sacrificing baby and me? Would you?"

I took my handkerchief and wiped her eyes.

"No," I wrote. "No, dear friend. You are right. We should lose more than sight and hearing if we lost one another. I like you very much."

"Perhaps you won't like the sight and sound of us when the sun comes back," she wrote.

"I think I shall," I wrote. "Tell me just what you are like. What is the color of your hair? How old are you?"

"I shall not tell you," she wrote, "because you like me now, and perhaps you would not then. If the sun never rises again I can look just as you like me to look, and be just as old as you wish. Now shall we go on?"

We walked on for a long time, and at last we came to some railings. As we felt our way by them we met a woman coming along in the other direction. We felt one another with our hands and accepted acquaintance. She was a very intelligent lady and understood our writing.

"It is Kennington Park," she wrote; "I am looking for my son. He went out for more provisions and has not come back. Have you met him?"

"No," I answered. "Can we sleep anywhere?"

"My house," she offered, and took us there.

We stayed with them for two days. Their name was Roberts, and they were a very pleasant family. We learned to know them all by touch, to find our way all over the house, and even to do work in the dark. We used to sit, "talking" upon one another's faces. I liked them all; but I liked Alice best.

The son came home soon after we arrived. He brought a lot of provisions. Mrs. Roberts managed to keep house in the dark, and even made a cake and baked it. She was a cheerful, brisk lady, and she declared that, in time, we should get on very well without the sun. "One's family and friends are all that really matters," she often wrote.

Alice wanted to get to her family, and I offered to take her. So on the third day we took a stock of provisions and started off together. We left the baby with Mrs. Roberts. (She afterward adopted him, as his parents were never found.)

We lost ourselves in the first few minutes and could not find anyone who could understand our signs and direct us. Indeed, we met very few people at all, though now and then we found dead bodies. (Most people stayed in their houses, or those to which they had come, during these days, we learned afterward.) We found many dead horses in the shafts of the vehicles they had been drawing.

The temperature had grown appreciably lower during the last two days, and I feared that the cause which had stopped the sun's light so suddenly was stopping the heat from him in a more gradual manner. We could not find a place to rest during the first "cold time"; but in the succeeding "warm time" (these terms had replaced night and day in our vocabulary) we found a deserted railway station and slept in a waiting-room. We had finished our provisions and could not find any shops open for a long while. People had evidently locked themselves in to keep their eatables for themselves, knowing that they could not replenish them. We came to a fruiterer's at last, and took a few vegetables from the open window, but the proprietors came out and drove us off with sticks. My hand was cut, and Alice thought she had a black eye.

"But you can't see how ugly I look," she wrote, She seemed very cheerful, and I grew much attached to her. I took her to be about twenty (I was then twenty-eight), and I fancied she would have dark hair and black eyes. Her features felt as though she must be pretty.

We ate our fruit and still felt hungry. We found one shop open, but it contained only sweets and tobacco. We took all the chocolate we could find, and I took some cigarettes. We wandered on till we came to open gates. From the size of the gateway we judged them to belong to a large house, and went in, hoping to get something to eat. We were quite lost by now.

Presently we found a "shelter" and concluded that we were in a park—possibly Battersea. We could not find the way out, and felt the "cold time" returning. Alice wrote on my cheek, "Very cold, hungry, tired, frightened." She wanted to sit down, but we were shivering already, and I dared not stop moving till we found a heap of small leafy branches cut from the trees. We laid down and covered ourselves with these as well as we could, and clung to one another for warmth. I could tell that she was crying, and I knew that my teeth were chattering with cold, though I could not hear them. I slept a broken sleep. When I finally woke all my limbs were numbed, and when the "warm time" returned we were too feeble to free ourselves from our covering for a long while.

We were sick with hunger and thirst, and walked about aimlessly. We came to the park railings, but she could not climb them and I was too weak to lift her. My mind was numbed as well as my body, and I did not think of following the railings to a gate, until we had gone away from them. We could not find them again.

We found bodies lying on the grass—three men, a woman and a dog. They had evidently been shut in and perished from cold and hunger—unless fright had killed them more quickly and mercifully. We ran away shuddering, till we came to a path. We followed it round and round and reached a café. Dead bodies were lying all over the floor. We thought they would have eaten all the food before they died, so we went away.

We were so weak from hunger that we could scarcely stand. The thirst was worse. We sat down and walked for a few minutes alternately. Then I slipped into some water, about three feet deep— I guessed a bathing pond. We drank greedily, and I wrung the water out of my clothes. Then we crawled away to a seat and fell into a sleep or stupor. I was roused by Alice shaking my arm.

"The darkness is moving," she wrote on my face. "Moving!"

I have often asked her to describe what she saw, but she can find no other words than this. To me it seemed as if the blindness of my eyes had gone, but they could not see through the darkness outside me—an overwhelming blackness that rolled upon us in black waves outrunning the black mist at the back. I could feel it, taste it— It almost stifled me, and my tongue swelled till it nearly filled my mouth, and I gasped for breath.

"The end," I wrote. "Good-bye. God bl—"

And suddenly the black waves passed and the world sprang upon us out of the dark! It was a bright day, and the sky was blue. A bird fluttered unsteadily in the air, and a man rose from the grass—staggered and fell. I scraped my foot along the gravel just to hear the sound. Alice grasped my arm till her fingers hurt. We turned to one another and saw—strangers!

Alice has never told me what she expected to see and what she saw, and I have never told her; but I think she expected to discover a handsome, well-groomed young gentleman, and I know that I had thought of her as a dark-haired, dark-eyed, rosy-cheeked, prettily dressed girl of twenty. She found a creature who looked like a tramp; a bent, unkempt, unshaken ruffian, who might have been forty. I saw a fair-haired, blue-eyed, white-faced, travel-stained—child! For she whom I had taken for the lady of my dreams was but a tall schoolgirl, of fifteen!

We sat and stared at one another. Our lips trembled when we tried to speak. I think we should have hurt one another if we had spoken, but the woman's heart in her childish body saved everybody. She took my hand and wrote on it slowly.

"Friend! Kind friend!"

And then I took her hands in mine and spoke. My voice was hoarse with thirst and weakness.

"God bless you, dear!" I said. "God bless you— This is 'only the sun and the sound.' *We* are the loyal and loving friends that we have been—that we shall be always."

"Always," she said; and we rose and walked forth to find the world, hand in hand.

It was Brockwell Park, we learned, and the people gave us food and drink; and in an hour we reached her home at Norwood. It was evening, and we were too tired to do anything but sleep. The next morning when I had shaved and borrowed new clothes I came downstairs, and found Alice bright and smiling and dressed in fresh white with a blue ribbon at her neck and another in her hair. She came forward holding out both hands to me.

"Why, child!" I cried. "How pretty you are!"

To my astonishment she burst into tears.

"I thought if I put on my best dress," she sobbed, "perhaps—perhaps you would like the— 'the sight and sound' of—of your friend."

"Dear," I said, "I shall like to see you and hear you as long as there is sight and sound; and even if they are gone, I shall like you!"

That is the end of my story of the dark days that men lost. You know as well as I that the astronomers reckon that they were seven; and say that the darkness and deafness were due to our passing through an etherless space which stopped light, and, in some way which they cannot explain, deadened the sound vibrations of the air. You know, also, how the earth was decimated and trade disorganized; how crops failed and hard times came; and how trouble made all the world friends, and strife ceased, and armies were disbanded. And so we came to these days of plenty and peace. Sometimes I think that the days of darkness were not in vain; and last night I almost wished them back.

I was leaving Alice's house, and she saw me to the door as usual. We have always loved one another as a man and a child may love, and now she has ceased to be a child, and does her hair up in a golden knob. I think her very beautiful.

We had just reached the door when suddenly the electric light went out. She gave a sharp cry, and in a moment she was in my arms— The light spluttered up noisily again, but she did not raise her eyes. And I did not let her go. Instead, I reached out one hand and turned out the light. Then I lifted her face and wrote with my finger on her cheek:

"I love you—love you—love you!"

She did not speak, but pressed my hand upon her face to feel her smile—the smile that lit my heart in the dark days, and lights it still!

# THE LONG NIGHT
## A STORY OF THE NEXT DECADE

Barely six months have elapsed since the great change in the revolution of the earth took place; but over a hundred books have already been published dealing with the causes of the change, the effects upon the physical conditions of the world, the disturbance of the calendar, etc., etc. These treatises contain elaborate tables showing the changes of temperature, the rate of mortality, the migration of population, and the damage to vegetation, buildings, and shipping during the long night in which the earth passed through the greatest crisis of its history; but I have searched them in vain for any picture of the life and sufferings of individuals during this terrible period. Thinking that such a record may be of interest to future generations, I propose, while the events are fresh in my mind, to set down what happened within my own experience.

Like most people, I first heard of the disturbance on the afternoon of September 20th. I was returning to my office after lunch when I found that a crowd had stopped the traffic in Ludgate Circus. I edged my way into it, and discovered that it had formed round some newspaper boys. A tall man had seized one of their placards and was flourishing it aloft:

EVENING POST.
THE SUN
THIRTEEN MINUTES LATE.
ELECTRIC
DISTURBANCES.

The papers gave little more information than the placard. The astronomers at Greenwich had found the sun thirteen minutes thirteen seconds late in crossing the meridian. They had telegraphed to other observatories, but had only obtained a reply from Edinburgh (where the difference was given as thirteen minutes fifty-one seconds) owing to some unknown electric disturbance which had upset the telegraph wires and cables. It was thought possible that this disturbance had affected the clocks, so that the lateness of the sun was only apparent; but the Astronomer Royal was not of this opinion. Special preparations were being made to test the matter at sunset, which was due at 6.5.

Most people treated the matter as a hoax or jest till the four o'clock editions came out. These reported that observations at Greenwich showed that the retardation of the sun's progress continued. Scientific authorities held that this was due either to a slowing of the earth's revolution, or to a change in the direction of its axis in space. The next editions announced that bombs would be fired at certain places five minutes after sunset. I went to Westminster Bridge to hear the signal at the House of Commons. The crowd seemed to find courage in numbers, and there was a good deal of chaff and some horse-play. Street vendors were selling an atrocious cartoon of a drunken man coming home to his wife. "'Tishn't me thatsh late, my dear," he said. "Itsh the sun." Others were hawking a penny pamphlet on the motion of the earth. Some workmen were arguing out the effects upon the eight hours day.

"If the bloomin' sun don't choose to 'urry 'isself," one said, "yer can knock orf by the bloomin' clock. Yer git more time orf, that's all."

"Wot's the good of more time if yer ain't got more money to spend?" another retorted.

"There won't be no more time," a third man insisted. "They'll shut at 'arf past twelve all the same."

A heated discussion upon closing time followed. A youth started playing a mouth-organ, and several couples danced to the music. At a minute to six the scene was like a fair.

When Big Ben struck six, however, the crowd suddenly sobered. The long hand crept on to five, and then to ten. When the quarter struck the crowd drew a deep breath. It sounded like the sighing of the wind.

"It seems very light." I observed to my neighbour.

"Horribly light," he agreed hoarsely.

The long hand crept on to twenty and twenty-five. The half-hour struck, and still there was no sign. Several of the crowd left to go home. They looked scared, and some of the women held their handkerchiefs to their eyes.

"Makes you wonder what's going on up *there*," said a man on my left. He pointed unsteadily to the skies till the umbrella dropped from his shaking hand. "Gets on your nerves, this waiting," he apologised as he picked it up.

"We can only be patient," said a pale man mildly. A hawker thrust a cartoon in front of his face, and he seized it and tore it across in sudden fury. "Get out with your foolery!" he shouted.

"Get out!" shouted the crowd, and the hawkers were hustled across the bridge.

A man who had been drinking from a bottle began singing a ribald song. The crowd handled him roughly, till half-a-dozen police-men formed round him and took him away. Then there was a dead silence till a quarter to seven struck. One could feel the crowd shiver, and a woman began sobbing.

"Come, come!" her husband remonstrated. "What's the use of taking on? Supposing the sun never sets at all, where's the harm?"

"Supposing it sets and never rises again?" she asked. Her voice was almost a scream.

A gaunt man got up on the parapet and prayed fervently that God, who spanned the heavens with His hand, would guide our little world safely through the changes of the universe. The woman stopped crying, and the men uncovered their heads. There were loud cries of "Amen" when he ceased.

Immediately after—at 6.50 almost exactly—there was a flash and a loud report. The sun had set, forty minutes late, at 6.45. The crowd melted slowly away, and I went home to Dulwich, where I lived with my married sister. Her husband met me in the hall, and whispered that he had told her that it was only the clocks that were wrong. She whispered to me in the dining-room: "I know, Fred, I know! I've seen the papers. Don't tell him, then he won't worry so much about me."

We tried to make conversation, but there were long pauses, and we kept glancing at the clock. They went to bed early. I sat up and smoked and paced the room, and wondered what Myra Davis thought about it. We had been engaged, but we had quarrelled six months before.

At midnight, by the clock, I went to bed. I woke before five, and got out to watch for the sunrise. It was due at 5.44, so it should begin to get light before five. If it was an hour late the forelight should commence about six. At half-past five the night was as black as ink. The electric lamps in the streets had gone out. I lit the gas and tried to read, but could not fix my attention on the magazine. Suppose the sun never rose again, as the woman had suggested? Suppose the earth had fallen from its orbit? Suppose it was being drawn, with gradually increasing velocity, into the fiery sun? I imagined these and a hundred other horrible things till my hair nearly stood on end. At a little after six o'clock I put out my light and peeped through the blind. It was still pitch dark. I wondered if Myra was peeping through her blind, and if *she* was frightened. She lived with her widowed mother at Upper Tulse Hill, and they had no male relative near.

The quarter went, and still there was no sign of the light. At seven, however, the inky blackness had turned to grey-black. I opened my window, and stood there watching the familiar objects appear one by one. My teeth chattered in spite of my thick dressing gown. The morning was colder than usual, no doubt owing to the longer night. As nearly as I could reckon, sunrise came at a few minutes to eight—over two hours late!

My brother-in-law was not down to breakfast. He had not slept well, my sister said, but now he had fallen into a doze, and she would not wake him. Her hand shook so that she spilt my coffee in passing it. When I rose to go she put her hand on my arm.

"They will be very lonely and frightened," she said. "I know it wasn't your fault, but—" She looked at me appealingly.

"It wasn't all her fault," I confessed. "If I thought that she wanted me I would go; but she'd be sure to say she didn't. Well, I'll risk it. Good old Sis!"

I kissed her, and went to Upper Tulse Hill.

Myra opened the door herself. She made a little choking sound, and clutched at my arm.

"I knew you would come," she said. "Mother is in Germany; and the servants left me last night. I thought it was the end of the world. . . . I wanted to see you first, and—and—oh, Fred!"

I stayed with her for half-an-hour, and made her cat some breakfast. She came to Herne Hill Station and saw me off. I arranged to go back in the afternoon and take her to my sister's.

When I got to the City I found most of the offices shut, and mine among the number. People were staying at home with their families to wait events. Only a few of the evening papers came out, and these at irregular intervals. A Cabinet Council was sitting to consider the situation, and a number of eminent scientists had been summoned to attend. Later in the morning a notice was posted up in thick black type:—

PUBLIC WARNING.

THE CHANGES IN THE TIME.

The changes in the length of the day are undoubtedly due to an unknown force, which produces a. progressive diminution in the revolution of the earth.

It is conjectured that this force emanates from a non-luminous and invisible "comet," passing the earth in a direction apposite to its revolution, but the disturbances cannot be completely explained on this or any other hypothesis. As gravity has not drawn the "comet" to the earth, it must be either immaterial or exceedingly attenuated. No danger need, therefore, be apprehended from collision, but serious electrical results are to be feared in the event of contact.

Upon this hypothesis the lengthening of the day and night will continue until the comet has passed out of range.

The lengthening of day and night will produce great extremes of heat and cold, increasing as the periods are lengthened. All persons are advised to make preparations for securing warmth during a night possibly of greatly increased duration.

Should the retardation continue at the present rate, the earth's revolution would cease at about 3.30 a.m. on the 28th September, when the British Isles would be upon the side of the earth remote from the sun. In such unfortunate event these countries would speedily become ice-bound and uninhabitable. The Government are making every effort to provide shipping for such a contingency, but it is impossible to obtain the full number of ships needed by Government action. Local authorities and private individuals are, therefore, urged to take every opportunity of securing transport.

In view of the purely conjectural nature of the information at present available, all persons are advised to refrain from flight until further data have been obtained. All available information will be promulgated immediately, but it must be borne in mind that telegraphic communication is greatly delayed by the electrical disturbances.

In spite of the notice everyone seemed preparing for flight eastward. I telegraphed to my brother-in-law advising him to go, drew out all my money (some £200) from the bank, which fortunately was open, and hurried to Tulse Hill for Myra. We packed a small handbag, and went back to town, arriving about five. There was a fresh notice up:

"Noon over three hours late at Greenwich.

"All telegraphic communication has failed."

We intended to take tickets at Cook's by whatever routes they advised; but we could not get near the offices on account of the crowd. At half-past five a notice was put up that every berth in every steamer was sold. We decided to go down to the south coast, in the hope of finding a vessel, or even a boat, for the Continent, proposing then to travel to the Mediterranean by train, and take a ship thence to the East. We tried Ludgate Hill, Cannon Street, and Charing Cross in turn, but the approach to each station was blocked by a frantic crowd.

We had some tea at a shop in Whitehall, and talked the matter over. Myra, who kept her nerve splendidly, suggested that we should buy cycles and ride down to Dover. We walked over Westminster Bridge, found a shop, and bought them. I tied the bag on behind mine, and we started. It was 7.30 then, and very hot. The sun evidently would not set for hours, unless some great catastrophe happened. The fear of this was always with us.

For the first hour the road was crowded with a hurrying mob; 'buses holding double their number; waggons and carts loaded with people and their goods; men and women with their children on barrows, or in mail-carts. One man had put wheels to a sugar-box to convey his baby. A little beyond Eltham we passed out of the crowd of pedestrians, but cyclists and motorists still flew by. The villagers stared at us in amazement. The proclamations had not reached so far owing to the breakdown in the telegraph. The sun had set a little before we came to Rochester, but the light was still good when we arrived there at half-past eleven.

Myra was too tired to ride any farther, so we put up at a hotel in the main street, called the King's Head. Most of the waiters and servants had caught the panic from the fugitives and fled to the coast, so we had to wait a long time for supper. We ate it by the light of our cycle lamps, as the electric light had failed. Then we went to bed. My room was in the front, and the noise of the unceasing traffic kept me awake for some time. Then I slept till eight. There was no sign of the dawn, and I dozed again till ten. It was still dark, and I felt so chilly that I doubled the counterpane. At eleven, the landlady brought a candle, and I dressed and joined

Myra in the coffee-room. A fire had been lit, and we sat over it after breakfast. It was pitch dark outside; no lamps, no moon, no stars. We decided to remain at the hotel till the sun rose—if it ever did.

Two motorists, who stopped for food, said that there was a horrible panic in London, and thousands of people who could get no conveyance were walking down. There was no fresh news up to the time they left.

A faint light began about two o'clock (just after lunch). We started soon after the half-hour. The temperature was nearly at freezing point. The sun rose just as we had wheeled our machines up Chatham Hill, and came to Jezreel's Temple. We stood watching it. The same thought occurred to both, and we shivered.

"If it is the last time," Myra comforted me, "we've seen it together." She touched my arm and smiled.

I had a puncture, and Myra's right ankle was weak. So we did not reach Dover till twelve o'clock—midnight of September 22nd, according to the old calendar. It was beginning to get very hot. The approaches to the pier were stopped by pickets of soldiers, and a young officer told me that I could not go any further. There were already more people waiting than could be embarked in a month, and there had been several fatal riots. The general was trying to get the women and children shipped first, but he feared that the mob would be too strong for the soldiers. "I'll try to pass you on, if you wish," he told Myra; "but I don't suppose you'd leave your—your friend? Of course not. I could see you weren't that sort!"

He advised us to make our way back towards the Isle of Sheppey, and try to catch a Flushing steamer from Queenboro' Pier, or a Government vessel at Sheerness Dockyard, where they had sent the ladies of the garrison. He gave us his card—Captain R. Winston, R.A.—with a pencilled introduction to the commandant at Sheerness. Then we shook hands and left him. He was frozen at his post during the long night, we learnt afterwards.

After a hasty meal we made our way to Canterbury, avoiding the main road as much as possible, as I did not like the look of some of the crowd on it. We both had punctures, and had to walk for miles before we found a repairing shop. So we did not reach Canterbury till after four on the morning of September 23rd (old time). It was nearly afternoon by the sun, and the heat was over-powering. Myra was exhausted, and we rested till half-past six. Then we took the main road, hoping to reach Sheerness before it was dark. The road was infested with roughs, and we passed several people who had been forcibly robbed of their machines. At Boughton a huge tramp threw me off my cycle. As he stooped to pick it up, Myra pluckily ran into him and rolled him over. I knocked him down as he rose, and regained my machine.

We reached Sittingbourne at ten o'clock, old time, just before sunset. I did not know the shorter way through the back streets, so we went on to Key Street. The inn at the corner, where we should leave the London road, had been sacked by a gang of roughs. They caught hold of us as we were passing, and took our machines. They tried to detain Myra, but I seized one of their sticks and kept them at bay while she ran on. Then I broke away and overtook her. Fortunately they were too drunk to run fast.

It was almost dark when we reached Bobbing, but Myra urged me to go on. She was weak and unstrung, and we walked very slowly. At about twelve she suddenly swayed and fainted. When she revived she could not walk for a long time, and then she had to rest every few yards. After several attempts she collapsed com-pletely. I sat down and let her sleep with her head on my knees. This was at 2 p.m. on September 23rd, old time. I tried to rouse her several times, but could not. At about four I must have fallen asleep myself. When I woke, my teeth chattered with the cold, and our knees were so numbed that we could not stand for some min-utes. I struck a match and found that the time was half-past nine. We stumbled along arm-in arm, but her ankle was painful, and we went very slowly. We lost the road several times, and once we fell over a heap of stones. No light was visible above or below. It grew horribly cold, and my moustache was frozen stiff. After some hours of wandering, Myra could walk no longer and became unconscious. I crouched under the shelter of a hedge, holding her in my arms. I was drowsy and almost senseless with the cold. Then I heard a dog bark, and carried her toward the sound, painfully and a few steps at a time. Presently I saw a candlelight in a window about fifty yards away. It took me ten minutes to carry her so far. When they opened the cottage door we fell helplessly inside.

The old couple who lived in the cottage—it was at Iwade—rolled us up in blankets, and fed us with spoonfuls of milk with coarse spirits in it. As soon as we felt a little warmth we fell asleep. When I woke they had come downstairs and lit the fire, and were getting breakfast. They had double clothing on, and looked like Esquimaux. They had never felt the cold like it, they said. It was after seven o'clock of the morning of September 24th, and the sun had been down for twenty-one hours. It was surely the end of the world, the old woman quavered.

After breakfast we shivered over the fire for an hour. Then a pale light streamed in at the window. We saw the fields and trees white with the snow and frost. It was one o'clock before we thought it warm enough to venture out. Patches of snow were still lying in the shadows, and there were dead sheep and horses in the fields. Near the ferry bridge we saw the bodies of a man and woman among the straw beside a haystack. Thin sheets of ice were floating on the river.

We reached Queenboro' Pier at half-past three, on what should have been the afternoon of September 24th, but the sun was still low in the east. A steamer was about to leave the end of the pier, and a huge crowd was struggling to get upon it. Hundreds were trampled under foot, and many were pushed off the pier into the water and drowned. Ten times the proper number were aboard already, an old man told us. They were beating back those who still tried to get on. When the vessel began to move, men and women jumped after it, and fell into the water. One man threw his little child right among the people aboard. At last the vessel was out of reach, and the crowd gave a shriek such as I hope never to hear again.

We went on to Sheerness and found Colonel Lemain, the military commandant—a courteous, grey-haired old soldier—and presented Captain Winston's card. The colonel was very kind, and said that he would gladly have given us a passage if he could, but there was not even a steam pinnace left. "A good many people are trying to reach the Continent in rowing-boats," he told us. "I'll put you in one with some respectable people, if you like; but I don't recommend you to go. If you don't reach the Continent before night you will be frozen to death. If you do I don't suppose you'll find a train. If you find a train, it couldn't get far enough east to save you except by the mercy of God. *That* can save you here. The great thing is to provide for keeping warm during the night. I am sending out pickets to bring in all the fugitives who have no home; and I've commandeered all the public buildings and hotels, and am laying in provisions and bedding and fuel. They're a pretty rough crowd, so far as I've seen yet. You'll be better in a private house, and the small rooms are warmer. There's 58 Marine Parade. Major Peters lived there, but I sent him off in a steamer with his family, as his wife was ill. I'll assign that to you. Let me know if I can do anything more. Good-morning."

We thanked him and made our way to the house and took possession. We found food and drink and a change of clothes. We slept during the heat of the day (which was thirty hours from sunrise to sunset). When it grew cooler we took a walk through the town. We met the colonel, and he took us to see the arrangements for the refugees. There were nearly two thousand, mostly from the slums of London. He had gathered them together in the neighbourhood of "Bank's Town," in the Victoria Hall and attached buildings, the two big workmen's clubs, the Royal Hotel, and Trinity Church, and kept them there with armed sentries so that they should not pillage the town.

When the sun neared the horizon, Myra and I said good-bye to the colonel, and went back to our house. We selected the dining-room for our winter quarters. I laid the fire and carried up a large supply of coal and wood, while Myra filled the cupboards with food and drink. Then we collected all the blankets and rugs in the house. Then we sat at the open window and watched the sun set. It was three o'clock in the afternoon of September 25th, old reckoning.

The twilight lasted for at least two hours, and it was still very hot after the prolonged day. A few people strolled up and down the esplanade, and presently a little group spoke to us, and we went out and joined them. One was the dockyard schoolmaster, and he had some knowledge of astronomy. He reckoned that the force acting on the earth was one which reduced the rate of revolution of a point on the equator by about five miles an hour, and that it would bring the earth to rest an hour or so before the next sunrise, if it went on at the same rate; but he had an idea that the force would diminish as the earth was stopping, so that the sun would crawl on to our longitude. In this case we should have perpetual day instead of perpetual night. We need not give up hope till midnight of September 28th, he said, some eighty hours after sunset.

We went to supper with him and his wife and some friends. After supper we tried music, cards, story-telling, and half-a-dozen other amusements, but could not fix our minds on any. We did not like to part company, and after many hours we had another supper; and our host then advised us to get back to our houses, as he doubted if he had sufficient food for us all.

The rain had frozen in the road, and we slipped and fell several times. It was pitch dark, and I had to crawl up the icy steps and strike matches to look at the numbers on the doors. At last we found our house, and went in shivering with cold. The electric light had failed, and we had only one candle, which we wished to save, so we used the fire, which I lit, for light as well as warmth. It was pleasant for a time sitting on the hearthrug, holding hands. We decided to keep a diary, and I jotted down the events in a little blank account book with the stump of a pencil, by the light of the fire. I think these rough entries tell our story better than any account that I could write.

19½ *hours after sunset.*—Returned to house. Freezing hard outside. Lit fire, and put on overcoat and winter jacket. Icicles on window, visible by firelight.

22 *hours.*—Noticed we had forgotten kettle. Fetched from scullery. Water inside frozen in solid block. On melting discovered kettle had burst. Found smaller one. Breakfasted.

28 *hours.*—Woke from doze very cold. Lunched.

33 *hours.*—Cold increasing. Made huge fire. Chimney caught alight. No damage. Had to open door to let out smoke. Cold air almost unbearable.

40 *hours.*—Several mice came out and sat in fender. Myra nervous, but would not let me drive them away. Fed them with crumbs. She slept on sofa, and I in armchair.

44 *hours.*—Frost cracked a window-pane. We should probably have suffocated in our sleep if this had not happened. Stuck brown paper over pane with marmalade. Windows thick with ice. Breakfasted.

50 *hours.*—The front wall suddenly gaped in a huge crack, just over the cupboard, doubtless from frost. Fetched door-mat from passage at great risk from cold. Cut it in pieces and filled cracks and poured in water which froze, and stopped them up except for some tiny holes. We thought these were necessary for ventilation, as we were both very drowsy.

56 *hours.*—Woke by Myra putting coal on fire, which was nearly out. Cold unspeakably terrible. Took an hour to boil water. Myra started to make mittens for our hands and masks for our faces out of old flannel. Found work very difficult through numbed fingers.

58 *hours.*—Myra completed masks and mittens. A great comfort.

60 *hours.*—Sun due to stop. Prayed. We wish to set down that we have been happy together during this awful time.

64 *hours.*—Saw faint light through window. Thought dawn coming.

65 *hours.*—Planet four times size of moon rose over sea to N.E. Sea apparently frozen, but could not see plainly through frost on glass. (We did not then know the moon had come permanently nearer the earth.)

67 *hours.*—Terrific crash from direction of sea. Myra fainted. (This, of course, was due to the ice falling in, when the moon drew the sea from underneath it. We thought it was the dissolution of the world.)

68 *hours.*—Planet disappeared.

80 *hours.*—Fire low. Had to crawl on hands and knees to make it up.

83 *hours.*—Air full of specks of bright light. (Generally ascribed to luminous tail of comet. Continued as long as I noticed.)

86 *hours.*—Decided to lie near fire, so that we could make it up without moving.

90 *hours.*—Myra crawled to cupboard and placed provisions within reach. We have can of water in fender.

104 *hours.*—Made up fire. Cold killing us.

108 *hours.*—God—mercy!

The pencil dropped from my fingers after I made the last entry. I remember very little afterwards.

We kept saying "good-bye" to one another. At last she did not answer. I made a tremendous effort and put some coal on, and kissed the mask over her face. Then I think I fainted.

When I roused there was a faint light at the window, a white light, not like the light of the big moon or fiery dust. I thought at first that I dreamed it. Presently I saw the face of the clock, then the hands—three o'clock. Five days since sunset, and now the sun had risen—in the west!

\* \* \*

You can read in the books how the day and night shortened again till we came to the present solar day of 28 hrs. 11 mm. 51¼ secs.; how the seas and tides changed with this and the drawing nearer of the moon, so that there was water where continents had been, and fresh continents grew out of the sea covered with the bones of monsters of the deep; how many were killed by the cold (and in the east by the heat), and some survived, and life for those who lived was changed. But the books leave out the greatest thing of all—the change that happened to thousands and thousands who went through the long night—as it happened to my dear Myra and me—the widening, deepening, and strengthening of our love by the troubles that we had passed through together.

# THE SHADOW
## A STORY OF A FUTURE DAY

### I
#### HOW THE SHADOW CAME

There were three of us who knew the truth about the shadow that came upon the earth. God will remember that we bore the horror of it and said no word. Henryson died a week ago, and Vassall is dying. Henceforth I shall bear the burden alone; I shall walk among the men and women who are branded with the shadow, change words with them, shake hands with them, lean on them in the little things of daily life. I shall know that they will do evil and see it done. The truth will tremble on my lips, and yet they will make no sound. At least I can write it down.

It was on the 12th of March, 1907, that the explosion happened in the laboratory of John Denton, F. R. S., whom some called the greatest scientist of modern days. I was the surgeon on duty when they brought him into the hospital ward. He was unconscious from concussion of the brain and spine, and the end was only a matter of time.

The papers attributed the calamity to an experiment with high explosives. That was true, so far as it went. Vassall told me the rest. He was a high official at the Home Office, and he came post haste to the hospital when he heard that Denton was there. Henryson, the specialist in "shock" cases, arrived a few minutes later. He was a friend of both, and Vassall had summoned him by telephone. They were in a state of intense excitement, though I did not judge them to be excitable men. They whispered less softly than they intended, and my ears are keen.

"I warned you both," Henryson declared. "You can't outrage nature beyond a certain point. Can you tell how far he had gone with the preparations? You've been there, haven't you?"

Vassall shook his head. "The whole house is a wreck. Even the lodge which stands a hundred yards off is damaged. Heaven grant it's all blown up; but I don't know. Will he recover consciousness?"

Henryson examined the prostrate form carefully.

"I fear so," he said at last.

They looked at one another meaningly, and then at me.

"He may say things that must not be repeated, Dr. Fielding," Vassall warned me. "There are grave reasons for silence; political reasons."

"Human reasons," Henryson corrected. "There must be no babbling nurses. We will watch him in turn, the three of us. You can manage that, Fielding?"

"I *can*," I said; "but I should like to know a little more about it."

Henryson looked at Vassall. "You can trust Fielding," he said; "and if you couldn't you'd have to tell him, all the same."

Vassall coughed and cleared his throat. Then he told me the story in a dry, unemotional voice, as though he were dictating an official minute.

"Dr. Denton was the inventor of the process of branding criminals by ether-rays, which excited so much controversy and finally turned out the government. They were to be marked with a shadowy letter and number, for purposes of identification, you will remember. We should have preferred to mark them obviously to warn people against them; but we conceded to popular clamor that the rays should be applied in some inconspicuous place. Personally I thought it the most valuable idea of the century. I think so still. However, the public wouldn't have it.

"Denton was grieved at the abandonment of the scheme. So was I. He was not a man who struck at trifles. Neither am I. We decided to work the process ourselves. His first idea was to brand convicts from a distance, somewhat in the manner of wireless telegraphy; but the difficulties were insuperable. So many prison officials would have had to be taken into confidence that the matter was sure to leak out. Therefore he conceived the idea of generating and loosing upon the world a large quantity of the rays, which would automatically settle upon persons of criminal intention, and brand them. I approved of this scheme. Henryson disapproved."

"It would have branded the whole world!" Henryson cried. "You and me and Fielding—all of us. Criminal intention! We all have it; but most of us fight it. Who shall say that it will prevail till it does? God and man judge us by our deeds. You promised me not to do it."

"We recognized Henryson's objection," Vassall corrected him calmly, "and promised not to use the rays until we found which would act only upon persons of marked and preponderant criminal tendencies. The original rays would mark the skin of anyone with whom they were brought in contact—good, bad, or indifferent. Denton found, however, that they could be modified so as to act only in certain cases; and that their selection of persons was governed, not by the nature of the skin, but by the temperament of the individual and the physical organization which is so closely connected with this. At last he invented a variety, which he termed the malfactory rays, having a special affinity for the criminal classes. By experiment with a dilute form, which marked temporarily and almost imperceptibly, he found that, out of 100 cases, 37 were undoubtedly criminal, 32 were probably so, 19 were doubtful, and 12 were wrongly marked, as far as we could judge. Henryson insisted that we must improve upon this result before freeing the rays, and Denton was experimenting to this end when it happened. Poor old Denton! If ever a man labored with an unselfish desire to benefit society it was he. You will help us to suppress it, Dr. Fielding, if only in the interests of other people? Suppose some unscrupulous person got hold of the idea, for example."

"I will help you to suppress it," I agreed, "in the interest of other people; not from sympathy with you or the injured man. I consider the project a diabolical one."

We arranged to watch Denton in turns, and I took the first spell. He did not stir, or open his eyes, and I fed him by injecting concentrated nourishment. Henryson relieved me at four o'clock.

"Nothing has happened," he announced with a sigh of relief.

"What did you expect to happen?" I asked.

"I didn't know. You see he had accumulated a huge amount of the rays—you can't make them in small quantities—and if they had been set loose? But I suppose they were all destroyed by the explosion. You were right when you called it a diabolical project. I ought to have stopped them."

"You really believe they could have done it?"

"I *know* they could. Well, well! You go and have your tea."

My tea was waiting in my little room as usual. I sipped it while I read the afternoon paper. I was pouring out the second cup when my eye caught a paragraph in leaded type, under the late news.

> THE BRAND OF CAIN—ASTOUNDING MARK ON A MURDERER.
> At Bow St. Police Court an extraordinary blackish-grey mark suddenly appeared on the face of the man Smith as he pleaded "Not Guilty" of the murder of Maude Farringdon. Her sister, who was in court, shrieked out that it was the brand of Cain. On being shown the mark in a looking-glass, Smith lost all control of himself, and called out, "I did it! I did it!" The court was adjourned for a medical inquiry into the state of his mind.

I dropped the teapot, which broke upon the table, and rushed down to Henryson. I do not recollect how I told him; but I think I could only point to the paper. I remember that he kept pacing the room and muttering, "The Judgment Day! The Judgment Day before its time. Good Lord deliver us!"

We telephoned for Vassall, but he had started before the message arrived. He brought all the evening papers. One of them had a facsimile of the mark. It was like a blotchy four-leaved flower, like this:

"There's enough of the cursed stuff to brand all Europe," Henryson said, after a long silence.

"If it only brands murderers and evildoers the world will be better for it," Vassall retorted. He tried to speak confidently, but his voice shook.

"It won't," Henryson cried. "You know it won't, Vassall. There will be the doubtful cases; and the cases of those who are innocent. Suppose it marks some of your own friends? Your mother, your sister, the little niece you are so fond of, who is just going to be married—?"

"Don't," Vassall cried suddenly. "Don't!" He put up his hands as if to shut some sight from his eyes. "The explosion must have destroyed most of it. A stray ray has escaped, that is all. Send a boy to get the next edition, Fielding. Whew! It's hot."

It was a cold day for March, but he mopped his forehead.

There were three more cases in the next edition. A lawyer of repute had been marked as he sat in his office, advising a company promoter about a prospectus. His client was marked also. A lady living in Cromwell Road, South Kensington, had gone out shopping at noon, and arrived home at three. She did not know that she was marked till the housemaid opened the door. She had been hysterical since, and could give no account of her movements.

The following edition reported twenty cases. The last edition gave nearly a hundred. All sorts and conditions of people were attacked, and under every variety of circumstances. Two low women were marked as they fought in a courtyard, and two society ladies as they whispered scandal over afternoon tea; a missionary as he visited in a slum, and a brute as he kicked his wife; an employer as he gave witness against an embezzling clerk, and the clerk as he stood in the dock; a prominent member of the Stock Exchange as he closed a deal, and a Cabinet minister as he answered a question in the House. One or two of the victims had almost lost their reason with fright.

"They must have intended doing—something," Vassall said; "but we don't know that they would have done it." He had altered his tone since Henryson suggested that his own friends might be attacked.

"The evil that will come would have come anyhow," Vassall persisted. "You would only add to it. Some of those who are branded may repent. Some of them may be quite innocent. Some of them may be your friends, and Fielding's, and mine. You shan't do it, Henryson."

"I will," Henryson shouted. "I shall go and tell the police, the press—everybody."

He made for the door; but Vassall seized the poker from the fender and sprang toward him. He stopped suddenly, dropped the poker, and stood pointing with a shaking hand to the looking-glass. A blurry, shadowy black, four-leaved shape had come upon his forehead. He swayed a little, and I took his arm and helped him to a chair.

"Mark or no mark, Vassall," I said, "here's my hand."

Henryson paused with his hand on the door-handle, and looked at us both over his shoulder. His face twitched.

"The mark ought to have fallen on me," he said in a slow, hushed voice. "You were right, Vassall. I swear by the shadow to keep silence."


II

How the Shadow Stayed

Three hundred cases were reported in the morning papers, and the leading articles discussed the matter at length.

"They must have meant to do something," Henryson stated; "but Heaven knows if they would have done it. They are entitled to the benefit of the doubt."

"They will do it," Vassall said. "We shall see if we watch them. We can't help watching them. If only we didn't know."

"Isn't there any remedy?" I asked. My voice sounded listless. I hadn't slept all night.

"If there is, only one man can find it." He jerked his hand towards the unconscious man on the bed. "'Can't you doctors bring him to for a moment? Henryson? Fielding?"

We shook our heads. We could only wait for nature. Interference meant death.

About this time one of my fellow doctors suggested to me a connection between the shadow and Denton's experiments. It was common gossip at the clubs, he said.

The next morning the rumor was in the papers. A mob howled around the hospital in the afternoon. The following day there was a larger mob, but it was kept back by a couple of dozen policemen. Vassall had obtained them through the Home Office. He sat beside the unconscious man with a revolver in his pocket. Henryson and I had revolvers too. We always carried them now.

In the afternoon the mob threw things and broke some of the windows, but fortunately they had no great supply of missiles. Then they threatened to lynch Denton, and made some ugly rushes. The police had to take refuge within the hall, and we barricaded the place as well as we could, but the mob brought straw and tar-barrels and threatened to burn the building. Vassall addressed them from a window, and reminded them of the harmless and helpless patients, but they only hissed and howled at him. They were an evil-looking set of ruffians, and most of them were marked upon their faces with the shadow. We stood at a side window with our revolvers, ready to shoot anyone who tried to fire the pile, and ultimately some troops arrived from Chelsea Barracks and dispersed the crowd. Vassall proposed to make a clean breast of everything to the prime minister in the morning, and ask for a permanent guard. Denton must be saved, he said, if it took all the troops in the kingdom. He was the only man who could dispel the shadow, if *he* could.

In the night Denton recovered consciousness for a few moments. Vassall told him what had happened, and asked if the shadow could be removed, and he nodded feebly. But when we asked how it was to be done he could only mutter incoherently. He made signs for writing materials, but after he had scrawled a few rambling marks on the paper the pencil dropped from his hands. Then he died.

To mingle with the people who were not marked unnerved me even more. I felt that I was a traitor who had not warned them against the evil in their midst, though Heaven knows I did it for the best—I feared them, too, suspecting that they were marked in some hidden place. So I dropped away from my friends, till at last I mistrusted all men; and all women—but one.

The one was Margaret Landon; and she was the reason why I did not run away from the world, like Henryson and Vassall. We had been friends for three years, and we were growing better and better friends. We knew what it would come to, but we were both busy with our work (she was an artist) and had not hurried the inevitable. Now, however, that the shadow had come, I wanted to shield her from the evil that I could not warn her against. About a fortnight after Denton died I called at her house and proposed to her. She accepted me very frankly.

"You have made me very happy," she said. "Do you know, I have been foolish enough to wonder if you liked someone else better. You seem to have changed so lately. You have been worrying about something, haven't you? Tell me about it, dear."

"I have been overworked," I apologized, "like most doctors. That is all. Well, I *have* been worried. It is—the shadow that has come upon the world."

"Is that all? I shouldn't trouble too much about *that*, dear. It is distressing, of course, if it shows, and if people mind it. Some call it a beauty-spot, you know. It's becoming quite fashionable. In

Paris they are beginning to wear shadow patches. Would you like me to wear one?"

She glanced up at me with her eyes laughing teasingly. She looked very young that afternoon, almost childish.

"Don't jest about it, Margaret," I begged. "It is horrible—horrible. You don't understand."

"Horrible?" she shivered and held my arm a little closer. "Is it anything *bad*, Fred? Anything that would make you feel differently to—to anybody? If I were marked?"

"Don't," I said sharply. "Don't speak of such a thing. It wouldn't mark you because—" I stopped quickly.

"Because your skin is too fair," I said. I had to say something. "It is nothing really, Margaret—just a foolish prejudice of mine. Humor me, there's a good girl. I dare say I am unreasonable; but I hate it—*hate* it!"

She drew her hand from mine and looked at me strangely.

"I am sorry that you hate it, dear," she said quietly. "So very sorry. I could cover it skilfully with my paints; but I'd rather hurt you than deceive you—and perhaps you love me more than you hate the mark." She drew her sleeve back a few inches from her wrist, and there I saw—what I saw! Merciful God, don't let me think of it! I shall go mad—mad! I stared at it and made no sign.

"It makes no difference to my love of you," she whispered pleadingly. Her eyes were moist and shining.

I did not decide for myself between Margaret and the shadow. The room seemed whirling around, and I could not think for myself. They fought it out between them in my mind; and Margaret won. I raised the slim, white wrist to my lips and kissed the disfiguring mark; and then she lost her calm and flung herself into my arms. I caught a glimpse of my face in a mirror, looking over her fair hair. It was working horribly. I wondered if I had gone mad, or was going. When I got back to the hospital I fainted, and they told me I must take a complete rest. So I went away.

I spent a week with Vassall. He was almost worn out from his unceasing labors in the laboratory, but brave and cheerful. He intended to devote his life to finding a way of obliterating the shadow, he declared, and when I retorted that the memory would remain, he said that no one had any right to remember the intention of evil, when no evil was done. "I bear the brand of Cain," he said, "but I am not a murderer. The mark makes me charitable toward men, because I misjudged Henryson. I would kill him rather than let him ruin the world by divulging the secret."

"Sometimes I think I shall have to divulge it or go mad," I confessed.

"Then go mad," he said, setting his lips squarely.

That was the conclusion of all our discussions. We could not lift the evil from the world, and by disclosing it we should only make others suffer as we suffered. Therefore we must suffer alone.

When I left Vassall I went on to Henryson. He had taken to mission work in a low slum, crowded with marked men and women, and had turned his house into a refuge for them, hoping to keep a few from doing the evil that they intended. About three per cent. of "his poor people" were wrongly marked, he thought. "And none of them are wholly bad," he protested. "The shadow has taught me a lesson, Fielding. You will not be so unhappy if you learn it too. It is to look for the good in people as well as the evil. The shadow isn't so terrible when you do that." Like Vassall, he was cheerful; but he had aged greatly, and he was troubled with a cough that seemed to tear him to pieces. "But I do not matter," he said, "or you. It is these poor people that we must think of, and those on whom they prey. Let us give our all—our lives, if need be—for the world."

It did me good to be with these men; and I went back to my work determined to look for the good in those who were branded with the evil. Instead of avoiding them I made friends with them; and if I could not trust them, I acted as though I could. But some of them cheated me, others robbed me. Two made a murderous assault upon me, and I was laid up for a fortnight. After this my horror of the shadow and those who bore it grew deeper and deeper. I shuddered with dread of Margaret even, when we were alone; but she was good to me; so very good to me, and I loved her. Nothing could alter that. When I was about again, after my injury, I asked her to name the day for our wedding. She hid her face on my shoulder and whispered it. I was glad she did not look at me.

It is within a week now; and I love her above all things; and I am sick with fear of her. There is no one to help me, no one to take counsel with. Henryson died a week ago, and Vassall is dying. They called it brain-fever and overwork, but it was the horror of this cursed thing that killed them—the horror of it.

Day by day I see the warning of the evil to come; and day by day I see the evil come after the warning. It is I who am branded with the brand of Cain; for I know and I make no sign. If I do not speak I shall go mad; and the world will go mad if I speak. Well, I will *not* speak. They kept the secret and died; and so will I—

I am feeling very ill to-night, and my temperature is high. It is the beginning of a fever, I think—I must destroy what I have written, so that no one shall see it if I die. Where was I?—Oh! The shadows.—They are all over the paper, you know. They—

III

How the Shadow Went

I remember that the world reeled away from me as I was finishing the story that I had written. The world sprang back on me suddenly in a private ward of the hospital. At first it was only a window-frame and painted walls, and an ache at the back of my head. Then I began to recollect; and then I saw Margaret. I knew that a long time had passed, because she had grown so thin and pale. She was dressed all in white, with a gold brooch that I gave her at her neck; and I gave a little cry of delight, because she was such a fair thing to see. Then I remembered the shadow and tried to cover my eyes; and she saw that I was awake, and bent down over me and kissed me, and cried a little, very softly. I liked her to kiss me, even if she bore the shadow, and I smiled, and tried to speak; but the sound would not come at first.

"You must keep very quiet, dear," she warned me. "Don't try to talk."

"I must," I protested feebly—my voice seemed to come from a long way off. "The paper that I wrote. Where is it, Margaret? The paper?"

"All your papers are in your room, dear. It is locked and I have the key. Now you must go to sleep. You can trust me, can't you?"

"The key," I said. "The key! Give it to me!"

She brought the key and put it under my pillow. Then she kissed me again, and I went to sleep. Whenever I woke I felt for the key. It was always there, and I got slowly better. She was very gentle with me, and humored me in everything; and the doctor said that she had saved my life. "You would have worn yourself out with your ravings," he said. "She is a good woman, Fielding; and you are a lucky man."

"A good woman," I echoed; but the memory of the blurry shadow on her wrist came up with my memory of Margaret. I set my teeth and put the shadow against Margaret, and Margaret against the shadow; and Margaret won.

"Roll up your sleeve, dear, and let me look at the shadow," I asked when she came in. There was a pink rose on her breast, and another in her hair, and the roses were coming back to her cheeks, and her eyes were soft and shining. She was as fair as—she is. There is nothing else like her.

"You are not strong enough to bear a shock yet, dear," she said.

I laughed, and my laugh had a ring for the first time since Denton came to the hospital.

"All the shadows in the world cannot shock me if they are on you," I told her, "my dear!"

She sat down beside me, and stroked my hair for a while before she answered.

"There is no shadow upon me any more," she said slowly, "or on anyone. The mercy of God that blots out our transgressions!"

"There is no shadow on my heart," I said boldly, and I raised myself on one arm and put the other round her. "Only a great white thought of you, sweet Margaret."

"You do not even ask how the shadow came," she asked, with a great light in her eyes.

"I do not care," I told her. "You are—you."

She laughed a little and cried.

"I am yours—not so good as I would wish to offer you. But it was because—I loved you so much," she said. "When you changed at that time I thought you cared for—someone else. There was a bad rumor about her. I did not believe it; but I meant to tell it to you. That was how the shadow came. But—" she lifted her head proudly— "*I never told you, dear*—We are not just one mean or evil deed that we plan; not all the mean and evil things that we plan. They are only the shadows—Our tears wipe them out, and the memory of them—God sets white marks for the good that we do—Hark!"

She rose and opened the window. A sound of music and singing came in, and the ringing of church bells and the scent of flowers. The sunlight played in her hair; and she lifted her arm like a saint pointing up the long, long way to Heaven.

"It is a day of thanks for those who bore the shadow and are clean," she said. "They do not know what it meant. We shall never let them know. They will have no memories to hurt. We shall remember—and honor those who wore the mark of their temptation and did no wrong.—Dear love, it is a world of temptation and ill-resolve; but God gives us strength to overcome."

"Margaret," I cried, "Margaret." I struggled to rise, but could not; and she flew into my arms.

"You shall give me a little white flower," she whispered, "to wear hidden on my arm—for token of the love of a brave man that keeps a woman good."

But I gave her a little black misshapen flower, uncertain of outline as the shadow had been, and told her to wear it that all might see. The sun shines brightest where the shadow has been!

# THE ANNIHILATOR

I

Harvey came into my room with a remark about the weather; sat by the fire, put his feet on the fender, and warmed his hands. The beginning of great things is so trivial.

I happened to be reading the *Evening Standard*, and I went on with an article in which I was interested. When I turned the page, he spoke.

"Put your newspaper away," he said. "I will show you how to make news instead of reading it."

I laid the paper down.

"If you think I am going to invest money in any of your inventions, you're mistaken," I warned him. He laughed. "Unless I see my way, of course,"' I added.

Harvey was a genius in some ways, and I had always fancied that he would hit upon something worth taking up some day. That was why I kept up our acquaintance. He was not in my set.

"You're going to see your way." He leaned forward and wagged his forefinger at me. "You're going to see your way so clearly that you'll risk your money, and your life, and your soul—if you have one."

"Never mind about my soul," I told him. "What am I going to risk the other things for?"

"For whatever you like to take from the world," he answered. "You ran have Westminster Abbey for a smoking-room, if you choose!"

This time it was I who laughed.

"You won't laugh when I've shown you," he said quietly. There was something that gripped me in his quiet. "We shall sit in my laboratory and say to the world, 'Pay or die!' 'Obey or die!' The world will pay and obey."

"Where do *I* come in?" I asked.

I thought that he had gone off his head from experimenting and studying sixteen hours a day, and that I had better humor him for a time.

"I require an assistant."

"Why me in particular?"

"My choice is limited. I know so few people with brains. You happen to have the qualifications I want. I don't think you have many scruples. You are an excellent photographer. You possess a good deal of courage. It's a hanging risk."

"Scientific piracy, eh?" I said, still thinking to humor him. "What form does it take?"

I struggled to suppress a laugh.

"Words are no use," he told me. "You wouldn't believe them. If you would, you'd be a fool, and no use to me. Come to my laboratory and see for yourself. *You won't laugh then!*"

I looked at him hard while I considered. There was a risk, of course, in trusting myself in a madman's den; but I am not a nervous man—well, I wasn't then. My nerves have gone a bit since. There might be something in the invention; and if he was too mad to profit by it—well, I wasn't!

"All right," I agreed. "I'll come."

We went.

He had three rooms at the top of our flats. One was larger than the other two put together, and he used it for a laboratory. We went straight there.

There were all kinds of machines and apparatus that I don't understand. They included things like cameras, and a contrivance that struck me as a queer double magic-lantern. He called it the annihilator.

"What does it annihilate?" I asked.

"Anything; at least, anything of which I have the—the real pho-tograph—I call it the psygraph. It's a photograph of the thing it-self—what it is, not just what it looks. Here's one." He opened a cupboard and took from a pigeonhole a piece of waxy-looking card-board. It bore an indented impression of a vase. "There's the origi-nal," he said, and indicated a common blue-and-white thing on a side-table. "Go and look at it. Take it in your hands. Hold it for a minute."

He placed the psygraph in the slot of a brass stand facing the lens of the annihilator, and turned a faint bluish light upon it for a moment. The vase that had been in my hands was gone.

"It's a trick!" I cried. "It's a—an infernal trick!"

"It's infernal," he agreed; "but it isn't a trick."

He moved a lever of the annihilator. The blue light changed to a pinkish yellow; and the vase was back in my hands!

I gave a start and a cry. The vase dropped on the floor at my feet, and smashed to pieces. There was a chair near me. I stumbled to it and sat down.

"It's not *natural!*" I cried.

My voice sounded childish. I shivered violently, and Harvey gave me brandy. I drank it and rallied my skepticism.

"It was an illusion," I declared, trying to laugh, "but it's clever. How did you do it?"

"It was an illusion in a way," Harvey stated. "The vase was there, all the time; but you couldn't find it by your senses. Nobody could. You want more proof before you risk your money—and other things? Give me your watch."

I detached it and handed it to him. He took a psygraph of it with one of the things like cameras—recams, he termed them. Then he handed it back to me and put the picture in the slot.

"Look at the time," he said. "Take it exactly."

"Twenty-seven minutes to ten," I announced.

"Now put it in your pocket. Well?"

"It's gone!" I cried, feeling my waistcoat.

"And yet it's there; and the works go on! We'll wait a minute or so." He strolled about the room, laughing his curious soft laugh.

"Now we'll bring it back," he said presently, and turned the pinkish light on the psygraph. I felt the watch in my pocket again. I took it out and looked at it.

"Twenty-four to ten," I stated; and he nodded.

"It was going all the time, you see. The effect was on you rather than on the watch."

"Exactly!" I commented; and he laughed again—that curious, evil laugh.

"I take your point," he said. "You want to be convinced that I can banish it from everybody's senses before you 'see your way.' Very well." He went to his cupboard and fetched out another psygraph; an indented picture of a man. "Do you know him?" he asked.

"The Home Secretary," I said. "You don't mean—you aren't going to—"

He did not answer, but put the waxen card in the slot, and turned on the bluish light.

"Look at the papers to-morrow morning," he said. "Then come to me, and we'll arrange things. We'll own half England by this time next week!"

"But—"

"Don't be a fool! You can't make omelets without breaking eggs. We'll have to get rid of a few people to frighten them."

"You can always bring them back?" I inquired feebly.

"I can," he said; "at least, I think I can. I haven't tried, because—the watch went on, you saw. *So will the man*. I knew what the watch would do while it was out of sight. I don't know what the man may do. There may be a sort of attraction between him and his psygraph. He may be able to come here and watch us. We must have our power firmly established before we risk bringing any one back, with knowledge to balk us. You must make up your mind to that, Brownlow."

"It's murder," I protested. "Well, not exactly. They—go on. We'd bring them back some time. It's only a—a temporary inconvenience."

"That's the way to look at it," he said cheerfully. "Anyhow, it's the only way to our end. That's the empire of the world, Brownlow!

Look in the papers to-morrow morning, and then come to me. You'd better go to your rooms now and get to bed."

"Yes," I assented. "Yes!"

I felt sick, and my legs trembled under me as I walked down-stairs.

## II

Every one knows that it was on the evening of Thursday, October 26, 1912, at a quarter to ten, that the British Home Secretary vanished in the middle of a speech on the Female Enfranchisement Bill. He was combating the argument that women should not vote because they cannot fight.

"Brute force has become a negligible thing," he said. "We wage war with the powers of nature, not with our own; the great unseen forces that compass us round, and—"

And then he went, like a light that is put out. It was a curious thing that his handkerchief, which lay on his seat, went, too; but his hat remained.

The panic which ensued was such as had never been known in recorded history. One member, more courageous than the others, got up to propose an adjournment; but the rest struggled and fought to get out of the house. Several were killed in the crush, and two people in the gallery were said to have died of fright.

I met a stranger in the street, when I took a walk early the next morning. He stopped me and talked as if we were old friends. People were like that at first. Afterward everybody suspected everybody, and held aloof from all but intimate friends. This man said that the annihilation of the Home Secretary was an outrage, and probably due to the anti-suffragettes, who were leagued with scientific people. Discoveries, he declared, had gone far enough; if he had his way, he'd burn all scientific books, and the scientists with them.

I laughed when I told Harvey; but he looked grave.

"That is one of the dangers that we have to guard against," he said. "If we don't frighten them pretty badly, they'll do something of the kind; and they *might* drop on *us!* We must go on at once. I say 'we.' I suppose you see your way now?"

"Yes," I said. I had almost made up my mind to say "no"; but I was afraid of Harvey. Besides, it was a big thing.

Under his orders I spent the morning and afternoon getting psygraphs of people and places that we might find it necessary to "annihilate." I always contemplated bringing them back again. I wouldn't have done it, but for that.

In the evening we typed the famous letter to the *Times*; the "annihilator letter," which announced that a new power had taken possession of the world, and intended to govern it, and that those who did not promptly obey its decrees, or who encouraged resistance to them, would be removed, as the Home Secretary had been.

Parliament sat as usual, and both houses put aside all business to discuss the method of fighting this "new power." It was decided to reenforce the London police by soldiers, and to pay a house-to-house visit, and make everybody account for himself or herself; and a royal commission was appointed to investigate the matter.

We had expected something of the sort, and Harvey had planned to interrupt the debate before any course of action was approved. But it had not occurred to us that Parliament would forego its staid customs to the extent of leaving out the answers to questions, or that the proposals of the government would be agreed to practically without discussion. So a warfare against us was organized before five members of the cabinet—three members of Parliament and two peers—vanished from among their fellows.

This led to a stampede of the houses; but the remainder of the cabinet reenforced themselves by co-opting half a dozen prominent members of the opposition, and met at once at the Foreign Office. Troops were ordered up by rail, and proclamations were posted that the domiciliary visits would begin the next day, and that all persons using scientific laboratories would be placed under temporary arrest, unless and until specially licensed by government.

It was necessary to obtain the earliest information about the action taken against us. I mingled with the crowd in Downing

Street. At about eight o'clock I saw the members of the recon-
structed cabinet proceed on foot toward the Houses of Parliament.
The crowd cheered them, and I cheered with the crowd and followed. There were more cheers from other crowds in the distance;
and the people round me said that they were cheering some brave
members of Parliament and peers who were going to a special
meeting of both houses that had been hastily convened to take further measures to apprehend "them science chaps what's doing it."

I tried to turn back to warn Harvey, but I was jammed in by the
crowd for a time, in the space in front of Westminster Abbey, where
a meeting was taking place. The speaker at the moment was a
woman—Lady Constance Harford, I was told; the *fiancée* of the
vanished Home Secretary; a tall, slim, pale-faced, high-bred slip
of a woman, dressed in black, with a wonderfully sweet, clear voice.

"There was never a time of trouble," she said, "but woman suffered most. We want to suffer with our men! We want to save our
men who are left; to avenge our men who are gone. I vow"—she
turned my way; and I thought that her face was that of a tortured
saint— "I vow before God that I desire that more than anything on
earth. I am not speaking to you only. There are those here who
will report my words and spread them through this land. What can
you do for your men, women of England? I'll tell you. You can re-
view in your minds the people whom you know, and omit none.
Think if there is one whose occupation is suspicious; one who stud-
ies and experiments; one who has a laboratory; one who has what
looks like a laboratory, seen through a chink in the door. One who—"

The pressure of the crowd had been bearing me away; and
after this I could not catch her words. I backed slowly out of the
crowd, and when I was clear I took a taxicab and went straight to
Harvey.

"I am afraid of that woman," I said. "She'll rouse the crowd to
search; and when they find your apparatus—"

"Don't lose your head," he said; "we're a mile off and more;
and a crowd of a few thousand can't search London in a night. You
must get a psygraph of her to-morrow, and we'll put Lady Constance Harford to—to 'temporary inconvenience.'" He laughed as
usual. "Meanwhile, I'm nearly out of—never mind what. It produces

the blue light. I'll make enough in ten minutes or so. Take a cab back, and have a look at the Houses of Parliament. You'll see something!"

"You mean—you have a psygraph of them?"

"Yes." He laughed again. There was something devilish, I think, in his laugh. It always seemed to freeze my blood. "When the clock strikes ten," he added.

I took a taxi back to Westminster Bridge, and edged into the crowd round the place where Lady Constance had been speaking. A man was speaking now. He was pressing the same point; that every one must make himself or herself into a detective to denounce suspects.

"Take nobody for granted," he begged; "not your father, or your mother, or your brother, or your sister, or your own familiar friend. The letter to the *Times* was posted in London. The arch criminal has a typewriter; and he has scientific apparatus." Ten began striking. "He—or she—is a person of scientific attainments; a person without religion; a—my—"

I suppose he said "My God!" But his words were drowned in an awful, unspeakable cry. The lighted clock, the huge tower, the noble buildings were gone, as quietly and quickly as a picture from a screen; and where they had stood one saw clear sky. It was a fine night; and the stars twinkled there. I remember wondering vaguely whether man was the greater, or the stars.

After the cry the crowd swirled like a live, mad tide. I was whirled round and round, elbowed and struck. A heap of people who fell—most of them were killed—grew so large that, under the lee of it, I could take shelter from the human waves. The speakers were just on the other side of the heap, and, as the crowd tried to avoid it, they, too, were saved from the very worst of the crush; but when the man who had spoken mounted his stool and shouted to the people to keep cool and go slowly, he was rushed over and another heap formed gradually over him, as happened whenever any one fell.

Lady Constance mounted on something and begged the crowd not to rush, and then everybody would be safe. Her voice was no longer music, but a rough scream, and her hat had gone and her hair hung loose. She was knocked over, too; but the tail of the crowd had come. I fought through it, using my fists, and tumbled a little heap aside and pulled her out. I helped her to her feet, and supported her while she got breath. That was the second misfortune to our plans. If I had let her be smothered—it really did not occur to me—Harvey and I would be masters of the world to-day.


### III

She was only bruised and shaken, she declared.

"I am glad to find *one* brave man," she told me. "We few who are brave have need of one another, Mr. —"

She looked at me.

"Randall," I said. It was the first name that came into my head.

"Mr. Randall, let us see if we can save any one."

We rescued a good many from the heaps. As they recovered they went on with the rescue; and I went with Lady Constance toward the ruins of the Houses of Parliament. I say "ruins," but there was no debris. The superstructure had disappeared. The foundations were unharmed, not being included in the psygraph.

The assembly itself had not been annihilated, but some were killed and many were injured by falling to the ground, or into the cellars, when the masonry disappeared. And, yet, according to Harvey, it was still "going on." Everything that ever was or will be goes on, I suppose; only we do not know.

I worked with those who were uninjured in recovering the rest. Lady Constance seemed to direct it all. She went down into the cellars herself and carried injured men upon her slender shoulders. Her jacket was torn and she was disheveled. She did not look the high-bred lady now, but very much a woman. She had a color, and she was very beautiful.

"Come and see me to-morrow," she said, when our work was done, "if we are both left. There will be work to do. If one of us is gone—God bless you! Come and help!"

"Yes," I said. "I—I am a reporter. You want to rouse the people. Well, popular enthusiasm centers round a personality; especially a woman. I shall describe what you have done to-night, and—let me come in the morning, and take a photograph of you to go with the article."

I meant a psygraph!

"Very well." She sighed. "If I seem to have a power to move people," she said, "it is because I try to do what *he* would have done. Say that in your report. A good man lives when he is dead. Good night, Mr.—my friend."

She gave me her hand; and a kind little smile. I pressed her hand in both mine. That was the third mistake in our plans; the one that was irreparable.

I told Harvey what had happened; what he would want to know of it. He said that I had done well. He did not agree that I had made a mistake in rescuing Lady Constance.

"The effect of removing her will be much greater," he said; "but it had better be done quickly. You must get the psygraph early in the morning. She is dangerous."

I went to her house in Park Lane at ten o'clock. I found the newly chosen prime minister—the old one had vanished—and several members of the cabinet there. She introduced me, and they shook hands.

"I believe you are right in your proposal, Mr. Randall," the prime minister said. "This is the time for a popular dictator; and Lady Constance is likely to outstay me. The annihilator, as he calls himself, does not appear to attack women. Photograph her by all means."

"With your permission," I said, "I will photograph you all; and if you will give me any message to circulate with the photographs it shall go out."

He gave me a long message to the people; but Lady Constance smiled it aside.

"Say this," she told me. "Do your best and bravest. God will do the rest!"

Then I "graphed" her; "graphed" them all. I would come back, I promised, to take my part in the work, when the photographs were distributed to the papers.

IV

I found Harvey in the laboratory working in a passion, turning the blue light of destruction on to one psygraph after another. Some newspapers lay round him on the floor.

"They are ordering up the whole army," he said, "to seize every one in London who can't account for himself, and to search everywhere and into everything. The United States is proposing to send over assistance. I've psygraphs of three of the Cunarders. *They'll* go! The president of the French Republic is holding a council to consider sending help." He put a regraph in the slot.

"There goes the president!" he snapped; and the blue light shone out. "Have you got her?"

"Yes," I said, "I'll develop them now. I've some others, too."

I told him their names, and he nodded.

I went to the little sink in the corner, and developed my plates. The process was a rapid one, taking only a few seconds.

The picture of Lady Constance was very clear. I watched it come out as the acid ate into the waxen card. The psygraphs, as I have said, were indented. The lines seemed to eat into my heart, as the acid ate into the wax.

"Look here, Harvey," I said abruptly. "You told me I could take what I liked from the world. I'm not going to back out, or spoil the business by mawkish sentiment, but—give me your word that you will bring her back some day? I dare say I'm a fool."

He turned round to me, and regarded me curiously, and not unkindly.

"Oh, I don't know!" he said. "What a man wants is—what he wants. Yes, I will bring her back. I want you entirely with me, Brownlow, and I am not afraid that you will be mawkish. Give me your word not to restore her till it's safe, and I show you how to do it."

I gave him my word, and he showed me how to produce the yellowish-pink light that brought things back to our senses—the things that "went on" all the time. He illustrated the process with a chair that stood in the laboratory, and a barometer that hung on the wall.

I gave him the psygraph of Lady Constance. He put it in the slot, and turned on the blue light. It looked as if she was crying. Then I suppose I fainted.

When I came to, Harvey hurried me out to take more psygraphs; and he locked up his rooms and went out for the same purpose. It was necessary to do enough to disorganize the whole administration, he explained, and to stop the domiciliary visits, or we should be undone.

I had been out for an hour, when newspaper boys came by, on bicycles, carrying bundles of papers and shouting:

"Special edition! Annihilation of War Office and Admiralty. Disappearance of French President and Lady Constance Harford. Two thousand scientists arrested!"

Others called out: "German Emperor offers an army!" Some sandwich men were distributing handbills advertising the departure of numerous vessels to France, and of special trains to the provinces. The return halves were to be available "on the restoration of lawful government, or within fourteen days thereafter."

I returned to our flat at one o'clock, as agreed; on the way I met parties of police taking away persons suspected of science. I recognized Professor Runton, the electrical expert, and the chemist at the corner of our street, among them. When I reached the street itself, I found that it was lined with soldiers, and that parties were visiting the houses. An officer stopped me, and examined my camera. He called a sergeant of engineers.

"There's something queer about this apparatus," he said. "You're in the photographic section, aren't you, Johnson? Look at it."

The sergeant saluted, and inspected the camera; and then the plates that I had taken.

"It's not photography, sir," he said; "and I see a 'positive' of Lady Constance Harford." I was carrying it about with me for security. "It's cut into a sort of waxy card; and the papers say that she has disappeared!"

"Take him to the commission at once," the officer said. "Don't waste a second;" and they hurried me off.

I looked up at the window of the laboratory—our flat was only a few doors away—and saw Harvey covering us with his camera. It flashed upon me that he would "graph" us, and then wipe out the party—myself and all! The plate of Lady Constance would go; and then he could never restore her, and she would "go on," wandering as a disembodied spirit, till the term of her life was over.

I think I went mad for the moment. I struggled to get free; shouted that I knew the annihilator, and would tell them everything; implored them to hasten and seize Harvey before he could destroy us all.

"And Lady Constance!" I cried. "And Lady Constance! He can't bring her back without that!" I tried to snatch the psygraph from the sergeant's hand; but half a dozen men seized me and carried me by my legs and arms and waist.

"I believe we've got one of them!" the sergeant said.

And then the sergeant and the men were gone from the world, and I dropped upon the pavement with a thud. It was in St. James's Square, just outside Cleveland House. My "camera" lay on the pavement beside me, and the case of finished plates. The regraph of Lady Constance that had been in the sergeant's hand was gone. I gathered up the things, and set off for our flats—they were in Jermyn Street—at a run.

I found people running out of it, and they shouted to me not to go there. All the searchers who went that way, they shrieked, had been annihilated. I went straight on, and into the laboratory, and dropped into the armchair. For the moment my strength had completely gone.

Harvey looked at me with a friendly smile, and went to the sideboard and got out the brandy.

"That was a narrow squeak, old man!" he said, almost with affection. "I happened to see you, and got a psygraph. Of course I cut you out, and the camera and plates, before I annihilated." He poured out the brandy with a soft gurgle. "A very narrow squeak! I think we're safe for a while now. I've been graphing searchers all the morning, and I've wiped out thousands. They won't come this way for a bit. Come, pull yourself together and drink it. You'll be all right in a minute."

I drank the brandy, and dropped back in the chair.

"You have wiped out the psygraph of Lady Constance," I said. "We can't bring her back."

It was only possible to take one psygraph from each "photograph," so I had no duplicate.

He puffed out his cheeks and blew. He had that way when he thought.

"I can bring the psygraph back," he said slowly; "but I don't know where it would reappear. The—the ghost, we'll say—of the man who had it may wander. I suppose he could carry it about with him. I don't know. He might drop it at the moment. I really don't know. I'll cut it out of the psygraph of the group and restore it separately. Go round to the place where he disappeared, and see if it returns there."

I left him cutting at the psygraph with a marvelously fine fretsaw, and went back to the square. I stood staring at the pavement where the sergeant had disappeared. The psygraph was not there—and then it was!

There was a piece of skin—the tiniest scrap of nail and flesh—adhering to it. The fretsaw had not been quite exact. The psygraph was cracked slightly. Harvey said that this would not hurt Lady Constance, and did not matter.

"And now," he said, "put it away for a little while. Some day you shall bring her back; when you can offer her the queenship of half the world!"

"You are merciful to my weakness, Harvey," I said; and he laughed as usual; but there was a touch of softness in the laugh.

"A man wants—what he wants," he said.

"We've wasted half an hour—and that may lose the empire of the earth—over a woman! Well, you'll find it harder to rule her, perhaps! Now, Brownlow, we can't waste any more time. The next day or two will settle the business, one way or the other. Let's have a council of war."

V

We sat down and we lit our pipes and discussed this struggle of two men against the earth, as if we talked over a matter of daily business.

"It comes to a question of bluff," Harvey pronounced. "The destruction of the searchers round this quarter, and here only, has given them a pretty clear idea where we hang out. If they knew how the business was worked, they would rush in on us faster than we could graph them and blot them out. It would be a matter of ten minutes! But they don't know. They think that we can destroy every one and everything, at any rate, in London, at any moment. So they won't come, unless a great leader arises. Even then it will take him some time to get the command and to rally them. Look out of the window. The street is full of people with traveling-bags. London is running away."

"Yes," I agreed. "We shall have time; but how are we going to use it? They will rally—say at Aldershot. In a day or two they will form up an army."

"Exactly. We will find the rallying-place, and go there and graph them; and when the army begins to march, it will vanish. There will be no more armies after that! Then we shall dictate terms. When these are accepted, we will travel about getting psygraphs of fleets, of arsenals, of national assemblies, of notable buildings. In a year or two, when we have collected enough, we shall be prepared to deal with the inevitable insurrection. There will be one, and one only, I think. Then you and I will be emperors of the world! We shall find a few trusty ministers to take psygraphs for us, I expect; but one of us will have to watch beside the annihilator for a few years; perhaps till we have sons to trust. It's a hard task to rule the world; but it's worth it."

"It's worth it!" I cried. I seemed to feel my eyes gleam.

We went out that afternoon taking psygraphs of the bridges, and of groups of buildings and streets. Small pictures were sufficient, Harvey said, and we took great blocks of places and great crowds of people. We learned that an army was concentrating at Aldershot, as I had guessed. We went there at night, and in the

early morning we "graphed" the troops as they mustered in bri-
gades, and were reviewed. They were going up to London the next
day to "rush the annihilator," gossip said. They intended to draw a
ring round the locality where the government rightly believed that
he operated, and to make short work of every one whom they found
in that area.

At Aldershot they had no suspicion of photographers, and we
were rather welcome, as recording an historical gathering. We
hurried off from there to Portsmouth, where a great fleet had gathered, and took the whole harbor; some fifty British war-ships, and
about as many of other nations—principally French and German—
which had come to render assistance against the annihilator—two
men with some apparatus! The "photographs" were very small; but
it was not a question of size, Harvey said.

We arrived back at our flat late in the evening, passing through
deserted streets all the way from Battersea. The trains did not cross
the river from fear of the annihilator.

We posted a communication to the papers, saying that the annihilator was aware of the preparations against him, and that, if
these were not abandoned, he would destroy the army, and also
the fleet, British or otherwise, now at Portsmouth, as a further
warning. After that every one in the country would be destroyed
unless the government made a complete surrender to his will within
four-and-twenty hours. A white flag was to be hung from Nelson's
Column in token of surrender, and an envoy was to be sent to
Piccadilly Circus to treat.

We supped and had a walk through the deserted streets. Then
we went to bed. In the morning we rose early and went out to take
more psygraphs. We saw signalers across the bridges, and heard
bugles. Some artillery was stationed on the far side of Westminster
Bridge.

"They're going to shell us!" Harvey predicted. "We must get
back and strike our final blow. They won't fight again, you'll find!"

We ran all the way; but as we passed the place where the War
Office had been, a shell fell in the neighborhood of Charing Cross
Station. From the sound of falling masonry it must have worked

great destruction. The Haymarket Theater was badly damaged by another shell as we passed; and another ruined a house close to ours.

We ran up-stairs, and set to work with the annihilator. In a few minutes the firing ceased. It never started again.

Harvey stood at the machine turning on the blue light. I put the psygraphs in the slot, one by one. We did not say a word till we had finished with every psygraph of the field army and the fleet. He shivered with excitement, and swayed on his feet when we had done.

"Emperor of the world!" I saluted him, and bent my knee.

"Emperor of the world!" he gasped, pressed his hand to his side, fell in a writhing heap upon the floor—and died!

## VI

I think that the shock of poor Harvey's death disturbed my mental balance for a time. I took his body to another room, and covered it. Then I went back to the annihilator, and strolled up and down the long room aimlessly for about an hour. I told myself over and over that now I was the sole ruler of the world; that I could impose my own terms; that the nations of the world would accept them without a struggle.

They would have done so. It only wanted a few hours' courage. I lost the whole earth for lack of that. *I was afraid to be alone.*

I fancied that the ghosts of those who had vanished were all round me—the people who were banished from sight of earth, and who still "went on." They seemed to cry to me to bring them back. Why, I asked myself, should I not bring them back, and still make my own terms?

I wrote a proclamation, typed a number of copies, and put them out in prominent places, stuck on chairs in the middle of Whitehall, in Trafalgar Square, on the great bridges, and elsewhere.

I had shown my power, I said, and I gave the world one chance of submission. I would bring every one and everything back. If they did not yield to my wishes, they and more should vanish again; and this time they would vanish never to return. My wishes were three: ten millions of money; a complete amnesty; and Lady Constance Harford for my wife. They were to send her to me alone, and with the bond of the British government for amnesty and payment. Failing compliance within six hours, or in the event of molestation previously, England would vanish, I threatened. I signed this "The Annihilator."

Then I went back to my room, put the psygraphs in their place, one by one, and turned on the yellow-pink rays of restoration— first on Lady Constance. I remembered Harvey's fear that they might reappear beside me, and was prepared to change the rays and annihilate any one who did; but none came.

I left the search-parties who had come to our neighborhood till the last. I heard their shouts in the street, and went to the window and looked out. I found them going on with their search, as if nothing had happened. The officer took my proclamation, and read it out to them. There was a silence when he finished, and the men looked at one another.

"Men," the officer said, "if he'd only demanded money and an amnesty, I couldn't ask you to risk your lives. It's more than risk. But he asks for the bravest lady in England. We're Englishmen. Come on!"

They came on.

I rushed to the annihilator, and turned the light of destruction on their psygraph. I laughed as I did so; but my laugh stopped suddenly. Their shouts and running did not cease. I heard the front door go down. I heard them on the stairs. *Harvey had not warned me that you could not use the same psygraph a second time!*

I turned the light on fuller and fuller. I shrieked. It was with rage, not fear. Afterward it was fear. The door of the laboratory went down—

"Take him alive!" the officer called.

They took me alive.

They tried me the next day, in the House of Commons. The new cabinet were my judges. Lady Constance was one of them—the first woman in England to hold high political office. I did not plead, and I made no protest till she had to vote for my life or death.

"I have lost the world for love of you," I told her.

"God has many ways to take care of His world," she said. "He chose me as His instrument. May He have mercy on you—death!"

And then I buried my face in my hands. The votes of the others were enough. She might have spared hers.

They have built a high gallows that overtops London; and there, to-morrow, I die; and perhaps "go on." Everything goes on, I think. And I signed myself "The Annihilator!"

The warders will come in if I laugh so loudly.

# THE CLOUD-MEN

## FOREPRINT FROM THE LONDON NEWS SHEET OF MARCH 9, 1915

GOVERNMENT NOTICES

This newspaper is published under the authority of the News Act, 1915, which directs the printing of a single newspaper in the United Kingdom. Under the provisions of the act, the paper will be exclusively devoted to the plain statement, without colorable matter, of important events, and to articles useful to the community.

It is provided by Section 3 of the act that the communication of false news is punishable as follows:

First offence—two years' penal labor.

Second offence—five years' penal labor.

Third offense—death.

Readers are reminded that the Unprofitable Employment Act has been repealed only to the extent indicated above. The writing or perusal of fiction, therefore, remains a penal offense.

The census of the United Kingdom, taken under the Act for the Settlement of the Population, has been completed, with the following results:

Males, total . . . 51,504
Males, unmarried (age 20 to 60) . . . 9,212
Females, total . . . 52,214
Females, unmarried (age 18 to 50) . . . 8,901

Under Section 2 of the act, persons between the ages specified who have not arranged marriages by April 1 next will be paired by the local committees appointed under the act.

A list of the centers selected for the concentration of the inhabitants of this country is published on page 4. The inclusion of Edinburgh and Dublin is provisional only, and depends upon sufficient persons desiring to reside in those cities. Choice of residence in the selected centers can be allowed only so far as is compatible with the public welfare. For instance, the necessity of a coal supply will require a certain population for Newcastle. Forms of choice will be distributed during the week.

The consultative committee of the governments of Europe, North America, and Japan has decided that the capital penalty must be enforced for the second offense of wilful idleness, as, in the present crisis, this despicable crime threatens the continued existence of the human race.

### Local Government of London—Notices

The weekly train for the North wills start at 10.15 on Saturdays in future. Free passes may be obtained at the council offices, on good reason for the journey being shown.

Persons taking possession of vacant houses should affix a notice to the front door, stating that they are in occupation. Otherwise the houses will be liable to be reappropriated.

In consequence of the universal disarmament, a large number of naval and military uniforms are available for conversion into workmen's clothing. Applications should be made at the office of the clothing committee.

A *crèche* has been opened in the building in Whitehall formerly known as the War Office.

### Editorial Notices

We desire to publish articles describing the experiences of any persons who came into close contact with the so-called Cloud-Men. Photographs will be especially welcome.

The following article is by Mr. John Pender, now superintendent of the Food Bureau. He and his wife, Mary Pender, formerly Melville, are the only persons known to us who have survived first-hand acquaintance with these terrible beings; but it is thought that there may be others.

*The Experiences of John and Mary Pender*

I

It is common knowledge that a great darkness set in during the later weeks of August, 1914. This was ascribed to the formation of clouds of exceptional thickness, and to their gradual descent toward the earth. At the time this was attributed to abnormal atmospheric conditions, although scientific authorities differed greatly as to the nature of the disturbances.

It is now believed that the clouds contained elements from some extinct world, dissipated in the form of gaseous matter and encountered in the journey of the earth through space. This question will be dealt with in a later article by Dr. John Dodd. I shall confine myself to my personal experience of these elements as reincarnated in terrestrial forms—adopting Dr. Dodd's view—and to the disastrous events which I actually witnessed.

At two o'clock upon the afternoon of Friday, August 30, 1914, I was walking in the Strand, to the east of Bedford Street. Some newsboys were making a great clamor. One placard said, "The Clouds Alive—Descent Upon Paris—Great Slaughter." Another said, "War of the Worlds—Wells Justified." There was a great rush to secure papers, and, consequently, I did not notice what was happening around.

I had just obtained a paper, and was standing under an electric light to read it, when I heard a great shouting. People near me screamed and ran, and I looked up and saw the clouds descending into the roadway, in long, thick rolls. They fell upon the vehicles and their occupants, and upon groups of foot-passengers, and appeared to smother them.

I dropped the newspaper, and turned and ran in the direction of Charing Cross. I was thoroughly unnerved, not only by the shrieks, but by the abrupt manner in which they ceased wherever the clouds fell; and I find myself unable to recall the exact impression which they first produced upon me.

I was soon stopped by a barrier of vehicles which had jammed together, a number having come into collision and overturned, in their attempts to escape. Other vehicles followed till they were brought up by the blockade, and I had difficulty in finding standing space between.

I was one of a group of about ten who took refuge among the debris of two wagons and an overturned motor-bus. A very good-looking young lady, who was one of the party, seemed much distressed, and I talked to her. She said that the clouds reminded her of the unearthly visitants in some of the tales of one Owen Oliver. I had not then heard of him, but I believe him to be one of the persons very properly convicted by the present government for wasting his time in writing fiction.

I suggested that the clouds were only a heavy—and possibly poisonous—vapor; but the young lady declared that they were alive, and were deliberately killing people; and a white-faced man said that that was certainly so. He had seen a cloud settle on a bus near him, and, when it left the bus, the passengers all had the appearance of having been drowned.

A woman sobbed that she had just bought a new mantle, and it was "so greatly reduced" and "such value in the materials." A loafer tried to snatch my watch, and I knocked him down. A flower-girl started singing and dancing. I think the fright had unhinged her mind.

Then the clouds began to descend on us, and most of our group smashed their way through the overturned motor-bus. I should have gone with them, but the young lady fainted; so I remained, supporting her on one arm.

The clouds were of a blackish-gray color, and appeared to be of stouter material than vapor. Their size varied. I do not mean merely that they differed from one another in magnitude, but that the same cloud expanded and contracted, rising as it drew out and falling as it drew in. Their proportionate dimensions remained the same, the shape being that of a cylinder with spherical ends, and the length about twice the diameter. When they first hung overhead the diameter was usually about twenty-five feet.

They had a black, diamond-shaped patch in front, which I believe to have been an organ of vision, and eight small circular patches at the sides and the other end, which were, I think, in some mysterious way, the sources of their horizontal movements. From time to time they made a faint whirring sound. Afterward I had reason to believe that this was a kind of musical language, depending upon the pitch and quality of the note, and not upon the articulate sound, which was always the same—whir-r-r-r! At least, it seemed so to me. My wife thinks that there were four kinds of whirs, and three different ways of rolling the r's in each. However, she agrees that the language depended partly, if not wholly, upon the pitch.

The clouds came down one by one upon the vehicles near us, and the knots of people jammed between them. The victims shrieked until they were enveloped; then all sound ceased. When the clouds left them, they had the appearance of drowned persons, as the white-faced man had said.

I will not dwell on the subject. The sight is one which most of my readers have seen. Let those who have not be thankful!

I crawled under a wagon and a cab, dragging the young lady, and reached a shop-window, just as a cloud fell upon us. I had hoped to get to the shop-door and inside, but could not. This was our salvation, probably; for it was clear, afterward, that the clouds searched the houses.

As we were being wrapped all round, I smashed the plate-glass with my fists, cutting myself rather badly, and put our heads through the opening. The cloud did not enter inside the glass, and we were able to breathe. We were enveloped to the necks by what felt like a heavy, wet blanket—a blanket that seemed to be, in some horrible way, alive—for about five minutes. Then we were left.

My limbs were limp and helpless. I slipped down on the pavement, with the young lady's head resting on my shoulder, and stared at the tops of the vehicles, which were all that I could see. The busses were full of "drowned" bodies, lolling against one another. A wagon-driver on a high seat had fallen forward, but his legs still held in the apron, and he hung head downward, leering horribly. A dead horse was at my back. I leaned against it.

It was very quiet now. The shrieks, that ended so suddenly, came from farther and farther away.

After a time the girl opened her eyes and looked round. She tried to speak, and could not. Neither could I.

I opened my lips after a quarter of an hour.

"The Lord have mercy upon us!" I groaned.

"Amen!" said the girl on my shoulder.

She had not moved except to clutch at my jacket.

I held out my hand to her. When she was about to take it she saw the gashes that the broken glass had made, and cried out piteously.

"Hush!" I said. "They may have ears!"

For I never doubted that they were alive after the wet monster had touched me. It felt like a blanket that was all fingers!

She nodded, took out her handkerchief, and bound my cuts gently. She asked in a whisper how I had done it, and I told her in a whisper how I had broken the glass, and why.

"Thank you," she said. "That isn't much to say for a life, is it? I mean more."

She looked at me and tried to smile. It was pitiful, very pitiful.

"Life isn't much to be thankful for now," I said; "except—that there is *some one* left. There is no one else, I think. We will help each other."

"We will help each other," she said.

Her voice and look were those of a steadfast woman; and so she proved.

Presently we crawled through the vehicles and the "drowned" people till we got into a restaurant. We found "drowned" waiters and customers there. Mary—that was my companion's name—sank on a seat. She would not have cried, I think, but I put my hand on her shoulder.

"Cry, dear woman," I said. "It will help you."

She sat with her face in her hands, and her body quivering, for a while. Then she wiped her eyes with my handkerchief, and smiled the pitiful smile.

"You are good to me," she said.

We ate and drank, and then we explored the upper rooms. The people in these were "drowned," too; and those in the other houses that we entered, creeping stealthily from one to the next. We heard the whirring sound sometimes, and saw the cloud cylinders pass by. Most of them were high above the houses, and were going toward Whitehall. We noticed a sound of firing from that direction, and guessed that soldiers were trying to defend the War Office—which, as we learned long after, was really the case.

After a few moments the firing ceased. Soon after that, the electric lights went out. They had been going for several days, and probably the power had failed; or one of the cloud-cylinders had fallen on those who controlled it—some brave men who stood at their post till the end. There were many such.

## II

We stayed in the house for two nights and a day—a day that was no different from the night—groping about in the dark for food, and sitting on a sofa, leaning against each other, when we slept for a short time. She was afraid to be alone, she said. I did not say that I was afraid, but I was.

After that time—it must have been the forenoon of the 1st of September—the darkness decreased to that of a dull twilight. We peered from the windows, and saw none of the cloud-rolls about, and heard no sounds. So we ventured out.

We got into the side streets, which were less obstructed, and into Whitehall. We then went over Westminster Bridge—it was strange to see the vessels drifting helplessly on the river—and wandered on till we reached Camberwell Green. We saw no sign of life all the way; men, women, children, horses, dogs, cats, even birds, were all "drowned," as I call it. The clouds had fallen upon humanity, and the dependents of humanity, and wiped them out.

The girl cried sometimes; but she was very brave. She told me about herself as we walked along. She was Mary Melville, a mistress at a high-school.

"And I shall never see my little girls again," she said. "They were such dear, naughty little girls, and I loved them so much! I liked to think that some day they would be good women."

We went into a house, the door of which was open. We found meat and drink there. She slept on a sofa while I watched; and then she watched while I slept—after breakfast we went on. We did not know where we were going; but we could not rest.

In the Peckham Road we met a man. He was dusty and travel-worn. His eyes blinked, and he spoke as if he were half asleep. He had walked up from Rochester, he said. The cloud-men—that was what he called them—had "wiped every one out," he told us. He had crept between two mattresses of a bed, and so escaped their search. He was going to Piccadilly Circus to look for his "girl." She was a waitress in a restaurant there.

"We were going to be married next month," he said.

Then he burst suddenly into tears. He was a big, strong fel-low—a fitter in the dockyard, he said.

A large party of soldiers had encountered the cloud-men on Chatham Lines, he told us. They had come upon a handful of the survivors running over Rochester Bridge. They had scattered some of the cloud-men, at first, by explosive shells; but the cloud-men had expanded into thin vapor, which the shells did not seem to harm, and advanced upon the army in that form till they had en-compassed it in mist. Then they contracted into "things like long balloons," and dropped upon the soldiers and "smothered them."

I suggested that, as we seemed to be all of the world that was left, we should make an appointment to meet again in, say, a week; but the man from Rochester shook his head.

"If I don't find my girl," he said, "and it stands to reason I won't, I'll go into a chemist's and take what comes handy till I hit upon something that settles me. Of course, if I find her, we'll come all right. You'd like her; quite a lady in her way, she is—was, I sup-pose. She—I'll be making a fool of myself if I start talking about her. So-long, and good luck!"

"God bless you and help you," said Mary, "and—and you will find her here—or there."

She pointed to the sky.

"Here or there," he said. "That's it. Good luck!"

He went on at a tired trot toward the city; and we walked on away from it.

"To be left alone," Mary said. "To be left alone! It is an awful thing. Alone! If you left me!" I looked at her reproachfully. "No, no! I don't mean that, only—if anything happened to you—"

Her lips trembled.

"We are in the hands of God," I said, "my dear. I shall never leave you while I am alive."

"No, dear," she answered.

That was all our love-making in those days—that we called each other "dear."

### III

We found our way to Dulwich by the afternoon. At the station we came upon a collection of about thirty people. They greeted us as if we were old friends, and we greeted them so. They had taken refuge in a cricket pavilion, they explained, and the clouds had omitted to search it. Every one else in the place was "drowned," as they too called it. They were lucky to have one another, they said; "so many of us"—and some of the women cried.

One young fellow was an electrical engineer. He had ascertained by the telegraph that the clouds were settling upon all the large towns, and destroying the inhabitants. This applied to the Continent and America, as well as Great Britain. Now he could get no answer from anywhere.

We walked together toward Forest Hill, and found nine survivors in Dulwich Park. A black mist drove upon us there. It was "only mist," we assured one another, clinging desperately together. But it condensed into the infamous cylinders. Our company ran in various directions, crying out till the clouds settled upon them.

Mary and I ran hand in hand, till she dropped exhausted. I sat beside her, and lifted her in my arms. We kissed each other. Then four of the cylinders came up, and one lowered itself upon us. The damp folds were enveloping us; and then a fifth cylinder, with four white bands—which were, I think, the insignia of high rank—made a whirring noise, changing the pitch as if it sang.

This was when I realized that they had a language. The cylinder that was smothering us lifted itself; and the belted cylinder drew near and settled on the ground, and shrank till it was not more than eight feet long. It pressed against us as if it examined us. It felt about as hard as a sofa-cushion in its contracted form; a hard cushion that was all hands and terribly alive. It stared at us with its diamond-shaped eye. Then it "sang" again, and somehow I knew that its song meant that we were spared.

Two other cylinders pushed us on our feet, and held us, and urged us forward. They took us to a large house, and into a long drawing-room; and one stayed by the window, and one by the door, to keep us there.

So far as I have been able to ascertain, we were the only persons who were deliberately spared by the cloud-men; and many conjectures have been made as to their reasons. Professor Dodd holds that we were selected as "specimens" for a museum which the cloud-men proposed to establish; but, if so, I do not know why I was chosen. Mary, indeed, is, in my opinion, a singularly handsome woman; but I cannot claim any distinction of personality, except that I am a good deal above the average in size and strength.

We remained in this house—which, curiously enough, I cannot identify—for nine days, during which we had every opportunity of studying the cloud-men, as we came to call them; for the house and its vicinity seemed to be a kind of *rendezvous*.

I will give a few particulars which we noticed.

Their shape, as I have said, always remained the same, but their size varied greatly, and as it varied they appeared to be composed of quite different substance. At the largest, they seemed to be nothing but dark smoke, and one lost all perception of outline in them, except that the "eye" remained as a little dark cloud floating in the smoky mist. As they contracted, they took definite shape in the cloud-cylinders which I have already described, and which felt like a wet blanket; a blanket which divided and "flowed" round one like water, exerting a discriminating pressure, like that of countless fingers. When they had further contracted to the size at which the belted cloud-man had shrunk when he settled on the ground, they were, as I have said, of the density of a rather hard but springy sofa-cushion; but, in spite of their hardness, a good deal of their pliability remained.

One that was probably not full-grown sometimes played with us, pushing us round the room, and, though firm, he did not hurt like a hard substance. When they were resting, they grew much smaller—at the extreme, not more than a foot in length. They then looked like black metal, and were so heavy that Mary and I together could barely move them. They felt as hard as iron, and we could make no impression on them; but yet they could fold round an object and handle it without crushing or injuring it in any way. I have seen them hold a flower, the metallic substance seeming to divide as they did so.

When they were in this state a hissing sound came from the eight circular disks, which appeared to control their motion, whenever they moved; and their whirring was sharper and clearer. It sounded like the playing of a musical instrument in a chromatic scale. We even learned to understand the meaning of certain series of notes, and especially of one which indicated that we might go out from our room and find something to eat—a privilege only accorded to us after a good while.

We were very near being starved at first. There was no food in the room, and no water, except some in which flowers had stood. We were reduced to drinking that. We tried vainly to get by the sentinel at the door; but he always enveloped us and pushed us back.

After we had fasted for nearly two days, and the last of the foul water was gone, we persisted in trying to get out, and entreated and made gesticulations. At last one of the belted cloud-men came. He watched our gesticulations for some time with his one diamond-shaped eye, and he and our guards talked, or "sang," to one another.

Finally the guard stood aside, and we were allowed to go to the kitchen under escort. We found some stale bread and some good bacon there; also some tea and sugar—the milk was sour. We took back some biscuits and two large jugs of water. After that we were allowed to go there twice a day, and a number of cloud-men came to watch us. So far as we had seen, they did not take food—they appeared to lack mouths—and our custom of eating puzzled them.

We were beginning to lose the edge of our aversion to these extraordinary creatures, and to think that perhaps their cruelty had been due to ignorance of the nature of life and death; and then three things happened which brought back our fears—and worse.

The first was a sight which we saw from the drawing-room window, outside which the cloud-men often held what were evidently assemblies. A vast multitude of the cloud-rolls came along, contracted, and hung in a circle round one who seemed to be a prisoner. After some "talking" in their way, one of the belted men sang a fierce sentence; and then the prisoner wailed miserably. After this they drew back from him, watching him closely. He swelled slowly, wailing all the time, and then suddenly there was a flash, and he was gone! His fellows sang a kind of dirge; then expanded and floated away. Sentence had been executed.

If they punished others, they would not scruple to punish us, Mary said; and so it proved.

The second incident, which brought this punishment, was a frustrated attempt on our part to escape. The guard at the door was talking, in his singing way, to the guard at the window. Mary and I took the opportunity to slip out through the door. They overtook us as we were running down the front path, and pushed us back. One held Mary and the other held me, keeping us at different ends of the long drawing-room. I could feel that my captor was angry by the touch, and in a few moments he folded himself close round me, pressing till my bones ached. Mary screamed and tried to get to me, but could not stir.

After a while my captor covered my head and slowly smothered me, till I was at my last gasp. Then he released my head, but still held me firmly, while his companion treated my poor Mary in the same manner. They repeated this cruelty three times. When they released us it was half an hour before we had strength enough to crawl to each other; and after that they pushed us roughly as we went to and from the kitchen to get our food, and sometimes made as if they would smother us again, though they never actually did so.

We both became very silent and grave after this, and we used to kiss each other good-by before either slept, which we always did one at a time, the other watching—though I do not know what service there was that watchfulness could do; asleep or awake, we were equally in their power.

The third incident came about as a result of the second, I think, though this is merely a conjecture.

I fancy that our warders thought, from our depressed and silent condition, that we were dying—perhaps we were—and they were afraid of being held responsible for the loss of the valuable "specimens" entrusted to their care. Anyhow, they were less rough, and allowed us more freedom in going about the house; and one day we went into the dining-room. It looked out upon great fields, which we had not seen before. A large number of "drowned" people lay there, arranged in orderly rows. They had evidently been gathered together by the cloud-men. But, why? We talked about that for the rest of the day.

The next day we again went into the dining-room, unattended. We saw a number of cloud-men, in the cloud-cylinder condition of existence, come and settle upon the "drowned" people; each upon one. When the cloud-men rose, the bodies upon which they had settled had disappeared.

Mary turned a greenish color; looked at me; swayed slowly. I held her in my arms. My first thought was to try to make the awful thing seem less awful to her.

"After all," I said, "we eat animals. If I could get you out of this, they might kill me, and welcome. Oh, Mary!"

I sobbed like a little child, and the tears streamed down my face. Mary folded me in her arms and kissed me, as a mother might have done.

"Come," she said, and led me to the open window.

It was about ten feet above the ground. I lowered her down. Then I jumped.

I could have made the jump safely enough a fortnight before—could make it safely now; but I suppose my limbs had grown feeble. The fall damaged one of my ankles, and I could not stand. Mary lifted me up and held me.

"Go," I said. "It will be easier for me if I can hope that you have escaped. Let me say this first—if all the women in the world were back again, I should want only you—dear Mary! Now, go!"

She laughed a strange little laugh, like a child. Then she lifted me up and staggered on with me—on and on. Sometimes she fell. She always laughed that curious little laugh, as a young mother might with a little child.

Presently we heard the whirring sound from the house. We understood that it was a warning of our flight. I cannot tell how we knew this; but we knew. We looked back and saw the cloud-men rising into the air, expanding as they rose.

"Dear Mary," I said, "this is the end!"

She gave a fierce cry, like a mother defending her young, and tried to carry me farther. When she found that she was too much exhausted to bear my weight, she dragged me to a hollow filled with dead leaves that the long darkness and mist had brought off before their time. We burrowed under the leaves, and lay there.

We heard the cloud-men go by, "whirring" loudly. I suppose they did not know that I was hurt, and expected us to have run much farther. Anyhow, they did not search the leaves.

For hours we lay quite still. In the dusk we peeped out and saw a great concourse of the cloud-men; and presently we heard a loud song, which we recognized as the judge's sentence. Two flashes followed. Our negligent guards had met their fate.

We were tired, and we rested softly among the leaves. We fell asleep.


IV

When we woke and peeped out, the sun was shining, for the first time for many weeks. There was a huge gathering of the cloud-men about. They were not flying, but moving over the land. Some were small, like the shots of big guns; others were as big as sheep; others were as big as a bear; others as large as an elephant.

They kept changing from small to large. Sometimes they changed back again, but mostly they expanded and floated up in the air. One or two seemed to dissipate into black mist, and be drawn up in a long spiral into the sky. They whirred continually— "whirs" of anger, or was it despair? It seemed as if they tried to hold to the earth and were drawn away.

"They are going!" Mary cried.

She raised herself out of the leaves. So did I; and then the cloud-men saw us. Several advanced upon us, growing to the size of elongated balloons, and rising.

Most of them grew and grew, and went up into the sky; but one reached us and settled on us. It felt wet and cold. It twitched fiercely as it swallowed us in its embraces, and blotted out sight and sound. My breath was nearly gone; and then the suffocating cloud seemed to grow thinner. I could see through it. I could breathe a little. Suddenly it parted from us with a snap, like the breaking of elastic.

The sun was shining cheerfully, and we breathed God's good air. The cloud-men went up, up, in streamers of black smoke. The time came when the last disappeared. We laughed and cried— laughed and cried.

"I wonder if any of our world is left'" I said.

"All my world is left," said Mary. "All!" She held my hand; and I kissed her hand that held mine. "But we will look for the others," she said. "We will look for them—our own dear people of our own dear world!"

We found none that day. We could not go far, as my ankle was badly swollen; but in the afternoon Mary came upon a little truck. She put me upon it, on cushions, and wheeled me to find the people of the world.

After that we came upon some, day by day; first a mother and her child, who had hidden in a chimney; then a man who had been left for dead, but had revived—the only case of the kind which has come to my notice. It was like drowning, he said.

Then we met a husband and wife.

"We will quarrel no more," they told us; and they told that to all whom we met.

They do not. Even people who love each other do not quarrel now!

At Chatham we found a large assembly, including a train-load who had come down from London. The man who had talked to us in the Peckham Road was among them. Strange to say, he had found his "girl"—a pretty, fair-haired, laughing little thing. She and several other waitresses had hidden in the roof of their restaurant. They were so frightened that they remained there and starved for several days.

"When I heard Will walking about below and calling for me," she said, "I thought I had died, and gone to heaven!"

"How did you know it was heaven?" some one asked.

"Why, I knew Will's voice!" she answered.

"We are going to be married to-morrow," he said. "Every man ought to look after a woman in these times."

I thought so, too; and Mary and I, and many other pairs who have met during the reign of terror, were also married then, promising ourselves a honeymoon in easier days. For at that period we worked eighteen hours daily, moving up to London, and sending rescue parties all round to gather up the remnants of the scattered population.

If we had not done this, I believe that half of those now surviving would have perished. For many were afraid to venture out from their hiding-places in search of food, and others were too weak to do so. Some seemed to have temporarily lost their reason from fright and hardship. A pestilence was threatened from the unburied bodies of men and animals, and was only avoided by our clearing certain districts for habitation, and proscribing other localities until time had removed the danger.

Trade and production had stopped, and machinery rusted. Oversea supplies ceased, and accumulated stocks were left to rust and rot in the abandoned districts.

Through the hard winter which followed, all lived upon a dole; and many a time, as we waited for the return of the spring, we thought that the last day had come to the human race. The despatch of food-ships from America alone saved us, in my opinion. We had just strength to unload them—no more. I shall never forget the pale faces of the tottering men and women who worked at this.

Now, I hope and believe that we are through the worst. There is food enough—on this point I can speak with authority, as I have the honor to be m charge of the department concerned with our supplies—to last us for the rest of the year, with care; and I believe that we can organize husbandry and industry so as to make satisfactory provision for the future.

Practically all domestic animals were destroyed in England, it is true; but, fortunately, a large number of oxen in the Highlands escaped our ferocious visitors; and in Ireland and elsewhere the pigs showed a capacity of recovery from "drowning" which no other animal has exhibited. A few surviving specimens of sheep are being carefully reserved for breeding purposes; and though the horse is extinct, it is hoped to rear a race of superior donkeys from half a dozen which escaped. Moreover, we have plenty of motor vehicles.

The stores of clothing and furniture are sufficient for many generations, so long as we do not allow ourselves to fall back under the absurd dominion of "fashions." I have great hope that we shall escape this, although, even in the best of women, I notice that a tendency to elaboration and decorativeness in dress still unfortunately survives.

I am confident, however, that none will allow such petty vanities to interfere with more solid occupations. For nothing has struck me more than the noble manner in which the women have struggled to help in the reconstruction of a prosperous and united society—a united society of the surviving human race.

"Union" is the key-note of our future. The days of discord and war are over. Each in future will love his neighbor as himself. Each will work for all. Unborn generations, when in more leisured times they come to write the history of the world, will record that the clouds of selfishness and cruelty lifted from the world with the darkest clouds that ever rested upon it; as if the evil passions of humanity were concentrated in and departed with those diabolical spirits of evil whom we have named the cloud-men.

# THE SOUL MACHINE

## I
### THE UNKNOWN POWER

The blinds of the lecture-room were drawn, but a fussy little breeze had joined their enemy the sun, and the allies made sudden sorties through the flapping defences. In one of these incursions the light fell upon the upturned face of the girl in the front row. She was watching the professor—she always did—with a frightened, but not unwilling, fascination; and, as usual, he was watching her. She had, it occurred to him then, the look of a martyr; and her light hair, lit by the sun, passed very well for a halo. He was a very tall, very dark, very stern-looking man, and young for his position. People said that he would make a great name.

"All the known powers of the universe," he was saying, "are forms of vibration. The unknown power that we call the soul no doubt is like the rest."

A spectacled student noted the statements neatly:

Powers = vibrations
Soul = ditto.

A tall girl in black glanced impatiently at her watch. A bored youth dropped ink on his pad, and watched the blots spread. A dumpty girl drew the professor as a windmill with whirling arms. A bronzed man skirmished under the desk for a red-haired girl's hand.

The girl in the front row shivered. She felt that she was being drawn to the edge of the abysmal unknown.

"One by one we discover the secrets of the vibrations; and so we catch the powers, and make them our servants. *Some day we shall catch the soul!*"

The spectacled man added to his notes, and the bored youth added to his blots. The tall girl concluded that "Fred" must be waiting outside by now. The dumpty girl added a chubby soul dodging the windmill. The bronzed man looked at the red-haired girl as if he meant, "Some day *I* shall catch *you!*" The girl in the front row clasped her hands. The professor's eyes seemed to claim that *her* capture was completed.

"I can even fancy how we shall do it," he went on. "We shall keep guessing at the form of the vibrations—discovery always begins with a guess—and testing our guesses; and some day we shall happen to guess right. We shall make some contrivance that would vibrate in unison with the soul vibrations, if they existed; and we shall find that it does and they do, and then we shall set to work to capture them.

"We shall begin by connecting the vibrating contrivance with some mechanism to register the vibrations, just as the 'record' of a phonograph registers speech in the form of minute indentations or lines. The next step—and this is the difficult one—will be to turn this inexpressive record back into the thoughts which it represents, as a phonograph turns the lines and indentations back into speech. When we have invented this machine the first part of our task will be done. We shall have caught the soul, and its secrets will be secrets no more."

He paused. The spectacled student made more notes, and the blotter more blots. The tall girl once more consulted her watch. The dumpty girl touched up the "soul" so that it made faces at the windmill. The bronzed man tried to catch the red-haired girl in a primitive form of soul machine—the pressure of two big hands upon a small one. The girl in the front row looked at the professor with eyes like lamps.

"And then"—the professor leaned forward, and his eyes seemed to seize her— "we shall tame the wild force that we have trapped. The soul is the hardest of the powers to catch, but it will be the easiest to subdue to service. It is its very nature to realise in action what is presented to it as the thing to be done. The controller of the soul machine will only have to turn the machine backwards to impress his own will on other souls. The rule of the world will be in the hands of the man who invents the soul-machine."

He bowed to indicate the end of his lecture. The spectacled student hurried to his next class-room. The tall girl hurried to her waiting escort. The dumpty girl hurried home, and the bored youth to a music-hall. The red-haired girl hurried into the passage. The bronzed man overtook her and seized her.

"Caught, little soul!" he whispered almost fiercely.

"Oh, Jack!" she cried. "Be good to me!"

The girl in the front row rose slowly and gathered up her books. The professor glanced at her, and she put them down again. When they were alone he held out his hand. She hesitated, then gave him hers. They had not spoken before.

"I think we have got as far as vibrating in sympathy," he suggested.

"Sometimes," she answered, without looking at him, "I think that you have hypnotised me."

"I shouldn't call it hypnotism," he said. "When two minds—two anythings—vibrate in unison, the stronger sets the pace. That is all."

"And yours is the stronger." She drew a deep breath. "You wished me to stay."

"Yes."

"Why?"

"Is that so hard to guess?" he asked, rather awkwardly.

"Oh!" the girl cried sharply. "It isn't that. . . . Don't pretend."

"No," he said," I won't. We shall be good friends, I hope; but it isn't that. My life has bigger things than—friendship. I want assistance, and I chose you, because we are 'in unison,' for one thing; because I can trust you, for another."

"Because you are the stronger, and I *can't* be false, I suppose. I don't think I should be anyhow. Yes? What is it?"

"I have invented the Soul Machine," he stated. "It is in my private laboratory upstairs."

The girl quivered and looked at him with frightened eyes.

"The—soul—machine," she echoed.

"The soul machine," he repeated. "Up to a point, that is. It registers, but it does not reproduce—yet. It will, with your assistance."

"Am I the first victim?" she asked.

She spoke as an inquirer, not as one with a voice in the decision.

"No," he said, "rather you will be—part of the machine, I think. I shall not hurt you. Do not be nervous."

She clasped and unclasped her hands.

"You know," she said slowly, "that I have no choice; that I must obey."

"Do you wish to disobey?" he asked. She shook her head.

"You *have* hypnotised me, I think," she said. "I . . . It is as you said. My mind has to follow yours. . . . Be good to me—as good as you can be."

"I will be as good to you as I can be," he promised. "Come!"

She followed him upstairs.


II

THE FIFTH DIAL

The laboratory consisted of two rooms, one entered through the other. The outer room was filled with ordinary scientific apparatus, and lit by two windows that looked out upon a field of housetops. The inner room, when he opened the door, was quite dark.

"Some of the things are affected by sunlight," he explained. "I will turn on the light as soon as we are inside. Give me your hand, Miss—"

"Myra Hamilton," she said, staring into the darkness within. "Shall I ever come out again?"

"Of course! You don't think I am going to murder you in the dark, do you? I will turn on a little light first, if you are afraid. . . . There! Now come in."

She entered, closed the door, and stood with her back against it looking at the curtains that surrounded the centre of the room.

He pulled a lever, the curtains rolled back slowly, and she saw the soul machine.

A powerful electric dynamo stood at one end. This did not differ from other dynamos. The soul machine proper occupied a space of about twelve feet long by five feet wide, rose about five feet from the floor, and descended into a space beneath—a rotary apparatus with complicated attachments.

The central rotary portion consisted of an elliptical chain-band revolving on broad-flanged wheels. The band carried four and twenty discs of a whitish material, like alabaster, mounted on short stems. These, the professor explained, were the receivers that took up the vibrations of the soul, or group of souls, to which they were "set." The "setters" were a number of tiny-coloured electric globes— nearly a hundred—arranged in a double row on each side of the upper course of the discs or receivers. Silvered reflectors were placed behind them to throw their light upon the discs. They sensitised the receivers, he explained, much as light affects a photographic film, but with the important difference that the sensitisation could be "wiped out," and the discs used again and again.

The lower course of the receivers ran in a kind of tank sunk beneath the floor. A number of nozzles projected slantwise on one side. These, the professor said, emitted a powerful chemical spray upon the discs. The object of this was twofold. The impact of the spray caused the discs to rotate upon their axes in addition to their elliptical motion—much as the planets revolve in their orbits— which was essential to their function. Secondly, the spray wiped out the impression of one moment and left them free for that of the next.

The discs were carried round from left to right, coming up on the left from the pit, cleaned like a slate for their next impression, and taking that as the lights fitted them for it. They carried the impression to the far end of the machine toward a curious apparatus there. The professor called it the diaphragm. It stood upon a platform about four feet square poised upon a complicated arrangement of pulleys and wheels and steel balls running upon other steel

balls. The diaphragm itself was hung upon wires with similar elabo-
rations. It was about four feet long, about a foot wide, and perhaps two inches thick. It appeared to be a slab of cream-coloured
wax, convoluted like a walnut, or a huge brain spread out in the
form of a tablet. The wires were gathered up in a waxen globe,
somewhat like a spherical brain. Other wires ran from this to five
dials.

"These," said the professor, "are the recorders. Will you attend
to me carefully, Myra?"

"Yes," she said, "master!"

There was a touch of sarcasm in her voice as she uttered the
submissive word, and her eyes flashed with a light of their own,
for the first time. It had occurred to her that he could not make
her attend unless she chose.

"I understand, Myra," he said quietly. "Yes. You have a choice.
You cannot help obeying; but your obedience is of little use unless
you try to make it useful. It is for you to choose whether you will
assist me in the greatest discovery of all time. If you refuse you
can go—go now, and return no more. If you agree you will have no
more choice. You will be bound ever after. I give you fair warning.
Now choose."

They looked at each other for a long while.

"You could release me," she suggested, "at any time afterwards?"

"Yes; but I should not."

She drew a very deep breath.

"I think you *have* hypnotised me," she gasped. "I . . . Your slave is
ready, master. . . . I never thought to be that to any man. . . . Go on."

He shook her hand with some warmth.

"You will be my partner in the greatest work ever done!" he
declared. "Thank you! . . . Well, now you will attend carefully. The
diaphragm takes down the vibrations of the soul and exhibits them
in a kind of spectrum—bands of colour with little breaks between.
Certain colours stand for certain affections of the mind. Anger
widens the red. Disappointment darkens the green. Intense
mental exertion makes the yellow wide and faint. Pain brings out

certain dark bands; and so on. In that way we might tell from the spectrum with practice that a soul was, let us say, angry and dis-appointed; perhaps even that it was angry and disappointed be-cause it had failed in some hoped-for mental achievement; but that is hopelessly inadequate to show the real soul. The dials do not even tell us as much as that. They merely indicate the intensity of certain of the primitive colours, and therefore of the mental facts for which these stand. In short, the diaphragm at present *repre-sents* the soul, but it does not re-translate it into your mind or mine. That is our problem in the future. . . . Well, now you will like to see it at work."

The girl shrank away from him.

"Not me!" she begged. "Not me!"

"Not if you are frightened," he said composedly. "You shall see it at work on me. Then perhaps you will believe that it is harmless. Sit in this chair and watch. . . . This is the arrangement that sets the machine to its particular 'victim,' as you would call it."

He operated a keyboard that looked like that of a small type-writer.

"I have written down my soul characters," he said. "I will ex-plain them to you some other time. Now the soul machine can cap-ture *me!*"

He came back and stood on a marble slab beside the diaphragm where a number of levers jutted out.

"It can't catch you unless you stand there?" she asked.

"It could catch me if I stood on the top of the Himalayas!" he declared.

"Or if I lived in Mars. I stand here because it is the one place where I can both reach the operating levers and see the diaphragm and the dials. That is all. . . . Now!"

He pulled a lever. The electric machinery buzzed and crackled, and long bluish sparks sprang from one place to another. The little electric lights above shone out in a wonderful spangle of colours, some vivid, some bright, some pale, some barely visible, some apparently not lit at all; defects in his character, perhaps, the girl fancied. . . . She did not like the powerful black globe. It represented his cruelty, she told herself.

The band went round, and the spray hissed, and the discs revolved faster and faster.

"Look!" he cried, and pointed to the diaphragm. A spectrum like a many-coloured rainbow shone upon the convoluted slab; and the girl roused to sudden interest.

"What is that?" she asked.

"It is I," he said, "so far as this kind of diaphragm will represent me; I as I am at this moment; the extraordinary medley of thoughts and feelings that exist even in a comparatively restful mind. The dials show better *how* restful."

He nodded at the indexes, and she went up to them. They registered from 0 to 100 she saw, and the highest pointer was at 7 now.

"Think of things," she begged excitedly. "Think of things!"

"You shall tell me what to think of," he proposed; and the girl clapped her hands.

"Work a sum," she told him. "I will put it down on this slate. . . . There! . . . Now work it. . . . This first dial is going up 9—10—11. . . . What does it stand for?"

"It estimates intellectual work," he stated. "The second dial has gone from 2½ to 3¾ you may have noticed. That is the physical effort."

"The third dial has gone up a little, too. What is *that* for?"

"Effort of will. The effort to work a simple sum is small in an educated man. It has become a habit. . . . Is the sum right?"

"Yes. The fourth dial has gone up just a little."

"The satisfaction which I get from my good arithmetic! That dial represents emotion."

She made him rack his memory, compose a verse, hum a tune, think of a good dinner, and explain the changes of the spectrum and of the dials that followed from each.

"And now," she said at last, "think of *me!*"

Changes took place in the rainbow of colours and in the dials as before. They represented his effort of attention, his aesthetic appreciation of her appearance, his satisfaction at having her assistance, and so on, he explained.

"And the fifth dial has gone up from 1½ to over 4," she said. "What does that dial mean?"

"That dial?" he said. "Oh, it is rather a tentative one. I meant it to indicate personal regard, or affection as we call it, in its higher degrees. I haven't done much with it."

"I should imagine not," said the girl, "if you have only taken down yourself!"

"It's up to 4½," he apologised. "I really do appreciate your assistance, and—and I feel that we shall easily grow friendly, and—it's gone to 5—5½! It will go higher in time. If you wait—nearly six . . ."

"Please stop the machine," the girl said irritably. "I want to talk."

He laughed good-humouredly and stopped the machine.

"I should not have promised," she protested, "if I had known that you had so little regard for people. I should have been too much afraid of you. And I am. . . . The machine shows that you are hard and unfeeling. . . . I wonder if I can break my promise. I wonder."

"No," he said. "You cannot."

"You could let me."

"No, I cannot. Myra, don't you understand? The success of this machine means the regeneration of the universe. If ten thousand people had to be sacrificed it would be my duty to do it; and you are only one."

The girl swayed a little.

"Then I *am* to be sacrificed," she said. "Oh, I knew! I knew!"

"It depends on what you call sacrifice," he said. "I think, if you understand it rightly—but we will talk of that another time. Come at eleven to-morrow morning, Myra."

"I will not come!" she cried.

The professor looked at her, and her eyes and voice sank.

"I will come," she promised. Then she went. She kept saying one word over and over to herself on the way home. "Six! Six! Six!"

## III
### ELAINE

There was a feeling very like compassion in the professor's mind as he went toward the laboratory door. He expected to see a little black-robed, pale-faced figure looking at him with doubtful eyes. Instead he found Myra radiant in white muslin, with a bright flower-hat, and roses at her bosom, and pretty pink roses on her cheeks, and holding a gay little parasol. She smiled at his surprise.

"Decked for the sacrifice!" she said with a laugh that was not wholly a laugh.

"It is not a sacrifice," he protested, "if you will understand. . . . You look very sweet, child."

"The dial will go to six and a half," she said sarcastically. "Let's try."

"The dials must take *you* down this morning," he told her.

"No!" she cried. "I won't, *I won't.*"

"You must," he said quietly. "Come."

He went to the inner room. She followed him. She dropped the parasol as she went, and let it lie. She had meant to catch him in Eve's woman-machine of adornment and smiles; and her wiles, she told herself, had failed.

"Sit down," he said, and handed her a chair. She sank in it.

"I can't see the diaphragm and the dials from here," she objected.

"I do not wish you to," he answered.

He experimented with the "setter" that looked like a typewriter for a time, while Myra stared in front of her without looking round.

"Ah!" he said suddenly. "I've got you." She gave a cry. "Don't be frightened. I am merely going to take you down as I did with myself yesterday. I shall do nothing else to-day."

"And afterwards?" she asked in a dull voice.

"I shall not hurt you at any time."

"But—?"

"Hush! I will explain afterwards. Now we will begin."

"I want to see!" she protested, in the same dull, hopeless voice.

"Some other time you shall see, Myra. I don't want your attention distracted to-day."

He moved the lever—she heard it click—and the lamps flashed out and the spinning discs went whirling round; but she sat quite still as she had been bidden.

"Think of your schooldays," he commanded; "your prizes, if you took any. Try to remember some dates. The Magna Charta. Its chief provisions. Can you think out a proposition in geometry? The angles of the base of an isosceles triangle. Ah! You know it, I see. Now—attend carefully please. Tell me what I told you about this machine last night."

She told him. Then he put other questions, gave her paper and a pencil to draw; made her play as if on a piano; told her to sing a song. She sang softly the first verse of "She is far from the Land." She had a very good voice. Singing, in fact, was her accomplishment.

"And now the last verse," he asked, "not merely for the machine, but for your beautiful singing. . . . Thank you, Myra."

"It would be 6¾ now, don't you think?" she asked suddenly. "Won't you let me go now, and try it on yourself?"

"Presently," he said. "Presently. We'll see what *you* make of the fifth dial. You are of a warmer disposition than I, and we ought to get some interesting results. Think of some relative; one whom you like. . . . None you like much, I gather."

"They are dead. . . . When my mother—"

"I see," he interrupted. "I see. I'm sorry I asked you. Think of someone else. Think of *me*. Poor little Myra!" He laid his hand on her shoulder. She gave a cry. There was a snapping sound, and then a noise as if a spring was broken and a clock was running down. The professor sprang back and stopped the machine. He looked at the index of the fifth dial. It had gone to 100, and then the spring had broken. Myra rose and saw it, too, and stood wringing her hands.

"There is a difference between six and a hundred," she said in a voice that seemed to come from a long way off, "isn't there?"

"It would be more than six now, Myra," the professor said. It was he who flushed. The girl was very white.

"It would be—shall we say 7 or 8?" She laughed feebly. "Well, now you know why I chose to obey you. I am ashamed and sorry;

but—you know. . . . You remember Elaine, perhaps? 'I have gone mad. I love you. Let me die.' . . . It was really the *only* thing to do! I am ready for the sacrifice now. Let it be soon. To-day. What is it?"

"Come into the other room," he said hoarsely. He wiped his forehead.

"No; not the light of day! You must do it now. I shall die of shame, like Elaine, if you don't. I mean it. I am that sort. What is it? Tell me very exactly."

He wiped his forehead once more.

"There is only one diaphragm," he said, "that is adequate to receive the impressions of human souls and give them out as they really are. It is a human soul."

"Yes," she said. She was very calm now. "Go on."

"It must be a soul that will give itself up to the task; remove its own thoughts and feelings and will—or submit to have them removed."

"Yes."

"A clean soul with no stains that will not come out. You are that, Myra."

"Go on."

"A soul that I can control. There might be others, but . . . The final object of the machine is to put my desires—my best and worthiest desires, please God!—into the world, and make it better. The diaphragm to do that must be a soul that is not only all the things that I have said, but completely in sympathy with mine. There is only you, Myra. Shall the work be done or undone? I have no right to compel you, I see now. I give you back your power to choose."

He looked steadily in her eyes.

"I have told you," she said, "that I choose to die. I should die anyhow now you know how I feel about you. Oh, yes, I should. You think one doesn't die of shame, but there's such a thing as tormenting the life out of yourself! I'd rather die quickly, and—and please you."

"You will *not* die," he said. "You will merely lose consciousness of identity—entirely while you act as the receiver and reproducer of the soul machine, to a lesser extent at other times. You will eat and drink and sleep and feel, but I fear that you will not think very much, or remember very well, or do things of your own accord. It is a great sacrifice, of course, but you will not know what you miss; and your life will be more useful than a million ordinary lives put together. I will give you my utmost care. Do everything that can be done for your comfort—" He hesitated. "Myra," he said suddenly, "will you put off the—the sacrifice for a year? Marry me to-morrow, and let me endeavour to give you a year of happiness first."

The girl threw back her head scornfully.

"I would sooner die a thousand times!" she cried. "I cannot deny that I love you, but I hate myself for doing it. Hate—hate—hate! It is now or never. Kill my soul, my identity, whatever you call it, to-day, or *you never shall*. I will kill myself, if you do not, and escape you. I hate the idea of marrying you so much that I will not do it, though I believe that in the year I would win your affection, and make it impossible for you to—to kill me! It *is* killing. . . . Well, if you don't, *I* shall."

The professor groaned.

"It must be," he said. "It *must* be. I shall suffer in doing it, Myra."

"You *should* suffer," she said, "and perhaps— You *shall* do one thing for me. Before I cease to be Myra Hamilton and become an automaton, we will have one afternoon to know each other. You should know what you have destroyed to make a diaphragm! You shall take me up the river. We will talk of music, pictures, books, our hopes and our ideas of life. I will sing to you. We will be just two friends together. In the evening we will come back here, and then— We'll forget that now. Will you take me?"

"Yes," he said, "if you wish it." He shivered, and his voice shook.

"I wish it. . . . No word of love or marriage. Promise, on your honour."

"I promise."

"And no drawing back when the time comes. *I* shall not."

"And I dare not, Myra. You do not understand. It is to save the world; and the world is many millions, and you are only one."

"Only one, and valued at six degrees. Come—I am going to make that six into sixteen this afternoon, perhaps six and twenty. I want you to be sorry afterwards for Elaine!"

## IV
### THE NEW DIAPHRAGM

The setting sun was reddening the sky when the professor and Myra reentered the laboratory. She carried a great bunch of wild flowers that she had gathered. Some of her hair fell loose when she took off her hat, and made her look very young.

"And now," she said, "you shall make your new diaphragm. Will you remember that it was once rather a nice girl? You thought so this afternoon."

"Oh, Myra—"

"Hush! It has to be. It is fixed in your mind beyond altering. Don't salve your conscience by pretending to be overruled by me! It is fixed in my mind, too. Do it quickly. I am ready. . . . Hush! *Don't talk!*"

The professor moved the diaphragm from its slab, and set a library chair there. He heaped it with cushions.

"Sit there, Myra," he said. "You will not feel any pain. When the machine starts you will know no more—as yourself—until it stops. Then I shall take you home."

"Me," said the girl thoughtfully.

"Me. You call it that? Well, it will not know what it has lost, will it?"

"*I* shall," he cried with sudden passion.

The girl smiled over her shoulder as she went to the chair.

"I *think*," she said, "your fifth dial will go higher than six when you think of me. That is why I made you take me out this afternoon."

"Oh, Myra!" he groaned.

"That will be *your* sacrifice, you see. Will you arrange the cushions, and make the diaphragm comfortable? . . . Yes, it will go

higher than six, won't it?—when you think of your poor little soulless, helpless diaphragm? . . . That is *very* comfortable. Thank you!"

She smiled up at him without a tremor.

"I have the best part, after all," she told him. "I shall forget,
and you will remember. Good-bye!"

"Oh, Myra! Don't you see, I am like the signalman who must
send the train to destruction—a thousand lives—or upon his child.
The world needs your soul, and I— May I kiss you once?"

"Yes," she said. "I shall forget, and you will remember."

She lifted her face to his, put her arms round his neck like a
child, and returned his kisses—for there were more than one."

"Think of *this*," she said, "when you take down your thoughts
on your brand-new diaphragm. Good-bye! Please do it now."

She sank back upon the cushions with sudden weariness, and
lay there smiling; and a wonderful moment of beauty came to her.
The professor looked at her and felt very faint.

"Myra," he cried, "it is my duty, and I damn myself if I refuse
to do it; but I cannot!"

His face worked painfully, and he strode up and down.

"It is you who are damning me!" he cried, as if he had lost his
reason. "You vowed to help me—declared that you were ready. It
was all pretence. You meant to win me over with your fascinations.
You talked glibly of dying, but you did not mean it. You meant to
make me love you and marry you. I might have saved the world,
and now— I *will* do it!" He laid his hand on the lever, dropped it
with a groan. "After all," he said, "your life is your own. Go! It is *I*
who will die!"

She sat up in the chair and looked at him with her hand on her chin.

"My life is my own," she said, "and all that I have to give. I give
it gladly!"

She leaned forward, holding by the arm of the chair, and put
down a lever. Then the powers imprisoned in the machine fell upon
her suddenly, and she dropped across the arm of the chair. He
threw himself upon the levers wildly and pulled two together. The
room seemed to fill with lightning and thunder. The soul machine

fell to pieces. The boarded window blew out. He saw a calm evening sky, and then he saw nothing.

A pretty young girl, with her head and hands bandaged, brought the professor to his home in a cab. He was unconscious. A policeman who came with them told his sister of the explosion at the laboratory. They had found the young lady sitting on the floor, holding the professor in her arms, he said. She had been sensible enough at first, and had ordered the cab, but on the way she seemed to have gone dazed, and "lost herself."

The professor's sister drew Myra to her and kissed her.

"Who are you, dear?" she asked.

The girl stared blankly, and gave a laugh that had no laughter in it.

"I am the new diaphragm," she said.

## V
### THE SAVING OF THE SOUL

A fortnight later, when the professor was well enough to go out, he told his sister the whole story. She made no comment till the end, but he noticed that she shrank from him.

"There is only one thing that you can do," she said, after a painful pause. "You must marry her."

"God knows," he said, "I am willing enough; but Myra—"

"There is no Myra," his sister said. "You murdered her. God forgive you. I don't think He will. Myra loved you, and marriage is the best way to protect what is left of her. You will go away, of course, and leave her with me; but she has a right to your name. You must marry her."

"If she is willing—"

"Willing? If you ask her she will look at you and say, 'Am I?' . . . Oh, George!" His sister cried a little.

They said no more till they heard Myra's step in the passage. She had lived with them since the explosion.

She did not speak when she came in—she never spoke till she was spoken to—but when the professor's sister kissed her she returned the kiss and smiled.

"Would you like to go out with George, darling?" the sister asked, holding the girl round the waist.

Myra looked at the professor.

"Would I?" she asked.

"Yes," he said. "Yes, Myra. Run and put on your hat."

"Which hat?" she demanded helplessly.

"I will come and dress you, darling," the sister offered.

Myra followed her obediently. Presently she came back in muslin and roses. He had bought her a hat and dress like those that the explosion had spoiled.

"She almost chose them for herself," the sister claimed, with a faint hope in her voice, "didn't you, dear helpless one?"

"Did I?" the girl asked. She looked at the professor for instruction.

"Shall we go now, Myra?" he said.

"Shall we?" She always answered questions so.

"Yes, dear," he said, and then they went; and the professor's sister laid her head on the table and cried.

"Where shall we go, Myra?" he inquired, when they were outside.

"You know," she said.

"On the river?" he suggested.

"Where we went that afternoon? You remember, Myra?"

"Do I?" She looked at him doubtfully. "I don't think I remember, because—I am a diaphragm."

He groaned.

"Do you remember what that is?" he asked.

"No," she denied.

He groaned again.

"We will go on the river," he decided. "Oh, Myra, you smiled so that afternoon! Will you ever smile again?"

"Of course," she said, "if you tell me to smile."

She looked at him for her orders, and he made a sound that was almost a sob.

"We will go in a motor," he offered. "You like motors. . . . Well, you *did*. . . . I think you do now if you knew what you liked."

He hired a motor and drove it out into the country and along the river banks. Myra sat quite still with her hands folded. She looked at things if the professor told her to look, but made no remark. The blue sky, the sweet air, the green fields, the little children who tried to race them and clamoured for pennies, the hills covered with trees, the valleys covered with grass and flowers, the white-sailed boats—none of the earth's good things seemed to move her to thoughts of her own. She was just a soul diaphragm, it seemed, waiting for impressions from her master, and faintly reflecting his pleasure. For when he told her that things were good or beautiful she sometimes smiled faintly.

"*You* know," she agreed.

They came to the boat-stage presently and took a little skiff. He put her tenderly among the cushions and rowed till they reached a backwater, and there he stopped under a tree among the water-lilies. She had been so pleased with them a fortnight before.

"Would you like to gather some, Myra?" he asked.

"Shall I?" She waited as always for his orders.

"Oh, Myra!" he begged, "can't you *want* to do anything?"

"I want what you want," she said.

"Do you? . . . I want you to marry me, Myra. Will you?"

"If you tell me to," she assented composedly.

"I want you to love me, Myra."

He held her hands. "Will you?"

She frowned and bit her lips.

"If you want me to," she demanded, "why don't you make me?"

"I want you to make yourself," he entreated.

"But, of course, I can't!" she said. "How can I? I am only a diaphragm."

"Don't," he begged hoarsely; "don't." He dropped his face in his hands, and his body shook. He was haggard when he looked up.

"Myra," he said, "it's no use telling you, because you can't understand, but I want to say it. The machine shall never be made again.

I see now that it was blasphemous folly. We cannot save souls; they must save themselves. Neither can we destroy them. Some day—perhaps after we are both dead, Myra—yours will come back to you; perhaps, in God's goodness, to mine! Meanwhile I shall be punished enough, Myra. I shall break a little piece off my heart every day for want of the love that you cannot give me. Don't you understand a little, dear?"

There was silence for five minutes, ten; then, for the first time for a fortnight, Myra spoke of her own accord.

"Come and sit beside me," she said, in a sweet, steady voice, "and—yes, I think you may hold my hands. . . . No; you must not kiss me yet. . . . Listen! there *is* a soul machine. It is called love. Souls must save themselves, as you say; but love can show them the way. I learnt that as I sat in the ruined laboratory holding you in my arms. The floor shook, and I thought perhaps we should go through, and I wanted to fend you from the fall. . . . No; you must not kiss me yet. . . . I love you very much. . . . I thought, if he dies he will lose his soul—and if he lives, unless he gives up this wicked plan of his own accord. Perhaps if he sees me as I might have been, as a poor helpless, soulless creature, who was once a girl that he thought pretty and bright and sweet—I could see that you thought that—perhaps he will be sorry and save himself *then*. Perhaps he will offer his ambition, his name, his love—Oh! I wanted *that!*—to this poor hurt, helpless, foolish thing. . . . And then, I thought, I will love him so dearly, I will be so good to him, that he will be glad that he has only sacrificed a machine and not a soul—*two* souls. . . . I love you very much. . . . And now you shall kiss me!"

# THE SLEEP AND THE AWAKENING

PART I: THE SLEEP

I am to go to sleep to-morrow. It is the fifth of April, 1920, and I shall wake on the fifteenth of August, if the Chief Physician has calculated the effect of his new drug correctly, and if the Powers do not order him to prolong my rest—perhaps for ever.

In that event I should like the woman numbered 214,713, London, by whose side I shall lie, to know the part that I have played in her affairs during her four years' unconsciousness, and since the pest of green flies—if they were flies—sent all the world, except a few thousand people, to sleep. So I will write this brief account and put it in her hand.

My name is George Raynor. On Thursday, August 24, 1916, when the flies appeared, I was twenty-five years of age. I saw them first when I reached the platform of Dulwich Station at 9:15 in the morning; little green flies—so I thought—no bigger than a gnat. They were in great swarms. Men were beating them off with their hats, and women with handkerchiefs and scarves. Several people were lying on the platform, apparently asleep. They had not lost their color, and they breathed freely, but they were quite insensible. I was told that they had been stung by the flies, and that the unconsciousness was practically instantaneous.

The man who told me threw up his hands and fell immediately after. Others shrieked, staggered and collapsed every moment—always just after a fly had settled upon their faces. In a few minutes there was no one left standing except myself and a porter. He

179

had taken off his coat and was swinging it round to beat off the flies. He laughed like a madman, and I think his mind was unhinged by fright. Presently a swarm of the flies almost covered him, and he dropped in a huddle. I stood rooted to the ground and, shuddering, waited for my turn to come; but suddenly the flies went. I did not move till they had disappeared in green clouds afar.

They went like that everywhere, when their deadly work was done, and nobody saw them again, or discovered even a dead one left behind. I am therefore unable to give any exact description of them. To me they seemed to be just a swarm of greenish gnats; and they are generally termed "the green flies." On the other hand, scientists mostly say that they were not really insects, but a poison dust which acted through the lungs. I can not remember the reasons for this view; but it is supported by two plain facts: that no bodies of dead flies were found, though many seemed to be beaten down; and that no one has ever discovered any sting-mark upon the sleepers.

I searched the platform in the hope of finding some one who was conscious, or returning to consciousness; but all were in a deep insensibility. Some were smiling. Some were distorted with terror. Some had tears still wet upon their cheeks. Many had their mouths framed as if for a word that sleep cut short. Their limbs were not rigid or cold. They simply slept; some with open eyes and some with shut. The open eyes frightened me.

Among the sleepers I found a very bright young lady, with whom I had chatted at an At Home in Rosendale Road, but whose name I did not catch when we were introduced. Her hair had fallen loose and hung over her face—she had probably shaken it out as a shield, and this made her look childlike. She was, in fact, barely twenty. I had found her very attractive and had looked forward to meeting her again. She was lying in the full glare of the sun. I shook her, and held her up on her feet, but could not rouse her, so I carried her to the waiting-room, made a couch on a bench, with some dust-cloaks that people had dropped, put my cricket-bag for a pillow, and laid her there.

Several trains went through the station while I was doing this. The engine drivers had apparently fallen off, or become insensible.

No doubt the trains went on till they ran into something. All the terminals were wrecked in this way, as those who wake will see; for we have not been able to provide labor to repair them, except a single platform here and there. Most of the railway bridges are in ruins for the same reason.

I walked over the bridge across Thurlow Park Road, and along the embankment. I noticed many people lying insensible in the road and in the gardens of Croxted Road. At last I saw a lady walking out of a back door—a tall, severe-featured, gray-haired lady of fifty-odd.

"What has happened?" she asked quite calmly.

"It is a fly!" I cried. "A cursed little green fly! It stings people and kills them!"

I knew that my nerve was gone when I heard my voice—it seemed to scream.

She listened to my account without comment or sign of emotion. Her coolness steadied me. "Help me over the fence," she commanded, when I finished. "We will go to the station."

I obeyed her without question. I did not know that I trusted her even then, but it never occurred to me to dispute her leading, Her name was Constance Ashbury, and she was a widow. She had been nobody in particular till that day. Now she is the Chief Power of England, and Vice-Power of the Universal Council of the World. An American Jew, Abrahams, who formerly ran a hotel syndicate, is The Power of the World. If I knew how the struggle between him and her would finish, I should know better how my sleep and the sleep of the rest will end. If any one can save the world, he can. They say that he was once a thief and in prison; but if any survive to write histories, I think they will write him down as the best man on earth in our times.

Mrs. Ashbury and I went through the station to a train which had stopped on the other side. The drivers had apparently turned off steam before they fell asleep. The passengers were also asleep except three gentlemen in one compartment. One of them, a red-faced old man, was blustering about the delay. Mrs. Ashbury addressed herself to him and told him what had happened. He got out of the train and looked round and nodded.

"So the world is blotted out," he said, as if he merely stated a fact which did not concern him,

"Come and help make a new one," she proposed. "I think you are a man!"

"By —!" he told her, "*you* ought to have been one! Get away from here! A train's coming into us. Run!" And we ran.

Before we reached the station the second train dashed into the first, and both crashed down the embankment. I proposed going back to rescue the sleepers, but Mrs. Ashbury curtly forbade this.

"Sleepers are no use to us," she said. "We want live people to make a live world."

So we left the trains and those in them to their fate. That was when I began to fear her.

We found the horses at the cab-stand unharmed by the flies. (They did not touch four-footed animals anywhere.) We took two cabs and drove to Herne Hill—the five of us. On the way we met only four "Wakers," as they came to be called. Two joined us. Two refused to leave their sleeping families, and probably perished beside them, as many did.

Half a dozen survivors had collected at Herne Hill Station, which was almost annihilated by the collision of two trains. One of the half-dozen was a telegraph clerk. He had wired to other stations, and understood that the fly had appeared everywhere, all over the world, and that only a few persons in any town at home or abroad remained conscious. A German scientist had pronounced that the "fly" was a sort of radium venom, but that the sleepers would not die, only sleep for a long period—on the average, about five years. He recommended collecting them in public buildings till they woke.

"Wake to eat us up!" Mrs. Ashbury cried scornfully. "Who'll collect food for them?"

"Ye-es," the red-faced man agreed. "They will be a difficulty—unless they wake soon."

"If they don't wake soon," she said, with a quick look at him, "they mustn't wake at all!"

And then I saw what was coming upon the world.

There was a long silence after she had spoken.

"Well," the red-faced man said presently, "you're the best man of us. You'd better take command. What's to be done?"

She turned to the telegraphist.

"Telegraph all over London," she ordered promptly, "wherever you can get an answer. Say that all the survivors must meet at St. Paul's Cathedral, and that the immediate formation of a strong Government is the only hope of saving any one. Let the dead bury their dead. The living must leave them and look after the living. There will be no mercy for those who disobey! Say that!"

"In whose name shall I send it?" the telegraphist asked.

"Mine," she snapped, and the red-faced man laughed a short laugh.

"You will be the power in the land!" he prophesied; and that was how the new title came.

We found a motor-bus driver wandering about. She told him to drive us to town. He refused, saying that he wanted to go and look after his pals. She pointed to the trees in the Brockwell Park.

"Another word," she declared, "and we will hang you there!" And the driver went quickly to his place on the bus.

The telegraphist and I had a little knowledge of motoring. So we each drove another vehicle, hoping to pick up some more passengers on the way. Here and there among the thousands who slept in heaps on the pavements, in the roads, on the busses, everywhere, we found one whom the green flies had not attacked, or had attacked in vain. (We do not know how or why any escaped.) Most of these came with us, but some were drunk or mad, and laughed at us, or ran away.

It seemed at first that no women but Mrs. Ashbury had survived. We were twenty-two men before we found a second female. Then we came upon four at a street-corner, and five weeping girls from a boarding school. We were thirty men and twenty-odd women, and a few children (very few of the young escaped the sleep), when we reached St. Paul's Cathedral. About a hundred people were waiting there. Others came later—men, women and children. We were five hundred and thirty-seven adults when we met at two o'clock and elected the new Government.

Mrs. Ashbury took the chair and opened the proceedings. She seemed to dominate the assembly, and was elected "Chief Power" without contest. The red-faced man, four other men—a butcher, a tax-collector, a clergyman and a clerk—and a lady, well-known as a leading suffragette, were elected "Powers." Dr. J. B. Mason, the eminent specialist, was appointed Chief Physician. It would be the most important office in the Government, Mrs. Ashbury warned us.

"We shall have to consider how and when to wake the sleepers," she said, "or *how not to wake them*, if they sleep until we have no supplies for them! We will save the world, *if we can!* If not, *we must save ourselves!*"

So the new Government began, with the clear understanding that those who slept would, if necessary, be sacrificed. Some of the audience, like myself, shuddered, but no one controverted the understanding. For the moment it seemed to me to be reasonable—a law of self-preservation. I might have adopted it, and have been one of the Powers by now, for more were added afterward, and I had the favor of Mrs. Ashbury; but a little memory came into my mind. That little memory may destroy my body in the end; but I think it will have saved my soul.

It was just a recollection of a girl who smiled at me, when we talked at the At Home in Rosendale Road, and I asked her why she smiled at everybody.

"I smile for two reasons," she said. "I always think 'some day you may help little me'; and I always think 'some day little me may help you.'"

Now the helpful little lady lay sleeping with her head on my cricket-bag; and the Powers would judge whether she should have her chance to wake; and I would judge the Powers! That was the beginning of my lack of loyalty to the new Government. I knew well enough that a struggle with it almost certainly meant destruction. For it was the strong-minded and the strong-willed who escaped the fly, and the Powers were the strongest of these. Nevertheless, from the first I meant to make the struggle, if it was necessary, to help "little me."

The "Chief Power"—as they call Mrs. Ashbury—told me that I was to be her secretary.

"You are like my son who died," she said, putting her hand on my shoulder for a moment. "Remember that I would not spare my son, if he were disloyal to me now. You think I am hard? These are hard times; harder than the days of primitive savagery. Nothing but strength—hard strength—if necessary, fierce and cruel strength—can save the world; and I am here to save the world!"

Her eyes flashed, and she drew herself up. For a moment my admiration carried me away, and I felt tempted to believe in her and serve her blindly; but the thought of the little girl who loved to help, and whom she would doom so carelessly, came into my mind again.

"To save the world," I said. "Yes, but what do you mean by 'the world'?"

"The world is ourselves," she answered, "we who wake. I can save no more, I think."

I often wondered how far she held this belief and acted conscientiously upon it. I am inclined to think that at first she was honest; but that the love of dominion outgrew all other motives as she tasted power, and that later she was actuated entirely by her determination to rule the whole earth and to suffer the return of no old rulers. Anyhow, her policy, from the first, was to sacrifice the sleepers.

She called a "Cabinet Council" at once, divided the duties of the new State, and entrusted different departments to each of the "Powers." One was to select residences, provide food, and so on. Another was to restore communication by rail, so far as possible, and to collect motor transport. A third was to communicate with different places in the Kingdom and tell them to establish local governments and report as to the numbers surviving, and so on. A fourth was to communicate similarly with foreign countries and to propose a General Council. The fifth was to make arrangements to make sure that the supply of water and light did not fail. The sixth department, under the red-haired man, was the Police, to rule the country under martial law. She kept the fourth and sixth departments immediately under her eye, and issued a proclamation at once that no one was to return to his home, or to trouble about the sleepers. "Let the dead bury the dead!" she said, repeating her favorite maxim. "We have enough to do to save the living!"

I entered on my duties at once and sat at a table with her, writing letters and telegrams at her dictation. About eight in the evening, when there was a lull in the correspondence, I asked permission to go back to Dulwich for an hour or so, wishing to put the sleeping girl, whom I thought of as "little me," into a place of greater security. I was promptly refused.

"Once for all," she told me, "my work is your work, and my work is for the *living*. I like you the best of these, I think; but that will not save you if you disobey me!"

At midnight, when practically all England had accepted the rule of the Chief Power, and she was busy in arranging a general telegraphic council with the new Governments in other countries, she dismissed me. I got into a private motor that was standing in Ludgate Hill, and drove it down to Dulwich, passing through silent streets, with sleepers lying everywhere. I found the girl still resting peacefully. I brought her back with me, and took her to an upper room in the Chief Power's house, where my quarters were. As I was carrying her up-stairs I met the Chief Power. She turned pale with anger.

"Come to my study, when you have disposed of that useless lumber," she said very quietly.

I found her sitting at a table. She had a revolver in her hand.

"You have disobeyed," she said. "Your life is forfeit." She bit her lips and seemed to struggle with herself. "My God!" she cried passionately, "if you weren't so like my son!"

"Well," I said, "you loved your son; and I love the little girl whom I have put where she can rest softly. It is all that I can do for her."

"You can do *nothing* for her!" she contradicted. "Or for the rest of the sleepers. We can barely save the living world. You do not see what is before us. I do. There is no past, only a future. No future, unless we put aside everything but work to make one. There shall be no future for those who refuse!"

She half raised the revolver—lowered it again.

"No past!" I cried. "There is—your son!"

She gave a sharp cry. I stooped to spring upon her and take the revolver, but she covered me quietly, and I folded my arms and waited my doom.

"No," she said. "There *was* my son. There *is* you; and you are unfaithful. God help me, if you disobey again, for you must die! Go and sleep. I shall want you at six. You have wasted two hours of the rest that should have strengthened you to work for mankind—what is left—when mankind requires your best effort, and mine. Go!"

"Promise me first that you will not harm *her*," I demanded. She did not answer. "If you do not promise," I said steadily, "you must kill me; or I shall kill you. I warn you."

She threw the revolver to me across the table.

"Kill me!" she cried. "You will kill the rest of the world; and some day you will wish that you had killed yourself! Disloyal servant!"

I handed her back the weapon.

"I will be a loyal servant in all else," I offered; "only spare the girl."

She considered, biting her lips and blinking.

"The girl shall fare with the rest," she said, in a dull voice; "no better, and no worse. I will not harm her individually. Neither will I favor her. You, if you weren't like my son—*Go!*"

And then I went to my brief rest.


The next week was one of continual work. For eighteen hours a day I helped the Chief Power to deal with letters and telegrams about the new Governments. (She had come to leave the home Government to the red-faced man, and confined herself almost

188                                                    OWEN OLIVER

entirely to international affairs.) In England the rule of the Powers was accepted readily enough, and there was no reason to suppose that the local bodies were not carrying out instructions. The "wakers" seemed to be of the hard type of Mrs. Ashbury and the red-faced man—ready to ignore the claims of the sleepers and to care only for those who were "awake."

The difficulties were with the Universal Government. There were more people left in the United States than elsewhere. They were very concerned to save their friends who slept, and they carried the election of Abrahams for Power of the World, though Mrs. Ashbury ran him close and became Vice-Power.

She and Abrahams had an animated dispute over future policy. She wished to destroy the sleepers off-hand, and he to save them, although the doctors, including our own Chief Physician, agreed that they would not rouse for many years. They would sleep, they pronounced, and require no nourishment, only warmth and protection from the elements. They would not change or grow older, but wake in a year—three years—ten years—and go on with life where they left off.

"They will wake to starvation," Mrs. Ashbury telegraphed. "Supplies will decay. We have not the hands to sow or reap harvests. To preserve these people, who are, to all intent dead, is to perish with them."

"So far as we can foresee, yes," the Power of the World answered. "But the situation is beyond human foresight. We must take our chance. They have a right to theirs."

"Your judgment is warped by consideration for some personal friends whom you are not brave enough to sacrifice," she accused him.

"No," he answered. "It is my enemies whom I am not brave enough to sacrifice. I could trust myself to judge my friends."

"What do you propose?" she wired back.

"The sleepers must be collected, and placed in comfort in buildings," he telegraphed. "That is the first and most important work. The second is to provide for them, so far as we can, when they wake.

The third task is for the doctors. They must seek for some drug or process to lengthen the sleep if necessary, so that we can let them wake in detachments, as we are able to provide for them. Then they, too, must toil strenuously to provide means of maintaining more, till in time the whole world lives again."

"And then," she replied, "your rule and mine will be over!"

"Why not?" he answered; and when she argued further, he replied curtly, that her rule, as his, rested upon obedience. "As you want to be obeyed, obey!" he commanded. "That is my last word. You will disobey at your peril!"

Finally she obeyed. Left to herself, I think she would have defied the World Power, but her Council would not support her in that. The Chief Physician, especially, was against her views. He would find a drug to prevent the sleepers awaking all at once, he declared, and that was the best solution of the difficulty. The Suffragette lady—who preserved a good deal of womanliness, and was throughout the kindliest of the Council—supported him strongly; and even the truculent red-faced man refused to agree to wholesale slaughter of the sleepers until the necessity was absolutely proved.

"After all," he said, "it would, at most, only save our lives. That isn't much."

So millions of helpless slumberers owed their lives to Abrahams, the Jew—a man who, it was said, had been a card-sharper, a bucket-shop proprietor and a company swindler; and who now ruled the world—and would not take revenge upon the men who had imprisoned him!

For the second week we were hard at work collecting the sleepers and stowing them on beds, couches and floors—wherever we could place large numbers together so that they were easy to watch. Some, of course, had perished by accidents; and a good many from the attacks of dogs, who had become like wolves from hunger. It was necessary already to send out shooting parties to destroy them, and dangerous to go out alone at night. Cattle died in great numbers, and, as we were quite unable to remove the bodies, a pestilence set in. This not only killed some of the "wakers," but many of those who slept. We had not time to bury them, but sent ship-loads down the river and dropped them into the sea.

I moved the girl for whom I cared to the "sleeping location" in the War Office at this time. It was under medical care, and always sprayed with antiseptics, so she was less likely to take infection there. Also it was where the Chief Physician had his quarters, and he promised to look after her.

Our troubles increased during the Winter, and the wolves—as the dogs had become—worried us especially. Packs of them even ran about in London by day; and in many parts of the country the people were forced to leave the villages and farms and to collect in large towns. This interfered with husbandry, and when it came to harvest-time we gathered barely enough for the waking population. The same thing happened all over the world; and on the anniversary of the coming of the green flies Mrs. Ashbury sent a strong protest to the World Power.

It was evident, she represented, that we could never provide for the wants of the sleepers or be secure in the great areas that we now occupied, and must continue to occupy, so long as we were burdened with "dead people." The only safe plan, and the only way to organize labor profitably, was that those who were alive (she always spoke of the sleepers as dead) should concentrate in one or two parts of the world and abandon the rest. The sleepers must be left to their fate, or killed. She considered death more merciful.

The World Power replied: "I have never turned my back on a helpless man or woman yet, and I never will. We must work harder and do better next year."

I do not think that any one failed to work hard, but the people suffered and grew weak, and the next year's result was even worse. Great tempests worked havoc upon the crops in many places, and the wolf-dogs overran whole districts. Abrahams himself was attacked by them in the streets of New York and badly injured before he was rescued. There were hardly any cattle left now, so the wolves preyed upon human beings; and poison and shooting scarcely thinned their numbers. But for an epizootic disease among them during the Winter, and the death of many through some severe frosts, they would have annihilated mankind in Great Britain.

Mrs. Ashbury proposed to repeat her suggestion of the previous year to the World Power, but, instead of doing so on her own responsibility, she decided to strengthen her hand by the support of her Council; and the Council voted against her. The natural obstinacy of the red-faced man seemed aroused by our difficulties, and he declared that he wasn't going to "give in to a pack of dogs." The Chief Physician supported him. The sleepers were under his charge, and he seemed to have acquired a sort of paternal affection for them. He hoped to dance at my wedding with pretty little No. 214,713, London, he told me sometimes. She was the girl I have mentioned. He had had a number put at the head of each sleeper. I always went to see her during the two hours' rest allowed on Sunday afternoons. (This was our only holiday.)

The year 1918 was one of great sickness and distress and scarcity. In the Autumn, just after the insufficiency of the harvests was fully realized, there was a great alarm. Some of the sleepers, according to the Chief Physician and those who occupied similar posts in other countries, showed symptoms of awakening. In the existing state of supplies this could only mean a struggle to the death for existence, and cables passed all day and all night between the members of the World Council. At last a vote was taken between the proposal of the World Power that the sleepers should be inoculated with the drug which our Chief Physician had invented, and which, he claimed, would ensure sleep for one hundred and thirty-two days, and the proposal of Mrs. Ashbury that the sleepers should be chloroformed to death; after which the living population should be massed in England and certain districts abroad, leaving the rest of the world to wolves and pestilence.

I was sitting by No. 214,713, London, holding her hand, when the Chief Physician came and told me the decision. He was always a good friend to me.

"Abrahams has won by a single vote," he announced. "I—I wouldn't have done it, Raynor. I'd have chloroformed myself first!

Well, I shouldn't have used chloroform." He tapped his pocket. "Instaneous. Like one? We may come to it."

"Give me two," I said. One was for No. 214413, London. I wouldn't leave her to the wolves. She looked such a young, smiling creature. None of my hardships hurt me like that smile of hers.

The day before the inoculation of the sleepers was to take place I stole her away and hid her. It would be no harm for one to wake, I thought, and if she did I meant to try to escape to America, thinking that we should be safer out of the dominion of Mrs. Ashbury. I was discovered. The Chief Power spared me once more, but she swore, by her love for her son, that if I disobeyed a third time I should die. She also dismissed me from my post, and from all Government employment.

The sleepers were inoculated the next day, No. 214,713, London, among the rest. The Chief Physician let me in secretly to see that she still lived and only slumbered as before. He employed me among the watchers of those who slept, unknown to the Chief Power. I heard what was going on in the Councils through him.

There was a quarrel between Abrahams and Mrs. Ashbury all that year. She was undoubtedly intriguing with the rest of the General Council, and hoped to displace him. She had ceased to be human since she had sent me away, the Chief Physician said, and was completely dominated by the desire to be ruler of the world. He thought that things were safe while Abrahams kept his place, because she regarded the example of obedience as all-important, in view of her own possible supremacy; but he believed that she would finally supersede him. "And then it's all up!" he said.

The sleepers were reinoculated every few months, and the process was quite successful. But nevertheless an outcry, carefully fanned by the Chief Power, began for "making ourselves safe" by destroying them. Just as this was becoming dangerous, however, the 1919 harvest proved to be a particularly good one. The produce was said to be much more than sufficient to keep all who were "awake" until the next season; and more than enough, if it could all be sown, to secure food that year for everybody, including those who slept. Then Abrahams called the whole General Council to a meeting at New York and made his great proposal.

Let the harvest be divided into three portions, he said. The first and the greatest portion should be sown. It would produce sufficient, if the harvest was good, to maintain every one—wakers and sleepers—on an "emergency ration" till the next season. The second portion should be used to feed the wakers till they had finished the plowing and sowing and had guarded the fields till the beginning of Spring. Then they should be inoculated and join the original sleepers, to economize supplies until all should wake together to gather in the harvest. The third portion would provide a pittance to keep the harvesters alive until the new stocks were available. Enough wakers should always remain to guard the buildings of sleep from the wolves, and no more. So the whole world might live again, "by the mercy of God; and without this it would end anyhow," Abrahams said.

Some regarded the proposal as the salvation of the world; others as its destruction. At first the latter predominated. We might wake, they objected, to find the harvests had failed. We might wake to find no passage through the wolves at the door. We might never wake at all. The World Power agreed to all this, but he still urged his proposal in a brief address, which was posted up everywhere. "At the worst," he wrote, "it is only dying at one time instead of another; and, with our dear friends asleep, life is little to some of us. Go and sit beside those of yours who slumber and make your decision there."

That was how the decision was made, when the Council issued the referendum to the people. Those who feared to sleep went and heartened themselves with the sight of their friends and relatives who lay in long rows in hospitals and galleries and halls and churches and museums, and sometimes in large private houses— or rather houses that had been private possessions, for there is no property now. Many kissed their unconscious friends; and some cried that sleep was better than the unremitting toil and the lonely struggles and the bitter horrors of the last few years.

So the decision in favor of the referendum was almost unanimous. For the last few months we have been making our preparations. In some countries the wakers, excepting the few selected as guardians, have lain down and suffered the injection of the drug, and lie asleep. In England we begin tomorrow; and I am drawn by lot in the first batch. "The sooner to wake," the Chief Physician says; and I shall lie beside 214,713, London; and, so far as he can judge, she will wake soon after me.

"*If* we wake," I said; and he and I looked, at each other for a long time. For there are rumors of plots and counterplots in these days. The Chief Power has not been seen for weeks. Some say that she has gone to America to kill the Power of the World, or to struggle with him for the supremacy. Certainly many familiar faces are missing and if she has taken a shipload of followers she may easily overcome him, and the small band who watch with him. If she should, I think that only a very few of us will wake in her time, if ever.

For she will certainly have no return of old authorities to interfere with her own rule. The Chief Physician pooh-poohs the rumor—he has always been outwardly loyal to the Chief Power—but he has guarded, with men armed to the teeth, the Palace where our royalty and the members of the old Government of 1916 sleep.

"Yes," he said at last, "I have thought of that. If it were only my word to her, I would break it, and you, and others whom I trust, should not sleep, but wake and keep watch with me. But I have passed my word to the Power of the World that none shall escape the lot. He is the best and the wisest of us, and—and I think there is a greater Power over all, though sometimes I have doubted. We are in His hands, awake or asleep. The Powers of the earth will not prevail over God!"

In that thought I take comfort, and in that hope I shall lie down to my rest, holding the hand of the woman who is numbered "214,713, London," and placing this writing between us, so that, if she wakes first, she may know what I have set down. God guard us in our sleep!

PARTII: THE AWAKENING

I woke suddenly in a strange place—a long room with light oak carving. I was lying on soft cushions on the floor. A rug had been thrown over me, but I was dressed. There were two long rows of sleepers—men, women, and children—and a number was put at the head of each. Mine was "214,713, London." One or two numbers had a name underneath, but mine was not there. It was Elsie Anderson, if I remembered myself rightly; but my memories did not come readily.

My left-hand neighbor was holding my wrist. He was "184, Government, George Raynor." I remembered the name, and when I raised myself on one elbow, to take a good look at his face, I remembered him. I had met him once at an at-home. He was a nice fellow and I liked him. He had said that he hoped we should meet again.

Next I noticed a manuscript in my right hand. I pulled it out and read the title: "The History of the Years of Sleep: 1916-1920. By George Raynor."

I gave a sharp cry. If it was 1920, I had slept for four years! I made an effort to remember what happened to me. I was going to town for a singing-lesson, and there were swarms of little green flies at Dulwich Station. They stung people, and the people whom they stung fainted. I screamed and tried to beat off the flies with my handkerchief, but they flew upon me—and that was the last thing I remembered. I must have fainted; and the faint had lasted for four years! Perhaps longer, for more years might have passed since Mr. Raynor wrote the history.

How had I come to this place? Where was it? Who were the other sleepers? Why did he put the book under my pillow? Why did he hold my hand? I guessed that it was a big hospital or building where they had put the sleepers for their security; and I thought that Mr. Raynor had brought me there because he knew me, and that he held my hand because he expected me to be frightened when I woke alone. I *was* frightened—so frightened that I dared not move or call. For I did not know what might have happened in all these years, and something dreadful must have come again to send Mr. Raynor to sleep.

I lay still for a long time, shivering and listening. I heard no sound but the faint breathing of the sleepers. I thought that every one but myself must be asleep. Then I heard a howling somewhere outside, the howling of wild beasts. It came nearer and nearer, till at last it was outside the window. The window seemed to be a good way above the ground, but I wasn't sure. I clung to Mr. Raynor's arm and begged him to wake, but he did not stir. He and the rest were evidently in a deep faint or stupor. I gave a scream, and then I fainted, too. The noise had gone when I recovered.

As soon as I was able to rise I got up and staggered to the door, but dared not open it. I staggered toward the windows, but dared not look out. I feared to find the world in the possession of the howling beasts, or of some unknown monsters. I went and shook Mr. Raynor again, and called in his ear, entreating him to wake, but without the slightest effect.

I sat down again on my cushions—I seemed to have been made more comfortable than any one else, and I was sure that I had to thank Mr. Raynor for that—and took up the "history"; but I was afraid to read it and learn what horrible things had come to pass— perhaps to find that I was all alone. I prayed a prayer that some one might be still waking in the world and come to me. And then I heard voices in the passage.

At first I thought they came in answer to my prayer, but, after listening for a few moments, some instinct checked the call on my lips. I went cold with fear, and lay down hastily and covered my- self and the book with the rug, and pretended to sleep.

"They are enemies," I told myself. "Enemies! If they should come in—!"

They came in, and I peeped at them under my eyelashes. They were a red-faced, elderly man and a gray-haired lady, with a pale, handsome face and cold, cruel eyes. It was she whom I feared. I think I should have spoken to the man, if he had been alone, though I did not like him.

"Since you will see him," he said, speaking as if she had an- noyed him, "there he is!" He jerked his head toward Mr. Raynor, and she knelt beside the unconscious sleeper.

"He is due to wake in three days?"

"Yes," he answered: "and the girl the day after, according to the books; but the reinoculations do not always last their full time, you know. She might happen to rouse a day sooner; two or three days even."

"Oh, *she!*" said the woman scornfully. "She doesn't matter. She goes to-night, with the rest of them."

"You can't dispose of them all," the man protested. "We must have some to fight the cursed wolves. It's no use shaking your head. We must, I tell you! We needn't rouse them all, but I can't get along without a few thousand men. The beasts are getting too much for me. You know what it was like coming here."

"Yes, yes," she said. "You can have your men; but we don't want women; at any rate, not her. She dies to-night!"

"Very well," he said rather sulkily, "The women can go—those of this batch. You'll have to save some of the later sections, or you'll have a mutiny. But it doesn't matter about her in particular. She's just an ordinary, stupid, pretty girl, so far as I can see. The only point is that he has an infatuation about her. The important question is, what are you going to do about *him?* I rather like the chap, but—"

"I don't know," she said, rocking herself to and fro. "He has disobeyed three times. I gave my word that the third time he should die— He is so like my son!"

"I suppose," the red-faced man commented, "your son was like *you*. If he is, and he wakes and finds that you have made away with this '214,713, London' of his, he'll kill you! If you must wake him, why not wake the girl and let him have her? He'll be all right then. If you kill her and spare him, he'll be our worst enemy. I warn you."

"He'd be my enemy anyhow," the woman said bitterly. "He would not serve me as I need service, for his own life, or even for hers. They must go to-night with the rest of their batch. Keep 6,000 men—no women and children; 2,000 of them in London. The rest in the usual proportions. Telegraph at once. Yes. He must die. But he's like my son!"

She bent and kissed him, laughing a strange laugh. It reminded me of the howling of the beasts. Then she rose.

"My last weakness," she said. "It's over. I shall go on to the end now, do not fear."

"I've never feared anything all my life, except *you*," the red-faced man said. "Sometimes I think you're the salvation of the world. Sometimes I think you're the Devil! I don't know."

"I don't know myself," said the gray-haired woman.

Then they went, and I fainted again.

When I came to, I judged from the light that it was the afternoon. I felt weak and ill and very thirsty, and so terrified that I could not think properly. I believe I should have simply lain still and waited to be killed, if Mr. Raynor had not been before my eyes and if I had not felt sure that I owed my life, so far, to him.

"They shall *not* kill you!" I declared, and sat up and clenched my teeth and hands, and made myself consider what I could do to save him. I decided that the first step was to read the history, which would probably enable me to understand the situation better.

It was a long story—far too long to set down here; but the main points were these.

The fly—but some people said it was a poison-dust, not an insect—appeared everywhere, all over the world, August 24, 1916, and stung people into a dense stupor. Nearly all the inhabitants of the earth went to the sleep, the account said. Those who remained awake were almost all clever, cruel people. They formed new governments, and called the head people "Powers." The Chief Power in England was the gray-haired woman. Her name was Ashbury. She did not wish the sleepers to wake, because she wanted to go on ruling. So she proposed to kill them. The Power of the World, an American Jew named Abrahams, who had been a hotel-keeper and considered a bad and unscrupulous man, but who was really a good one, would not agree to this. But, when the sleepers seemed likely to wake, he had to inoculate them, to make them sleep longer, because there wasn't food for them.

He tried to grow food, but the harvests were bad, and the dogs, who had become wolves from hunger, overran the country. There were pestilences and storms, and those who "woke" were in great trouble; but at last there was a good harvest, and, after most of it had been sown for the next year, he thought it would produce enough to keep everybody. So he persuaded most of the "wakers" to go to sleep too, until it would be ready, so as to economize supplies. That was how Mr. Raynor came to go to sleep. He did not know if he would wake, for the Chief Power was plotting to depose the Power of the World, and if she did, she was sure to kill most of the sleepers.

He had rescued me, and the "disobediences" for which she wished to kill him were on my account. There was a Chief Physician, and he was a good man and had helped him, and liked me. He was one of those left awake. He said that he meant to dance at my wedding with Mr. Raynor. (The history made it quite plain that Mr. Raynor was in love with me.) He called me "pretty little 214,713, London." The sleepers had all been numbered, and I suppose the "wakers" had been numbered first, because Mr. Raynor was 184.

I decided at once that I would try to find the Chief Physician. The history said that he lived in the building where we slept. (It was the War Office.)

I opened the door and looked into a very long corridor, paneled with brown wood. It was quite empty. I lifted Mr. Raynor in my arms and staggered out with him, and went up-stairs. On the walls there were printed plans of the floor. There were only numbers on them, but one or two had been written across in red ink, "Captain of Guard," and so on. On the top floor I found "Chief Physician" marked on one.

I opened the door, and staggered in. Mr. Raynor was big and heavy, and I am only small. I was so exhausted that I fell; and then I heard a voice—a kind voice that did not frighten me. "2-1-4-7-1-3, London! Good girl!"

"Water!" I begged. "Water!"

"I can't move, my dear," the voice said.

I wiped my eyes and looked up, and saw a gentleman rather like my father, bound to a chair; and I got up somehow and tried to untie him.

"You'll never do it with those little fingers," he said. "There's a penknife in my waistcoat pocket; left hand; my left; the lower one. That's right!"

I cut the knots and he got up and staggered about, stamping and shaking himself to get rid of his stiffness. He asked if I had read the history, and I said yes; and he told me what had happened afterward.

Mrs. Ashbury had gone to America, with a shipful of armed men, to try to kill the Power of the World; but he had been prepared, and had taken them by surprise as they were landing, and defeated them.

So she and those who were left had come back in another ship. She had broken away from the other Governments, and those in England who did not agree with her had fled abroad, or had been killed, unless it was a party in Lancashire, led by a "Suffragette lady," who had been one of the Powers under Mrs. Ashbury, but would never agree to harming the sleepers. He did not know her fate. Mrs. Ashbury and her followers meant to wake only enough of the sleepers to fight the wolves—and perhaps a few women and children later—and to kill the rest. He had refused to help in the slaughter, and they had to get another doctor to help them. So they threatened to kill him with the first batch that very night.

"I'm afraid they will, little one," he said; "and you, too. We might possibly get away by ourselves; but not with—our burden." He shook his head at Mr. Raynor, whom I had lifted on a couch. "I don't suggest your going alone," he added, "because—"

"Because, if I would, I'm not worth saving," I said. "No. Of course I wouldn't leave him; and you wouldn't, because—he trusted you; and I do. But can't you wake him?"

"No; not till the three days are up. We must try to save him till then."

He considered for a long while with his chin on his hand.

"I can think of only one way," he told me at last, "and I fear it requires courage beyond your power, my brave little lady."

"If there is only one way," I said, "of course I must try. What is it?"

He did not answer my question at once, but thought again, staring at me as if he did not see me.

"I want you to understand the situation," he said. "It is fairer; and, besides, you may see some better plan. It would be possible to get out of this building. There are guards at the doors, but we could get through a window on the ground floor. There are thousands of empty houses where we could hide, if we once got away and if we escaped the wolves—and the human wolves, the followers of the Chief Power. If you and I were alone, there would be a chance; a poor one, but I think our best. With our friend here to carry, there would be no chance at all of escaping so." A howling rose in the distance, and he took me to the window looking down Whitehall to Big Ben. "Look!" he said; and I looked, and clung to him.

A large party of armed men—about two hundred—were coming from Parliament Street in our direction. Innumerable wolves—dogs of all kinds and sizes, and yet changed from dogs—were following. Sometimes they approached so near that the men faced round with fixed bayonets, or axes. Sometimes a few ran by the side of the party and snapped at men till they were stabbed; and then the other wolves rushed upon them and devoured them

"They go in flocks," he told me, "but they rush down all the streets in turn; and with our friend to carry we could never get away from them, or from the patrols. No, we can't escape that way."

"What is your plan?" I asked.

"We might hide in chimneys, or under the floors; but they would be sure to trace us. It's a poor plan."

"Yes," I agreed. "What *is* your plan?"

He looked at me again for a long while. Then he told me,

"That you should go back to your places," he said, "and let them think that they kill you. They propose to do it by injecting poison. If they have not changed its prescription—you must risk that—I can inoculate you with an antidote. It will take away all power to move, and a good deal of your sensibility; not all. You will suffer—suffer in body and in mind, my poor child, but you will live. In a day or so you and he will wake. You are both young and active, and he is bold and resourceful. They will probably give up watching the dead. You may escape then—escape, I hope, to a long and happy life together."

"And you?" I asked. "*You*, dear friend?"

"Oh, well," he said, "I had to die anyhow."

"I will take no chance of safety that you do not share!" I declared. "He would not, if he were alive—awake, I mean. I answer for his honor. And he shall not wake to find that I deserted you!"

"I shall go out and chance escaping the wolves," he stated. "You see, it would be no use inoculating myself. When they found me unbound and yet unconscious, they might suspect my plan, and—and make sure of me! Probably of you and of him, too."

"They shall not find you unbound," I said. "I will bind you as I found you, and inoculate you. Then I will inoculate him; and then myself. And when I wake—if I wake—I will come to you."

"Ah, my dear!" he said. "You are brave! But are you brave enough?"

"I have to be!" I said.

We ate and drank. Then we carried Mr. Raynor back to his place, and the Chief Physician inoculated him, showing me how to do it. He marked the place on his own flesh and mine when we went to his room. He kissed my forehead. "The good God strengthen you!" he prayed. Then he sat in his chair, and I bound him. "If we live, I will be a daughter to you," I promised, "and he will be a son." Then I inoculated him. He went quickly into a stupor.

"Hide—the syringe—before you—go—too—numb," he gasped faintly. Then he said no more. Even his eyes did not move, but they were open, and I believed that he could still see and hear.

"I shall be brave," I told him. "Do not doubt me."

I kissed his forehead, and went out into the deathly stillness of the empty corridors, and back to my place. I must have screamed if I had not bitten my lips.

The good God must have given me strength, as the Chief Physician said, for I never faltered in my resolution. I wrote on the history what had happened, so that Mr. Raynor might go and rescue the Chief Physician if he woke and I did not. After that I sat by him for it few moments, with my arm round his neck, and my face against his.

"I hardly know you," I said, "but you love me. And I love you. God help us, dear!"

Then I lay down, covered myself with the rug, dug the syringe into my flesh and pumped in the antidote. I only just succeeded in removing it, the numbness came on so quickly. Then I lay waiting; motionless, unable to stir an eyelid or make a sound, and yet dimly conscious of everything round me—more than dimly conscious of fear. The light grew dimmer and dimmer. I heard the wolves howl four times before I became unable to distinguish Mr. Raynor's face; once more, and then it was quite dark. I heard them howl three times more; and then the death-dealers came, talking to one another unconcernedly, as if they went about some routine task.

There were eight of them. Two women and a man carried lanterns. Three men had large syringes. A lad carried a pail of fluid from which they replenished them. The red-faced man watched. They went along the room in pairs, one holding the lantern while the other knelt by the sleeper and made the injection—two strokes of the piston with a pause between. One pair came to Mr. Raynor and another to me at the same time. I was too numb to feel pain when the great syringe dug deeply into my flesh, but it was well for me that I could not scream. As it was, I made a faint sound.

"Must have been near waking," the injector said, putting the rug over my shoulders again. "Well, she's safe for another four months." Evidently he had not been told that he was administering anything but the usual sleeping-injection. To the credit of my countrymen and countrywomen I would record that it is now clear that Mrs. Ashbury deceived them about her intentions, and that very few of them realized that she intended to kill the sleeping world.

"Make *him* quite safe," the red-haired man commanded, nodding toward Mr. Raynor. "He's a dangerous man."

"He's had the usual dose," the operator answered. "The Chief Physician always said that more was dangerous."

The red-faced man made no comment, and they passed on, finished their work, and went out. The wolves howled right under the window just then. Soon afterward I went to sleep. I felt as if a weight were crushing me; and I thought that perhaps the antidote had failed. I did not seem to care about myself—it would be good to be at rest, I thought—only about Mr. Raynor and the Chief Physician.

In the early light I woke in great pain. I remembered that the Chief Physician had said that I should suffer. I was glad that Mr. Raynor was unconscious. I thought that if I woke fully I should wake mad. Presently some men came in, and I feared that I should go mad in my stupor.

They did not look at Mr. Raynor or me. Some one called out "214,717" and "214,725," and they carried off two sleepers, both big men. I suppose they were selected to wake and fight the wolves.

"You can leave the doors open," the voice called. "The wolves won't matter now."

Then I think I did go mad for a time. I seemed to be struggling with a tempest of pain and fright, till I became unconscious once more.

I woke, still racked by sharp pains, to find the gray-haired woman kneeling beside Mr. Raynor. She was crying. I tried to call to beg her to keep out the wolves, but no sound would come. When she went, however, she closed the door. I forgot my pains in my thankfulness that we were safe from the wolves, and slipped back into sleep. Sometimes I roused a little at a pang of pain, or rather, after it. For I knew that I had been hurt, rather than felt it. Sometimes I dreamed of green fields, and brooks, and music. Sometimes I dreamed that stones were being heaped and heaped on me.

The dawn of another day was beginning when I became fully conscious again. The pains were not so violent, and presently they left me almost entirely. I could not hear Mr. Raynor breathe, but I thought that he did. The others were still—quite still. I could not speak, but I could move my eyelids. I blinked and blinked. Presently I could move a little finger; then all my fingers. Gradually the use of my limbs returned, and I sat up, aching all over—not violently, but with a kind of cramp, and feeling as if I had just come to from "gas" at the dentist's.

Mr. Raynor was still "sleeping." and the Chief Physician had said that he would not wake until some time after us. So I was not worried on his account, after I had ascertained that he really breathed—which was the first thing I did. I was too weak to lift him, and I thought that probably the guards below were gone, and the wolves. So I decided to go up-stairs alone and untie our kind friend, if he still lived. In case I should never return I wrote on the cover of the history and put it beside Mr. Raynor:

> I have gone for the Chief Physician. If I do not return, I shall have died. If we live, I will do what you wish. God bless you. 214,713, London.
>                                        Elsie Anderson.

The corridors were empty, but I felt, sure that I heard wolves upon the floors below, so I ran as fast as my shaking legs would carry me. I found the Chief Physician alive and evidently coming to, but not able to speak. I unbound him and rubbed his hands and bathed his face. In about half an hour he could just stand. Then I heard a sound in the corridor. *Pit-pat, pit-pat!* I shut the door, and the wolf came and scratched at it and whined and barked. It went away and came again. At last the Chief Physician stumbled to a cupboard and got two axes and two revolvers,

"Take some for him," I proposed; for, of course, I knew that we should go down to Mr. Raynor at all risks.

"He won't wake yet," our friend assured me. "It's no use burdening ourselves. We shall have to fight our way, I expect." He seemed quite cheerful at the prospect of the struggle. "Use the ax when you can, and take the revolver in your left hand. We'll settle this one first. I'll jam his head in the door. Get ready!"

He opened the door a little. The wolf—it had been a big bull terrier—forced its head through the opening, and I brought the ax down.

"That's one!" said the Chief Physician. "Come on!" And we went out. Strange to say, I had no fear; I felt like a machine.

There were no other wolves on the two upper floors, but some were coming up the stairs from the second floor, where Mr. Raynor was. They retreated before us, growling and snarling. About twenty waited at the foot of the stairs. We had to reach a door some twenty yards along the corridor. We shot three of the beasts, and the others fell upon them; then we made a rush and reached the room. One wolf tore my dress, but the Chief Physician killed him. Another got half through the door after us and caught the Chief Physician's boot, but I blew out its brains.

Mr. Raynor was breathing very faintly. The Chief Physician listened to his heart and felt his pulse. He shook his head several times, and I gasped for breath.

"I do not know the exact effect of the poison and the antidote on a sleeper," he said at last. "I hope he will wake, but—I do not know. I have done my best, Elsie.

"You have done your best," I said, "your very best, dear friend. But if he does not live I do not want to. Is there nothing you can do? *Nothing?*"

"If I could get a stimulant from my room," he said, "it might help him. There is nothing really wrong. It is a question whether his heart is strong enough to outlast the struggle between the poison and the antidote. The heart beats more feebly in the sleep, you see. Are you brave enough to be left?"

"I am brave enough not to let you go alone," I answered.

We went to the door, and peeped out. The wolves had gone. So we decided to take Mr. Raynor up-stairs again, carrying him between us.

We were half-way up the first stairs when we heard a terrific howling overhead, and the shouts of men, and a few women. The wolves had evidently gone up above and the "wakers" had gone by another way and were pursuing them in force. The fight for which the Chief Power had awakened some of the slumberers was beginning. Shots were fired, and we heard the blows of axes: the wolves seemed to be running along the corridor to the stairs.

"Back to the room!" the Chief Physician cried. But as we reached the corridor the voice of the Chief Power rose above the others, and with one accord we fled down the next staircase. For we thought that she might come in the room to look again at Mr. Raynor. We feared her more than all the wolves.

We reached the main hall, breathless and staggering with our burden; and then the wolves overtook us. They were too terrified to do any harm, but swept on like a sea, knocking us down on the slippery tiled floor and running over us. The pursuers followed in the rear, smiting with their axes, till the wolves were killed or had got through the doorway, running over one another, three, four, five high. Then we sat up, and the guards formed between us and the doorway, waiting for orders from the gray-haired woman.

She stood at the foot of the white marble stairs, with little streams of red blood running down them, and faced us. She was motionless, like the statue of some evil deity. Mr. Raynor opened his eyes and moved his lips. The Chief Physician and I knelt, holding him between us. He smiled faintly at me, and I smiled at him, putting my arm round him and drawing him against me.

"We live for a moment together," I whispered; "and perhaps—afterward." For I saw in her eyes that she would kill us.

There was a. long silence, and all waited with their eyes on her.

She moved her lips silently before she spoke. She addressed the Chief Physician.

"Traitor!" she said in a clear, stern voice. "Traitor to us all!" She turned to the rest, "He cabled to Abrahams!" she told them, and there was a fierce murmur.

"Yes," the Chief Physician told her. "I cabled to the Power of the World—your master and mine. It is you who are the traitor—traitor and murderess!

"Your Power of the World has not come," she taunted him. "He does not govern England, and you are a traitor to your country."

"You are a traitor to mankind," he answered. "He *will* come, and then he will kill you!"

"And now," she said very quietly, "I will kill you."

"I expected nothing else," he said. "But, if there is a spark of womanhood or humanity in you—" He was going to ask her to spare us, but she cut him short.

"There is none," she said, "for traitors! Kill them!"

The crowd advanced upon us, but she made a quick motion with her hand. "Take them outside," she commanded, passing her hands over her eyes. She sank on the marble steps with her dress dabbling in the blood, and the men seized us and dragged us through the doors. Our arms were round one another, and they did not separate us.

"All in vain," the Chief Physician muttered; "your courage; and yours!"

"And yours," said Mr. Raynor, "old friend!"

"No," I said. "Not in vain, not in vain, my dears! There will be an awakening!" And I kissed my lover and my friend, and they kissed me.

And then we passed through the doorway, and the wolves rushed upon us like a stormy sea. There were thousands of them— tens and tens of thousands, wolves that had once been dogs, all kinds, all sizes. They covered the wide road and more, for they ran on top of one another. They came from both directions, and from each way a great army of men and women pursued them in serried ranks, axes in hand—axes dripping red.

The guards dropped us and ran within the doors. The wolves knocked us down, as before, and swarmed over us; swarmed in heaps that crushed us and almost stifled us; rose like a great wave to the top of the doorway and fell in one wave after another.

I caught a glimpse of the marble stairway, and wolves were pouring down that, springing at the throats of those who tried to pass up it. I saw the gray-haired woman fall with a dozen holding her. Shrieks and shrieks and shrieks came from inside.

Outside, the men and women, coming both from Charing Cross and from Westminster, slew and slew. Every now and then a rush of the wolves—those that were not driven into the building or killed—swept them off their legs. The men and women closed up again and still slaughtered. I can see one little fair-haired woman now, smiting and smiting and smiting. She was a mistress from my old school, and she had always been such a gentle little thing; but the wolves had killed her child.

They killed the heap on top of us, throwing them aside as they slew them and smiting the next. We rose red with the slaughter, and a man, also red, held out his hand to the Chief Physician—a stout, panting, disheveled old Jew man, who seemed to be directing everybody.

"You are the Chief Physician," he said, "aren't you? They showed me your photo. I am Abrahams; I came at your call."

They stood there, forgetting every one but themselves, and talked, while the others went into the War Office to finish the last of the wolves. They would have slain the human wolves, too, I think, if any had been left; but there were none. They knew the Chief Power only by her dress.

The Power of the World told how he had come with a handful of men, at the Chief Physician's summons. If England did not rise to support him he must die, he knew. "We run that risk every day," he said, "and I believed in England." His belief had been justified. The people had gone over to him everywhere, as soon as they knew what Mrs. Ashbury intended; and though hundreds of thousands of sleepers had been poisoned under her orders—her tools mostly believing that they were merely using the sleeping injection—he had been in time to stop most of the slaughter.

About thirty thousand of the first batch of sleepers had already roused and joined him. He was clearing away the wolves and seeking Mrs. Ashbury and the remains of her Government—who, it seemed, had not heard of his arrival—"to clear them away, too." But their fellow-wolves had done it for him.

"We are saved," he declared, "if we can get through the next few days. We have to draft the people to their homes without losing trace of them, and to get the food supplies distributed to them. We must work, work, work! Nothing like work!" said the stout, disheveled, big old Jew man, who looked like a butcher. I had expected a noble patriarch, and I felt disappointed in him—then. Now I know that he is greater than all the rest.

Mr. Raynor and I had said little all the time, only held hands tightly and looked into each other's eyes.

"You are mine," he said. "Dear—I do not know your name, but you are mine."

"It is Elsie," I told him. "Yes. I am yours."

And then the Chief Physician touched the arm of the Power of the World.

"Here are two of our best," he said. "*They* will work."

The Power of the World held out his hands to us, and smiled; and then he seemed no longer an old Jew, and something more than a man.

"You are doing the best work in the world," he told us; "just loving! Never leave off, my dears!"

That was his text and the battle-cry that led us through the struggle of the next fortnight. "For the love of those who sleep!" he urged, when some grumbled at our privations. "For the love of those who suffered to save you!" he told those who woke, when their weakened bodies halted at their labors—for we worked till we dropped in those days. "For the love of your old leader!" he pleaded, when even we who were round him thought his counsels too hard.

His last words as Power of the World—in the speech by which he restored the old rulers and resigned all power and place—were the same.

"The best work in the world," he said, "is the work that all can do—just to love one another. I have done only that. But if you think you owe anything to me, who owe everything to my faithful followers; if you think that the waking of the world is due in any part to my efforts, make it a world of love and good-fellowship—a world that was worth making!"

And so, because all the world loved him, every country all over the earth passed one great law of peace and fellowship and good-will; and, to mark the fact that the days of war and strife were over, the calendar of the years was started afresh; and I, Elsie Raynor, formerly Anderson, wife of George Raynor, Secretary of the Traffic Reorganization Board, write this account in Year One of the Awakening.

# PLATINUM

My solicitors forward me yet another letter from the solicitors of Messrs. Jones, Evans & Jones, Dealers in Precious Metals, demanding the address of my brother-in-law.

I have again refused it.

The firm, which is a large and long-established concern with an unimpeachable record for integrity, threaten to proceed against him for obtaining money by false pretenses. Their allegation is that he sold them, as platinum, certain heavy matter, which, although it appeared to pass the usual tests for that metal, subsequently turned into a putrid organic mass of obscure nature, but anyhow valueless.

My solicitors suspect that they intend to plead that they made the purchase under hypnotic influence. The defense, in addition to a total denial of such influence, would be that my brother-in-law was not an expert in metals, but left it entirely to the buyers to test the substance, which he believed to be platinum, although he obtained it under peculiar circumstances, when shipwrecked in the South Seas.

His account of this will follow. It makes a big demand upon belief, and it is necessary to consider the evidence as to his veracity and character.

In general repute he was about ordinarily truthful. If he stated that he had met an elephant or a camel in the street one would believe him. If he stated that he had met a prehistoric monster or an archangel with a flaming sword, one would not.

He was always regarded as perfectly honest, although somewhat "sharp." I am afraid that his own view of the transaction exhibits the characteristic of "sharpness," but I cannot call it dis-
honest.

Mr. and Mrs. Pratt, who were shipwrecked with him, and who
appear to be most reliable persons, state that he hid several kegs
of rum which floated ashore, and consumed the spirit freely until
he had an attack of delirium tremens; that, in this condition, he
had delusions to the effect that certain slimy, mud-covered rocks
were live and ferocious animals; that when a volcanic eruption
forced them to leave the island in a boat which they had patched
up, he insisted on taking some half-petrified tree branches which
he termed "platinum" and "tentacles."

Even when he recovered from the D.T.'s, on the voyage home,
he retained this delusion and guarded them carefully. Except for
the rum and the delusion they speak highly of his actions. He was
very unselfish about the food, trying to stint himself to increase
the woman's portion, sharing the berries and shellfish which he
found, giving her an old blanket which came ashore, and also an
old chair for her cave.

He was more concerned for them than for himself when he
thought that the "platinum" (which he considered alive) was threat-
ening mischief, and he stood between them and an imaginary sea-
serpent, and he offered them a share of his imaginary platinum.

Against these charges I must record that he was never a drinker;
that the metal merchants evidently took the "half petrified tree
branches" for platinum, and that he has never meddled with hypnotism or mesmerism to my knowledge. I have known him from
boyhood. I am satisfied that if he hypnotized any one he did it un-
consciously.

My sister has been married to him for five years, and considers
him a compendium of the virtues, according to her letters from
Australia. They married hastily and left the country owing to the
trouble with the metal merchants. There are three babies and they
have a considerable farm and are prospering. He has the highest

reputation locally for fair dealing, she declares. Marie is an exacting person and entirely truthful.

I am clear that if he is a liar or drunkard or swindler she has not found it out. I never knew her fail to find out anything!

His story must speak for itself. I have tried to reproduce it exactly as he told it to me. Frankly I didn't believe it at the time, but five years longer in the world have convinced me that men err more in disbelieving than in believing.

I have left out names of places, latitudes and longitudes at his request. If ever Marie will let him, he proposes to seek for more platinum!

This is his story:

On the fifteenth day out the heavy wind sank, and the sea was like glass; hot glass with a long, wavering bend in it. There were sheets of lightning at night, and ghostly glimmerings at the top of the mast. The air weighed heavily upon one and I didn't sleep much.

In the morning there were spots of purple cloud in the bright sky, and the bends in the oily sea grew steeper and steeper. About noon the little clouds spread themselves out rapidly, and the sea looked like glassy mountains, and lightning streamed from the skies like great sheets of rain, and little sheets of light flowed from the ship.

Suddenly the steady mountains of water seemed to break to pieces. I was watching a tramp steamer climbing a sea about a mile ahead of us. I lost her as she went over the swell; and then I rubbed my eyes and looked for her in vain!

There was a strange roaring sound such as I had never heard before. The sea on the port beam rose to an enormous height as if an eruption had thrown it up.

A tiny green island on the starboard bow seemed to grow and grow out of the waves toward our ship. Then a broken precipice of water fell upon us. It smashed the deck cabins, crashed through the deck, shattered the bridge, snapped off boats and davits, and swept away women and men.

I found myself jammed between wreckage, but somehow un-hurt. I was one of four survivors upon what remained of the prom-enade deck. There had been about fifty people there a moment before.

The broken ship was borne by a torrent of unbelievable force and speed toward the island, a little green centre with vegetation and palms, surrounded by disjointed rocks and slime cast up by the earthquake.

I struggled out of the wreckage and helped the other three out. Two men got up from the engine room somehow a few minutes later. The rest were drowned, they thought. One of the three pas-sengers was a woman. She screamed and wrung her hands.

"It is the end of the world!" she cried. "Have mercy, O God. . . . Dear God!"

Well, that's what I thought she said. I was not sure if I heard it or read it on her lips. The torrent which carried us roared and roared, and we could not hold a conversation. We linked hands and stood in a line until the ship struck the shore.

We were very close to the land before the keel ran aground. The ship was traveling sideways, and our impetus and the forceful water behind, toppled the ship over on its side.

The woman, and a lad from the engine room, and I were thrown upon a spur of slimy land, and only bruised. Durrant, one of the other passengers, fell beside us, but he hit a lump of rock and was killed. Miles, the ship's carpenter, dropped in the water, but got out and climbed up to us. I do not know what became of the other man. We never saw him again.

The ship remained lying on its side for a few minutes, fending the torrent from us till its fury had abated. But for this we must all have been drowned. Then the ship seemed to melt away, except for a few fragments fixed upon the shore.

A corner of the forecastle was among these and we found bis-cuits and two barrels of water in it afterwards. The carpenter told us then that they would be there. I saw countless fishes thrown up on the new land; some dying out of water, some swimming in tiny pools.

"We shall have enough to eat," I said, "till a ship passes and takes us off. I've matches in my pocket, and they'll dry in the sun, and there's lots of broken wood. I daresay we'll find a few blankets in some of the forecastle berths in that bit of the bow, when we can get to it. Things might be worse, friends, and—"

"Look away, sir!" the engine-room lad screamed. "Look!"

He clutched my arm, and I turned toward the sea, and he pointed to a thing swimming there.

It was like a huge coil of rope, perhaps a couple of hundred yards long, not thicker than my thigh. It had perhaps fifty fins at each side; fins about half a yard long. Its head was like nothing I've seen; an oval mass, the shape of a Rugby football, only larger. It seemed to have a single eye at the end, and above the eye a large sting. The mouth was underneath—a long slit that went down the body some way, as well as along the head.

It had no proper features. That was the awful thing—the awful thing!

There was no neck; but the part of the body near the head was finless. It raised that part out of the water, and a portion of the finny part too sometimes. It was raising it then toward shore and swimming in.

We hid behind a lump of rock, and peered around it, and saw three sailors from the ship scrambling over mud and rocks and through pools in their attempt to escape from the creature.

It took one of them.

The other two hid somewhere. When the serpent swam away we called to them, and they came out. There was a creek between us. They invited us to come across inland away from the serpent and join them, but I advised them to come to us instead, and help us carry away what we could get from the piece of forecastle which was ashore, and they agreed.

We worked hard for two hours, securing biscuits and water, and a few odds and ends that will seem trifles to you, but were rare prizes to us; needle and thread, a bar of soap, two pairs of canvas shoes, three plates, a tumbler and four knives. I think that was all. Oh, no! There were three tobacco boxes with a little tobacco in each. One held the face of a girl cut from a photograph and stuck inside the lid.

Three men came to us at the end of that time; one of the pair who had escaped from the serpent, and two others. One fainted as we greeted him. One kept moving his mouth without sound coming. The third sat on a boulder and rocked to and fro with his face in his hands.

"Where is Bill Thompson?" the carpenter asked him.

"Oh Lord!" the man cried. "Oh, Lord— They've taken him, and two more!"

"The serpent!" I cried.

"No," he answered, looking up at us and his face was as white as paper. "Devils! Out of a hole in the ground. Hell's opened up by the earthquake. That's what it is. Devils made of lead. No eyes, no mouths, no faces, no anything. If the serpent comes back I'll stake out and pray that he'll take me. He's a natural beast to them! They're made of lead, I tell you, or iron."

The man who was moving his mouth found words then.

"Lead," he said huskily, "and it moves—lead that's alive."

We said nothing for a long time. Then the woman sat down, choosing a bit of clean rock, in her tidy woman-way, and folded her hands and prayed. She was a good woman, the best and bravest of us, and sweet-faced, very sweet-faced. God bless her!

"Now," she said quietly, when she had finished praying, "we are in the hands of Heaven. Let us go and look where these creatures are. Perhaps they will not come to this barren shore, and we can hide in a cave or among the rocks till a ship passes."

We crawled among the rocks and slimy hills till we reached higher ground and could see most of the island. The original island thrown up above the slime cast up from the sea by the earthquake looked very green and tempting.

Two of the newcomers wanted to go there, but the rest of us were against leaving the shore, and the stores which we had secured. So the two decided to go alone and explore the green island. There was no sign of the "leaden devils," and we supposed that they had gone back to their "pit." The mouth was smoking about half a mile to the left.

The men set out, and we watched them from our hill as they made their way across the broken, barren ground toward the next hill. As they neared it, four shapeless forms came around its side toward them.

I don't know how to describe the creatures except as leaden devils with metal tentacles. They had no permanent form at all, no features. They were worse than the snake, because that was always the same, and they changed and changed and changed.

There was a "body," so to call it, about the bigness of a cow. It was a dull lead color, except a whitish patch. I suppose that was the head. I don't know, the shape kept altering.

We called them the "leaden devils," but I don't think their bodies were metal. Outside there seemed to be a sort of heavy hide, like rhinoceros skin. I don't know what they were within, but they could not have been flesh and blood. Too heavy! Far too heavy!

They crunched the rocks in their track. Ugh!

They had about twenty tentacles apiece. One I know had eighteen, and another had twenty-one. These were metal rods, sometimes thicker than my leg, sometimes thinner than my wrist. That was when they stretched to the extreme. I suppose they were twenty feet long then. Most of them ended in a three-fingered hand.

The tentacles were solid platinum. I've tested them since. I can't say whether they were part of the creatures or mechanisms which they used, and how they stretched them and bent them and seized things with them I have no idea—but they did.

The four we saw made for the two sailors. They got over the broken ground by contracting and expanding their bodies and pushing and pulling with the tentacles. We could see and hear the rocks break with their weight. They moved faster than a man could run, and anyhow the sailors seemed paralyzed, and stood still without making a sound.

The devils seemed to roll upon them, and then they were gone. There were no traces left. I think they were eaten, but the things had no mouths, and—when I think of them I sometimes suspect that I am mad!

We crouched down on the hill behind some slimy seaweed; huge, fern-like sea weed, which I had never seen anywhere else. The devils lumbered on, smashing down everything in their path, and passed us. We went back to the sea-shore, holding hands like frightened children. I think most of us would have laid down and died, but the woman told us to do our best and trust the result to God.

We found an overhanging rock facing the sea with small shallow caves in it, and carried our provisions and bedding there. We rarely moved any distance from it for a week. The carpenter and the other sailor made one attempt at exploration, but the leaden devils saw them and chased them.

They caught the carpenter. The sailor reached us late at night. He had waited till dark for fear they should track him and find us also. He was a fine, courageous chap and would have died a hundred deaths for our sweet lady.

He had seen down the pit, he said. An enormous shaft came up it, and they ascended clinging to the shaft with their tentacles. He saw about thirty in all. Just before dusk most of them descended; but they left three guards.

One tentacle of each gave a light like electric lamps, and they flashed it 'round and 'round like a searchlight. Their shape when at rest was rather like that of a short, very stout fish, he said, and they were as big-bodied as an elephant. They drew most of the tentacles inside them then, and this seemed to make them swell.

On his way back to us he had found one of the ship's boats in a cave to our left, not a hundred yards away. There were oars and a mast and a sail in it, and, so far as he could tell by feeling in the dark, it was seaworthy. He proposed that we should inspect it in the morning, and, if it was sound, should sail away to sea and take our chance on being picked up.

The boat was not injured, we found, the next morning. We carried our provisions and water to it. We were struggling to push it across the slime to the water, and then—it was about noon—the serpent came again.

It rose suddenly out of the water about fifty yards from the shore, coming toward us with its head raised quite thirty feet. We ran to the caves, but it pursued us across the slime, using its fins as legs.

The boy fell and seemed to be too terrified to rise. We ran on a few steps. Then we all stopped with one accord and went back to help him. The serpent tore him from us. We clung to it till we were almost dragged into the sea.

Afterward we tried to launch the boat, but we seemed too weak. We rested in our caves for the remainder of that day.

The next morning we made another attempt with the boat, and dragged it almost to the water's edge. The sailor seemed to have the strength of six. He had fallen in love with the woman, though I did not think she guessed this, and was strengthened by his love for her. He was a magnificent fellow; a brave gentleman without learning. Pratt, the chap's name was.

He stood in front of the woman's cave when the serpent came again and chased us from the boat, but the woman ran out and tried to draw him back. The beast raised its head to strike, and then a great leaden devil crashed down from the rock above on the sandy slime, and came between.

The serpent tried to retreat, but the metal tentacles seized it, and drew it slowly forward.

I often try to picture exactly what happened, but can never get it clear, though I was not five yards away.

The "devil"—I do not know what else to call it—seemed to draw the serpent under it piece by piece, and presently the beast was gone, and though the "devil" moved away no sign of the serpent remained!

When it moved away it took the woman and the sailor imprisoned separately in its tentacles. They called good-by to each other; and when I began to follow them they entreated me to go back.

I still went on, however. I don't know why, as I had no chance of rescuing them. I think I was beyond hope or fear. I still followed them, even when another leaden devil came toward their captor.

It released them then.

Both of the monsters gave out a hissing sound, and the air round them seemed to grow warm. It was evident that they were going to fight for their prey.

I ran up to my comrades as the leaden devils were skirmishing with their tentacles, and took them away, first carrying the woman twenty or thirty yards, then putting her down and going back for the man, and then repeating the process. For this reason I cannot describe the fight. When the man was just beginning to stagger alone—he fell every few steps—the woman pointed back over my shoulder.

I stopped and rested then, and looked back. One leaden devil had lost all his tentacles. The other had two left and was trying vainly to move with them. Their bodies were both crushed out of shape—if any shape ever belonged to them—and were writhing convulsively.

"We will get the boat in the water and go," I said, but my comrades were too feeble all that day to help push it, and we had to wait till the next morning.

We rose at daybreak and crept out cautiously toward the boat. The leaden devils lay very still, with their tentacles strewn round them.

"I'd like to know what they're made of," I said. "I know something of metals, and the tentacles look to me like platinum."

"Or tarnished silver," the sailor said. "If we knew they were that, we'd take a few home!"

"Platinum is worth more than gold!"

He laughed aloud.

"Gold that you can tie in knots!" he cried. "It ought to be worth more. I could be a gentleman then!"

"You are now!" the woman said quickly; and he looked hard at her.

"And I could marry a lady!" he said.

"You can now," she answered very softly.

I took some of it—which I sold for seven thousand pounds. The others wouldn't have any. They seemed to think it was tainted. We escaped in the boat and were picked up just before we finished our provisions.

I offered a share in my platinum to the Pratts—she had a farm and he married her and I believe they're doing well—but they wouldn't take any. I think their privations and the glaring sun had unhinged their minds. They thought it wasn't metal, but petrified wood.

They had other delusions.

One was that my water barrels—I found two—were full of rum. They wouldn't have a drop out of these, only out of their own. A second delusion was that they seemed to forget the existence of the platinum monsters as soon as they were on board ship. I think the long days of suffering in the boat impaired their memories, and they thought the horrible events on the island were only delirium.

Anyhow, the tentacles *were* platinum, or Jones, Evans & Jones wouldn't have paid me seven thousand for them.

I suppose it's some peculiar organic form, which dies and rots, but that's their look out. . . . No, I didn't tell them how I came by it. They'd have wanted to put me in a lunatic asylum, old man! If it has decayed that's their bad luck.

I've got the seven thousand, and a little more that I had before. I'm not going to waste it on a law-suit. Marie and I always thought we'd like to travel, and we're going to Australia. . . . It doesn't matter whether you consent or don't, old chap. She's five-and-twenty, and knows her own mind.

They tested it and pronounced it platinum; and no jury would believe their yarn about it turning to putrid pulp.

They'd think it was a make-up to swindle me.

Do *I* disbelieve them?

No, I don't; but when I sold it, it *was* platinum.

# COACHWHIP PUBLICATIONS

## COACHWHIPBOOKS.COM

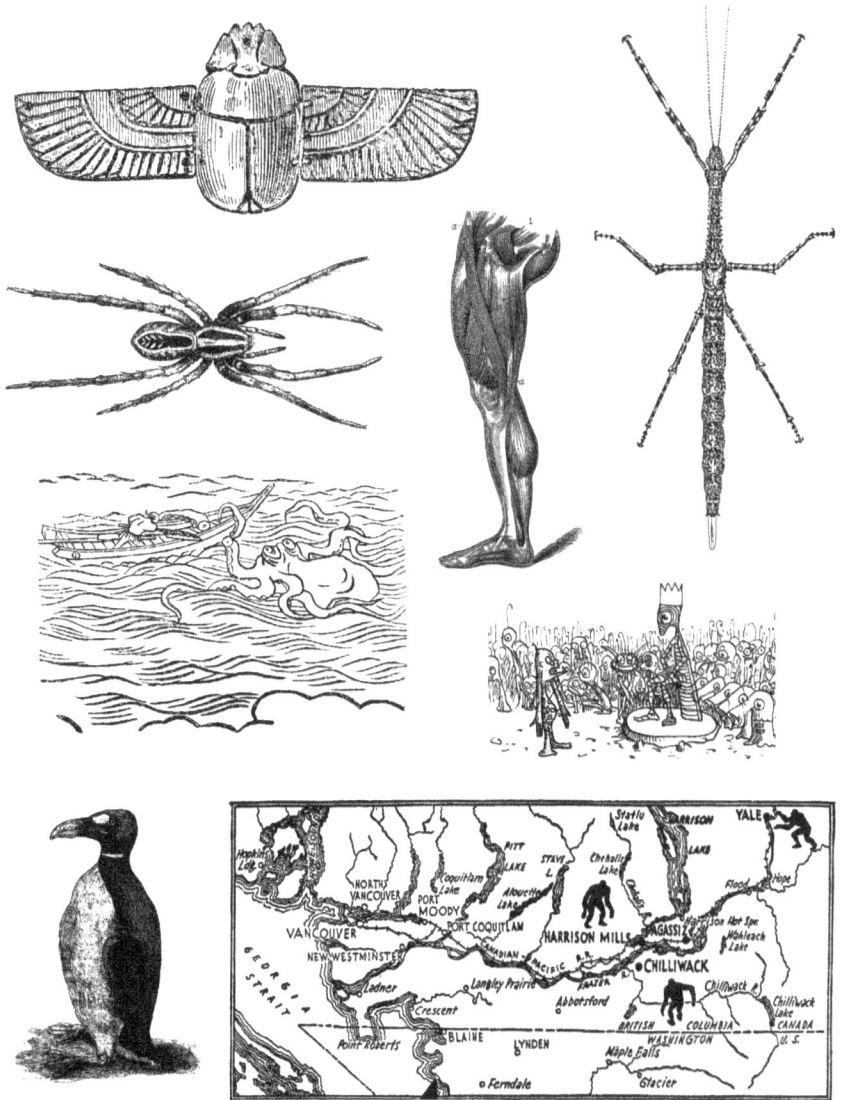

# COACHWHIP PUBLICATIONS

## COACHWHIPBOOKS.COM

BLACK SPIRITS
AND WHITE
RALPH ADAMS CRAM

TALES OF THE
SUPERNATURAL
JAMES PLATT

SHADOWS GOTHIC
AND GROTESQUE

*Shadows Gothic and Grotesque*
ISBN 1-61646-059-8

*Ancient Haunts:*
*Stoneground Ghost Tales / Tedious Brief Tales*
ISBN 1-61646-005-9

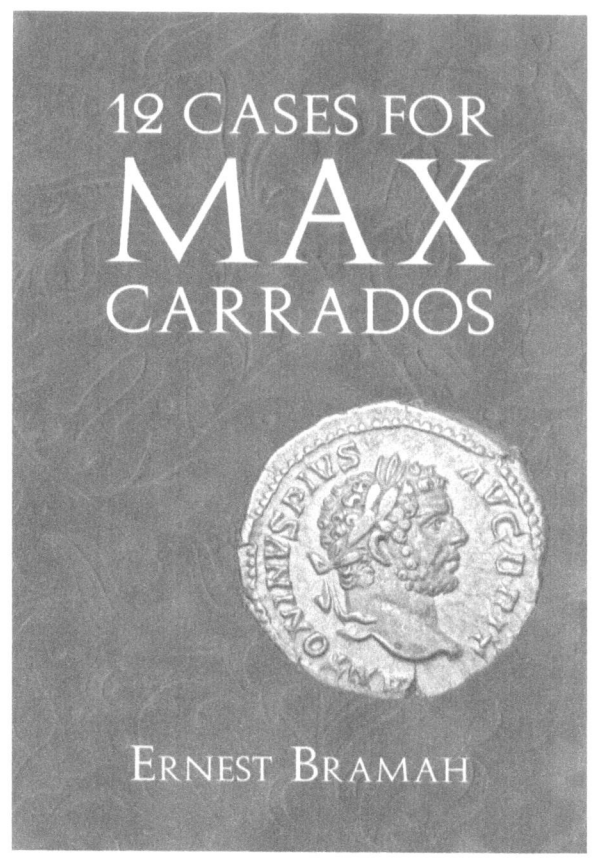

# COACHWHIP PUBLICATIONS

## ALSO AVAILABLE

*A Queen of Atlantis / The Devil-Tree of El Dorado*
ISBN 1-930585-74-8

COACHWHIP PUBLICATIONS

ALSO AVAILABLE

*Wulf: Tales of Wolves and Werewolves*
ISBN 1-61646-056-3

www.ingramcontent.com/pod-product-compliance
Lightning Source LLC
Chambersburg PA
CBHW020641260626
47157CB00008B/2861